FECKENMEYER'S MAILBOX

....

A DICK STRANGER CRIME NOVEL

T. E. VERNIER

To Dennis & Susan... Enjoy the "local color"! T. E. Vernier

First in the Dick Stranger Series
T&D Publishing
Tomah, WI

T & D Publishing
P. O. Box 123
Tomah, WI 54660 USA

www.tevernier.com
Facebook: www.facebook.com/tim.vernier.5
LinkedIn: T.E.Vernier/TimVernier

Feckenmeyer's Mailbox / T. E. Vernier -- 1st ed.
ISBN 978-1492365068

Printed by CreateSpace

Book Layout ©2013 BookDesignTemplates.com

Cover Photo:
"The Old Mailbox"
Used with Permission
Copyright © Joyce Kimble Smith, Photographer
www.joyce-kimble-smith.artistwebsites.com

Cover Design: T & D Publishing

Author Photo: T & D Publishing

Ordering Information:
Quantity sales. Special discounts are available on quantity purchases by corporations, associations, and others. For details, contact the "Special Sales Department" at the address above.

For Denise

Acknowledgments.

My deep thanks go to Terry and Kathy Hoffer for their sensitive reading of the text and for their caring editorial assistance. To Michael and Peggy Vernier, Susan Kohl and Rosemary Denson, Martin and Lisa Potter, Bob and Tina Hawk, and Leo Gordon – thank you for your encouragement, and for your confidence in the book, in me, and in my future. I am grateful to the many friends who kept asking about the book's progress, and who have patiently awaited its arrival. And to Pat McKeown and Dick Stranger, thank you for the inspiration to use Dick's name for my fictional detective. Above all, my thanks go to my wife Denise, for her patient review of the text, for her undying enthusiasm for the cause, and for her belief in me. I trust the book is worth everyone's wait.

– T. E. Vernier, 2013

ONE

....

. . . Dick was perched at his ebony baby grand, pounding out the lead piano part in "Rich Girl" Hot and heavy into it, he rose to his feet, kicking over the piano bench, -- a fate underserved by any piece of Steinway furniture – and he leaned down into the boom-mounted microphone, wailing . . . "your old man's money" . . .

Slowly, Dick realized that the aroma of bacon and hash-browns had overtaken whatever will one's nose has while sleeping, and he wondered who could be in his kitchen. After all, except for Jung, he lived mostly alone.

Fresh coffee. That was the limit. His left eye fluttered awake, but his right, as always, was mattered shut, and with a quick pull of the eyelashes, it too was open. Spring, Summer, Fall, it was always hay-fever season in Wisconsin.

And the piano dream. He was always at his best while playing the piano. If only he knew how to play in real life. Someday.

Dick gazed up from the bed at the painted tin above him, the only ceiling he had left intact when he remodeled the loft for living space. The master bedroom was a quiet harbor, and had the only full twelve-foot walls in the place, with all the others as half or three-quarter walls opening up to the exposed beams.

Rolling over onto his side, Dick could see the small black pads of two paws, fringed in beige fur, and a black nose on the edge of his tall mattress. Jung was a Cairn Terrier, and having performed his morning stretches after exiting his kennel, the little guy wanted companionship. And food. And outside. In reverse order. In fact, if things were urgent, Jung regularly let himself out of the soft-sided kennel, with a deft paw on the inner zipper slide.

Dick looked over the bed side to see a happily wagging tail and a big tongue-curling yawn, two ends of a sturdy and trim sixteen-pound beige and black package.

Jung. The collective unconscious. Carl Jung. Dick had been catching up on his philosophy reading when he adopted the abandoned puppy. Carl or Jung? He always wondered if people named their kids this way.

The bedroom door opened and Jung shot into the loft and headed for the kitchen space. Of course, no one was cooking bacon and hash-browns in there, and Dick Stranger had known it as soon as the night's fog had lifted. After all, he owned the café downstairs.

TWO

....

Dick threw on black sweats and white socks and padded out of the bedroom. He was a fit six-footer, a former runner who had graduated to a bike when the knees got too bad. His Italian background had bequeathed him good looks.

Olive skin, dark hair and eyes. Well-preserved for the high school class of 1984. Dick had been going through an Orwell phase right then, so the irony of observing the imagined versus the real 1984, and marking that time in history with his graduation, was not lost on him. Was he or was he not a product of 1984?

He drew a cup of hot water for tea from the 180 degree spigot on the kitchen counter. Instant hot water. The greatest aid to mankind since fermentation. Dick left the back door ajar, and Jung bolted down the rear stairs, whose bottom door held a doggy door to a small grassy and fenced back yard.

Another great invention. What would Ben Franklin think?

Gazing west out the huge arched windows on the Main Street end of the loft, Dick pondered downtown Woodstock, Wisconsin, home of the Fighting Woodchucks, twelve-time State Divisional Football Champions. And that was just since the new High School was built in 1975.

What was it about Woodstock that bred fans eager to don furry hats and fake woodchuck teeth to watch kids in all kinds of weather?

Somehow, Dick felt at one with the fans. He liked Woodstock, his home for over twenty years now. Drifting off a little, he was roused from his reminiscence by a knock on the apartment door.

The door unit was an old, old walnut affair, with equally old pieces of pebbly glass in the transom and door. The glass still had vintage large black-edged gilt letters I.O.O.F., gently arched and topped by the Odd Fellows logo. On the hallway plaster next to the door was a brass plaque: Truth is Strange Investigations, Richard Stranger.

A second rap on the door was supported by a female voice,

"Dick . . . oh, Dickie . . ." sounded up and over the transom.

Dick knew the voice. It was his client Trixie Shiraz, formerly known as Patricia Wellington. The Wellingtons had local banking money, and she had been able to control a tidy share of cash and bank stock. It was probably not a social call.

"Dick . . . Dickie . . . are you there?"

No choice. With the transom open he couldn't do anything in the loft that would not be heard. Jung, having let himself back in, skidded across the light maple floor and barked a noisy tail-wagging hello.

Dick dipped his fingers in his hot tea, swept back his hair, and calmly welcomed in the voice.

She was a very well-kept mid-40's, with thick shoulder-length honey-blond hair, and a yoga-toned horse-woman's and runner's body. Dick took it all in – her very presence invited hyphens. To-day she presented with sharply creased designer blue jeans, a white long-sleeve shirt with upturned collar and cuffs, enough silver jewelry to qualify for Southern Arizona, and black heels.

"Trixie, good Saturday morning. You know I get paid double on weekends."

"Oh Dickie, you'd never do that to a good customer like me. Oh, hi Jung!"

The dog stopped, raised his head to the top of her head and back down to the shoes, and resumed the wag.

Dick reminded her,

"But Trix, it's business."

And business it usually was with Trixie. Dick took a deep breath and was overwhelmed with today's fragrance. The new Chanel, he believed. Or was that Obsession.

Dick and Trixie, the Mrs. Boris Shiraz, had maintained a professional friendship as she purchased investigations of a few of her husband's staff, and for that matter, of Boris himself.

She also bought diamond jewelry from Dick, as he ran a small off-the-books loan and pawn business on the side. The jewelers in town were fairly old-school, and they refused to buy back diamonds at fair market value. Dick was a fair market kind of guy, and never had any compunction about delivering to a prospective seller the sometimes disappointing news about the difference between wholesale and retail in the diamond market. Somebody had to do it.

And Boris. Boris was also a diamond customer, supposedly unbeknownst to Trixie. So he was no stranger to Dick. Boris had suddenly appeared on the local scene about ten years ago, and swept Patricia Wellington and her money off their feet. He dubbed her Trixie at the same time, and made a further splash buying up real estate for development purposes.

About three years ago, Trixie was updating her estate plan with the bank's co-owner and attorney, and she felt that Boris deserved some post-marriage vetting. It was Dick's first retail detective case.

"Well, Trixie, I don't have a lot to report," Dick told her at the time.

"Dickie, he has to have some past. Like, we're all, you know, 40-ish."

"Trix, he's clean as a stolen Cadillac at a Chicago carwash. No history before he got here, but he does have an f/k/a. I checked it out too. Nothing."

"F/k/a? What's that?"

"Formerly known as. Detective-speak."

9

"So what is, like, my real married name?"

"Shiratski. I will admit, Shiraz is a bit more romantic."

"Shiratski. I would have enjoyed that."

It was easy money for Dick. A little background check, and nothing to report. He was in business.

Here he was three years later, standing in the kitchen area, with Trixie hustling herself to a seat by his windows, and she was asking for coffee from the kitchen.

Dick knew he should be polite and walk the coffee over to her, but he actually wanted to observe her walking across the sun-space for the cup. Oh well, be polite.

"Dick, I think something is wrong at the farm," she said, taking the cup. No diamond sale today, Dick thought.

"What's happening?"

"Well, first off, like, Boris is like distracted, you know? He's either at the store or on his cell all the time. And he's constantly gone to meetings."

She signaled quotation marks around "meetings" with her fingers.

"I can't believe he's got the, like, itch, with everything I do for him."

Dick knew he shouldn't touch that line.

"And Wayne . . . " she continued, pausing.

"Wayne Nelson?" Dick asked.

"Yes, him. He's still like keeping the place up some, but it's like all he does is think about the corn crop. He had some like consultants in, and now he's got Boris to spring for an irrigation system – we're in Western Wisconsin, for cripe's sake –, and our fertilizer bill is through the roof. And I only know that because Gilbert down at the feed mill was all full of it when I was there to buy some treats for my new Arabian."

"Wayne gets paid according to how good the crop is, right?"

"Well, yes, that's like part of it."

"Seems simple. I don't know about Boris, but it sounds as if Wayne wants a good crop so he'll get a bonus. Case closed, that will be five hundred dollars, please."

"Funny. Look, I'll pay you to find out what's going on with like the both of them. Like, period."

It took about five seconds for the mercenary in Dick to make a decision.

"Easy enough. Usual terms. You're the boss," he said, as the lyrics to "Rich Girl" played through his head.

Jung wagged his tail faster, and put his paws up on her knee.

THREE

....

. . . Dick was well into Elton John's "Honky Cat" at the piano, and he was absolutely maxxed out on the vocals, the place ringing with honky-tonk piano . . .

Jung's bark jolted Dick out of his reverie and to attention. They had just driven past his destination, an old service station that now was home to a small used car lot. Dick took a left, doubled back through the alley, and backed up the Cube Van to a tacky warehouse across from the station. The old blacktop in the alley cracked and popped under the tires, and Dick cut the engine, shutting off the radio and Elton John.

The old windows of the warehouse were papered over, but the windowless double height garage door looked brand new. It silently rose at the press of a remote. Dick aimed another remote at the security system and the red light stopped blinking. He backed the truck into the open area of the building.

It was spotless as a NASCAR shop, equally well-equipped, and the exterior windows did not exist to the inside view. Epoxy non-skid floor, the best mechanics' benches and cabinets, overhead retractable air lines and drop cords, electro-hydraulic above ground hoists, and full tilt video plus Sony's latest audio. Dick had spared no expense. As always, though, he liked to keep a low public profile.

Another click and the door closed. Dick inhaled the seductive aroma of fresh paint, cleaning supplies, oil, tires, and old cars. The building contained, among other things, Dick's small but choice car collection. His favorite, and most valuable, sat in a zippered bag. These bags were the latest and current fad in car storage. Special chemical treatment for moisture and corrosion protection. A soft inner cover plus a weather-proof yet breathable bag enveloping the entire car. The bag extended underneath, zipping at floor level.

The car: a 1968 Ferrari 330 GTC, 4.4 Liter V-12, 5 speed, Silver in color over Red leather. The vintage was from when Ferraris held gorgeous, voluptuous designs, nothing like the angular doorstops of the Eighties, Nineties, and beyond. Dick did acknowledge that these were matters of taste, and of course it was his own taste that was right. And he had to admit that the F12 Berlinetta from the 2012 Geneva Auto Show marked a return to style.

Dick yanked on the roll-up rear door of the truck and pulled out the ramp. Methodically, he unloaded and stocked into a lockable storeroom one hundred cases of red wines. Merlot, Cabernet, Sangiovese, and his favorite, Chianti. Each plain white box was stenciled with "Strangere Winery – Product of Italy."

Gathering up Jung, Dick reversed the arrival process and drove across town to the afterhours rental drop and parked the Cube Van. Jung scampered over to Dick's 1953 MG TD, Ivory over Tan leather, and waited. Dick put the truck keys in the drop-box and slid into the MG, resetting the switches to fire it up.

While a favorite car of Dick's, the MG was not his choice for night driving. Un-restored, the electrical system had that British character of having been made up as they went along at assembly. Plus the instrument lights simply did not work. One day, Dick would get around to it.

But the distinctive MG roar was addictive and the very British aroma of leather, rotting ash, and leaking petrol was seductive. Off to the garage behind the apartment they motored, the only two who ever handled the wine shipments, Jung's nose to the wind and hair slicked back in the night air.

FOUR

....

. . . Dick leaned back, extending his arms to the keyboard. Eyes closed, he meandered through "Candle in the Wind" with ease and grace . . .

Looking trendy and mysterious in his Bausch & Lomb Wayfarers, Dick was stretched languidly out on a park bench in the middle of Woodstock, just a few blocks south of the apartment.

Dick's collection of sunglasses had become a point of discussion among his friends. Did he seriously think, as he would state when challenged, that these things had collectible value? Or was he secretly trying to be fashionable? What message did the Wayfarers project?

He snapped back to the present when Jung landed on his lap and curled up for a nap in the sun.

The music stopped, but Dick continued to think of Antonina and where he sat today, one of their favorite reviewing stands for the parade of life in their town.

They shared hours on this bench, observing Woodstock's mobile life on its main street. The trucks of commerce, the vans of family pick-up and delivery, the full-size sedans headed for retirement coffee, the basic but slightly customized cars and trucks of the young, and the occasional Amish buggy.

The Amish had settled in the area decades ago from the East, during an economic crisis for family farms. Somehow having the money to buy farms, they then stripped the electricity and indoor plumbing from the homes, and set to plowing fields with horse-drawn equipment.

Trading in town was facilitated by horse and buggy, and Woodstock soon had hitching posts behind the hardware stores and in municipal parking lots.

The buggies themselves fascinated Dick. The design details of these daily drivers was determined by the Bishop, who decreed rubber versus steel wheel rims, windshields or no, placement of lamps, and so on.

But the buggies did leave something in their wake – the residue of horses. It was not too bad in town, but on the winding hills and valley roads that connected the many Amish farms, avoiding the odorous and slippery road deposits with your car required concentration and skill.

Yet, Dick and Antonina always stared at the buggies and waved at the drivers. At times the Amish and local cultures blended, with the Amish displaying a new stepladder from Wal-Mart or such, lashed with twine to the roof of the buggy.

Antonina was an Italian college exchange student, and she had stayed on in Woodstock with a combination of inertia and a lingering crush on her English Professor. The feeling was mutual, painfully obvious, and Dick Stranger was that professor. At twenty-five he had seemed both much older and yet contemporary with her twenty when they met. Flirtation, a few coffee dates, and two years passed as Dick purposely watched the teacher-student relationship expire, to be replaced with genuine affection, passion, and love. Soon they married.

Dick taught Renaissance and Elizabethan Literature, and Creative Writing at Woodstock College, the private liberal arts college in town, and he eventually retired after twenty years, taking an early out during a federal cutback in education spending. The financial aid and programs essential to maintaining a "cost is no object" tuition level dried up.

Antonina was with him for nearly all this time, and nothing could surpass her in his love for all things Italian. She had Sophia Loren-like sophistication and a significant build, yet was casual, approachable. Dick was sure he was inhaling fresh olive oil whenever he was with her. The passion of her convictions brought Dick to life. They were inseparable.

Frequent travel to their mutual homeland was a must, and Dick scored a number of research sabbaticals. He qualified by assuming extra class duties, and ended up with the College's Entrepreneurship Program. His strategy was to stay close to the center of the circle as the cycle of time off slowly spun around.

Florence and Siena drew him and Antonina particularly, and these sabbaticals normally involved thirty long days in libraries followed by a two hour per day routine to produce a publishable item, the idea for which usually was inspired by student's term paper. The freedom of the entire balance of each day was a planned bonus. No doubt, he thought, this was how all the great scholars found their critical muse, napping, enjoying the aromas of the olive and grape growth, testing the quality of the Chianti, eating prosciutto, viewing the countryside.

If not Florence or Siena, then Pisa, Padua, and Venice were the favored literary destinations. Antonina's family was still in Siena, and eventually she and Dick secured a tiny apartment there, a family heirloom of sorts, which allowed them to be in the city for the Palio di Siena horse races. The apartment was, naturally, located in the proper neighborhood, or contrada. Of the seventeen contrade, ten participated each year in the Palio, and when her neighborhood was in the race, Antonina could cheer and celebrate the anointed horse with family and with friends from her youth.

Just west of Siena, in the Chianti country of Tuscany, a villa also beckoned. Funded by inheritance, Dick and Antonina acquired a well preserved palazzo designed in the classic Tuscan style, stone and tile, and parked in the center of vineyards and olive trees. It was a working farm that had once been the central hub of a group of farm shares, each with their own smaller villa. Now by itself, the farm was operated as an agriturismo, or agricultural tourism site, and enjoyed sustaining acreage in addition to views overlooking the beautiful hills. Beautiful hills indeed, the property was named Bellapendio.

With Antonina's family close at hand, operation of the agriturismo posed no difficulty, as her brother and sister-in-law assumed management, showing an amazing knack for viticulture. Living in the villa, they were hosts to Dick and Antonina for the long summers and the periodic winter visits. The "owners as visitors" role was a charming turn of events, and every trip was indeed a vacation as Dick and Antonina held their own guest suite, and in the winery storehouse stood a well-kept Fiat Spyder for vacation use.

In order to qualify for the tax breaks and subsidies provided by the Italian Government, the agriturismo was required to feature guest quarters, and the Stranger party from Wisconsin took over the entire second floor of the palazzo. In the spirit, Dick and Antonina took time each day with the producing vineyard and olive grove, and tended blending and quality at the winery. The wine had become a favorite enterprise, and the product was special enough to rise above the Italian red wine surplus. Of course, many cases were for export to Wisconsin.

Dick gazed out at Woodstock, population 17,000, and dreamed back to the days at Bellapendio, and inescapably back to "the day."

His life had turned upside-down five years ago. He quietly stroked a sleeping Jung as it all played again, a highlight reel he could not turn off, the film on which he could not walk out. Antonina kissing him goodbye. Hopping on her bicycle destined for the farmers' market in the very park where Dick sat today. Fresh tomatoes for tonight's pasta. An anonymous tire screech in the distance. A police siren, and many more. Dick running from the yard of their Lannon-stone bungalow for Main Street. The sirens growing close, then silence. Running. And running.

FIVE

Dick sat on a stool at the Café bar. This was the aroma that woke him the day that Trixie dropped by to discuss Boris and Wayne. Jung sat quietly at Dick's feet, having somehow gained a Licensed Service Dog status after a couple of nursing home visits and a well-timed donation to the City Clerk's favorite charity. Jung really was irresistibly cute, and he had won over the City Hall staff when Dick plunked him down on the counter of the "Pay Taxes – Buy Licenses" window, with the Service Dog application tied around Jung's neck with a string.

Katherine K. Kaul, Bookstore manager, was seated to Dick's right, and to his left was Kenny Wisdom, Bar and Restaurant manager. This was a breakfast and lunch place that turned into a tavern at night. They were just there for the morning coffee.

Dick was running a clever reading, writing, drinking and teaching establishment on the ground floor of his apartment. It had all seemed so simple the first day he owned the building, three deep and narrow storefronts in old downtown Woodstock, Wisconsin, America. The stores had been opened up into a single expanse, high-ceilinged, full of supporting pillars and a fun-house riot of worn and warped and mismatched hardwood floors. Formerly occupied by a furniture liquidator, no maintenance had been performed on the site during the term of an old five-year lease. It was a sponge for cash.

A double-door entrance graced the dead center, and was flanked by a commercial staircase good for three persons wide. The stairs carried to the second floor. This creaking, shallow-rise, dark wood assemblage was a masterpiece.

Delusional as usual about its ease of refinishing, Dick thought the staircase alone was worth the building's price of admission. It was a full but gradual two story long affair with a generous landing half way up for the rest and leisure of second floor patrons. How totally quaint and last century, thought Dick, how historic.

After a year of being taught in fact the distinction between "historic" and "old" by his contractor, Dick held the keys one day to what he fondly called A Stranger Place.   Corny perhaps, but with the last name Stranger, Dick had grown up with puns. He was eight years old and living in Chicago when his Calabria-born-and-raised father changed the surname from Strangere to Stranger. Young Richard, or Enrique as his parents called him, was not so sure this was an improvement, but he had to roll with it. He was told it had something to do with not appearing in Southern Italy for a while, and Enrique seemed to understand.

Three related businesses occupied the first floor of A Stranger Place. Facing the building, the left or North third was Stranger Than Fiction, a new and used book store and news stand. The center was The Library, with a tall bar in the rear that doubled as a lunch counter. Plus a few tables flowing up to a lounge seating area in the front. This space was separated by a three-quarter wall, and was quiet area for reading and sipping.

The mahogany and brass bar furnishings gave way to the green and terra cotta and light maple décor as seen in popular chain coffee shops. This was referred to by most at the Café.

Dick's crowning play was obtaining a full restaurant liquor license for the place, plus a package license to support the final ingredient, The Liquid Muse, a liquor store that occupied the south third of the floor space.

The licensing required some heavy lobbying, and the clincher was five cases of a good drinkable Cabernet for Melissa Schwartz, member of the Planning and Licensing Board, wife of Police Chief Bill Schwartz, and committed red wine lush.

With separate retail entrances, easy walkways internally between shops, plus the central entrance for all three, whoever came in usually took in all the stores, and A Stranger Place took off. The latest books, and a real Rare Book department, poetry slams, live jazz on weekend nights, wine and beer making classes, plus a corkage fee program with The Liquid Muse for those who desired beverages not on The Library's list. It was a hit.

Dick nodded to Katherine and Kenny, and said, "Okay you two, how can we keep up this pace? We're a year into this deal and I'm afraid the honeymoon could end. We're crazy busy right now, but how do we keep fresh?"

Katherine, also known as Kate or Clan or Red, was taken aback.

"Are you saying we're not doing okay?"

Katherine was bookish by nature, eccentric in a good way, and carried her six feet with Bacall-like elegance. Green-eyed, red-haired, her posture inspired a picture of a young girl walking across the room with a book on her head. Now she did that for fun in the bookstore.

She was after Dick. Jung gazed at her with obvious affection,

Kenny Wisdom, Sage to his friends, and manager of The Library Café, answered for Dick,

"Kate, Kate. It's all okay. We just have to do something new to keep people coming, you know, staying in the lead. Look, we've got the loyalty cards, special coffee and drinks, but I think Dick's right."

Kenny was short and well-muscled, with grey eyes that held your gaze and a smile that could calm anyone. He was the one who had taken notice of Kate's initials and dubbed her Clan, which was about as far from her politics as Irish whiskey from wine spritzers. He worked hard, volunteered in the community, and liked cars. Dick's kind of guy.

Kenny was married to Pearl, who ran The Liquid Muse. Twenty years ago Pearl White became Pearl Wisdom. She was taller than Kenny, with a gigantic smile and curly brown hair. They worked together well, and lived together the same. She was busy with inventory in the store, or she would have been at the counter for coffee.

Dick appreciated Kenny's understanding and agreement on the future of the enterprise,

"Right. Look, I call this an Holistic Drinking, Reading, and Dining Experience. I just wanted to add a little lagniappe for our customers, you know, to keep the altitude up."

"Free books!" shouted Kenny.

Jung swiveled his head to look at Kenny, and wagged his entire back half.

Kate was aghast,

"Free books? We sell books for a living!"

"I love it," announced Dick.

So went the newest idea for Stranger Than Fiction and The Library. Brief discussion. Free books it was. And Ludwig "Jack" Bluhm would be in charge. This would be a surprise to Jack, but he was a good friend of Dick's, assistant to Dick in another enterprise and a skilled rare book buyer.

The plan was simple. Jack frequently had to buy entire lots of used books just to get the good ones, and the duds languished in inventory until Jack found a home for them, in fact gave them away.

These surplus books would be offered for free lending. Kate signed onto the program, but she already pictured herself more as a book collector than a librarian. The Free Book Program would add a lot of bother with low rate books. Mostly she wanted to agree with Dick.

Kate's high school teaching career had been shortened by a fling with an eighteen year old senior, and after examining her options she returned to university to pursue her PhD. She ran out of scholarships and other money, finished as an AbD, or All but Dissertation, and ended up managing an Earth Shoe store near the university.

Dick knew that Earth Shoes were in again, and Kate had never stopped wearing them. She was a believer. After a few refreshments at social events, Dick was occasionally overheard telling friends, "just don't get her started on their virtues unless you are prepared for a presentation worthy of Amway."

Fortunately, Kate inherited a chunk of money from her family's long invested bootlegging legacy, so she returned to her home town to claim her piece of the pie and to do what she loved, hanging around books and the people who loved them. She had financial resources, natural beauty, and intelligence. All she lacked was Dick.

SIX

·····································

Antonina, her bicycle helmet shattered, lay motionless next to the curb. The bicycle, wheels twisted and frame bent, was a few feet away. An ambulance approached as a crowd gathered. A hit and run.

Dick clung to her as best he could. As she was loaded on the gurney, Antonina mouthed "I love you" to him with a brief flash of her eyes in a moment of consciousness.

She did not survive the short trip to the hospital.

Oddly enough, a tow truck had been called along with all the other emergency vehicles, probably just routine. As Dick climbed up into the back of the ambulance, he noticed the tow truck driver, his friend Ellis, sweeping up the street, like at the end of a circus or vaudeville show.

Still on the park bench, Dick gazed blankly without seeing, and his mind suddenly fast-forwarded to today. He swept Jung up off his lap and, with tears in his eyes, hugged the little dog.

SEVEN

....

Antonina's accident started Dick's investigative career. The police had no leads in the hit and run in the days following the accident, and Dick questioned the Police Chief, Bill Schwartz,

"But Bill, don't you even know what kind of car hit her?"

Chief Bill had the look and manners of someone other than a Schwartz. In fact, he too looked a little Italian, maybe too fair-skinned to be full blooded, but he had the habit of talking with his hands and repeating himself. Good subject for an internet search, thought Dick for the first time.

The Woodstock Police Chief's office was in the oldest part of the Justice Center, the part which remained original when the new construction took place. This spoke to Bill's social skills and political clout with the City Council. 1950's green asphalt floor tiles, steel desk, paneling. On a credenza stood several shooting trophies and die-cast model police cars. The Chief's shoulder holster hung on the coat tree along with the uniform jacket. Too much time at the desk chair had led to a little too much of Bill at the belt line.

Dick, socially progressive but skeptical of bureaucracy, pictured desk drawers full of Little Debbie snack cakes and spilled powdered coffee creamer, and a police training phrase book full of evergreens such as "Book 'em, Danno."

"Sorry Dick, just nothin' from the skid marks, looks like a mid-size. Really, a mid-size."

"A mid-size! In a city like this? Let's just narrow it down to five thousand local cars, plus visitors."

"Hey Dick, the boys are doin' their best out there, checkin' the skid marks and all."

"Bill, what about the color or parts search."

"We got nothin' but skid marks."

Dick knew enough about hydraulics that he was about to blow an artery somewhere if this conversation continued, so he simply got up and walked towards the office door.

Boiling away, Dick had the instant of clarity to feel that he should be careful not to offend here. Too much, that is.

After all, he and Antonina had been to Schwartz's home several times for gourmet club, and he had personally challenged Melissa Schwartz at her own game, red wine consumption. There was no clear winner.

Door knob in hand, Dick resembled Columbo as he turned to the Chief and asked,

"One last thing. Mind if I look at the bicycle at impound?"

Increasing the distance between them, Bill leaned back in his swivel chair and swung his legs up onto the corner of the old government issue desk, displaying his parade polished police issue oxfords.

"Hell, be my guest."

EIGHT

....

Dick left in pursuit of a key for the impound padlock from the Department's front desk. He approached the lightly green-tinted bullet-proof glass and spoke into the little steel grate. Just like an old time movie theatre.

"Hi, I'm Dick Stranger. I'd like to get into the impound lot to inspect an accident vehicle."

The young officer had one hand on his pistol grip and ran the other through his one-half inch flattop tapering down to shaved side and back, as if this would buy him time to figure out if he missed the day of Impound Lot Procedures Training.

Keeping his hand on his Glock, the officer reached up to his epaulet and fingered the clipped on microphone.

Dick wondered to himself if the guy's badge was metal or plated plastic with "Junior G-Man" in raised letters. He had already noticed the name tag "Ofc. P. Justus."

Officer Justus' eyes were slits as he mumbled something back and forth. He turned to a cabinet door, swung it open, and pulled a key off an old cup hook.

Key in his palm, he officiously inquired,

"Who authorized you to go to the impound?"

"Chief Schwartz. I just left his office."

"Here's the key. Make sure it's locked when you're done."

Dick thought to himself, "Finished, young man, not done. Finished," but decided not to offend yet another policeman today.

"Okay, thanks."

No ID, no sign out register, the key was not even stamped "Do Not Duplicate." Perfect. Small town America.

Dick walked across the street and up three blocks to Hardware Hank, and had a key made for future use. You never know. Then back to the impound, which was a small chain link enclosure in a corner of the Municipal parking lot behind the Police Wing. Opening the padlock, he pulled off the chain and swung wide the gate across the cracked and dirty concrete.

Typical impound lot. At least twenty stolen and recovered bicycles stood under a canopy. The open lot included an old Caprice Classic with dubs, dressed to look like an SS, a couple of Grand AMs with blacked out windows, and an assortment of four damaged vehicles. In the far corner stood a VW Microbus that clearly was not from Wisconsin. Lacking rust, but with lots of stickers and a California plate, it probably commemorated the untimely end of someone's cross-country magical mystery tour. It had four flat tires. Dick made a note to watch for the police drug seizure vehicle auction.

Lying against the fence, just inside the gate, was Antonina's bicycle. The bright blue Trek had been specially equipped for her, with all the specific components as would befit a serious rider. Wisconsin built, it had been her joyful project to plan, order, and then operate. The precious project was badly tangled.

Dick gazed down at it. The crushed rear half-fender had a long streak of silver paint on it. He chipped at it with his fingernail and finally held a good sized hunk of paint in his hand. Then, a chunk of bicycle paint was also obtained. He carefully placed it all in an old Kit Kat wrapper he saw on the ground, folded the wrapper, and put it in his pocket.

NINE

....

Tossing the padlock key into the stainless steel tray beneath the glass enclosure in the Police Department, Dick bid Ofc. P. Justus good day, and walked back to his apartment to pick up the MG.

Next stop, Woodstock Towing & Recovery, Ellis Smart, Proprietor.

Dick roared up the gravel drive to the office and shop, trusting that the old brakes would stop the car yet one more time. Curb stops and a healthy overgrowth of arbor vitae looked like a good fallback plan. Fortunately, the old binders worked once again, and Dick stopped in front, prompting a beige cloud of dust to envelop the entrance. He headed directly to the shop, where the tow truck from the scene of Antonina's accident was parked outside an open stall door.

"Ellie! What's happenin'?"

"Well, Dickie Stranger, you've arrived without needing my towing services. What a change. And

Dick, I wanted to tell you again how bad I feel about Antonina. I don't know what to say."

Ellis actually did know what to say, and had said it well, as he had expressed many thoughts already, visiting Dick in the days immediately after the accident. Ellis and his wife were old friends of Dick and Antonina from gourmet club. Ellis was the family chef, a self-made literary scholar, and seasoned older car mechanic.

"Ellie, you've said it all. Don't feel that way."

"Well, I . . . "

"Ellie. Thank you. Today I have another favor to ask. Look, the police are only checking out skid marks from the accident scene. Didn't I see you sweeping up there?"

"Yes, I was. I didn't know why I was called in the first place, but I thought I would make myself useful. So I swept up. Didn't the PD already collect evidence?"

"Evidence? Evidently not."

"Honest. When they said they were leaving I took it at face value. Let's go look at what I swept up."

The big blue Rubbermaid garbage can was bungeed to the inside front corner of the wrecker body. Zip's Wreckers, New Hampton, Iowa. Nice truck, Dick thought. Popping the lid, Ellis said,

"Yours was the last sweep up. Everything else has been a disabled runner or an off-road accident. Here we are. Your accident data, sir."

Dick pulled out some silver painted grille pieces, a broken chrome headlamp surround, a plastic plaque of broken gold toned letters, and some dust from the street. Amber and clear plastic turn signal material, headlamp glass.

He knew immediately. Even with missing letters, enough was right there. Oldsmobile Bravada. He pulled out the Kit Kat wrapper and matched up the paint from the bicycle with a scuff that stayed on the headlamp surround. And, some vehicle paint had jammed into the crushed parts. Pewter, or whatever GM called it. Pewter. Blazers, Bravadas, half of them were pewter.

"Ellis, are you seeing what I'm seeing?"

"Bravada. But how do you find it?"

"Assume an amateur. I'm headed for the salvage yards. Haystack here we come."

Ellis said his normal farewell to Dick,

"Hey. Don't be a stranger."

TEN

....

Dick started with calls to GM dealers in a fifty mile radius of Woodstock. Next were the yards, but the character of many of these prescribed a personal visit.

The used parts cult. Secretive, functioning on a need to know basis. Exceptions to the attitude existed, and these better outfits operated like any professional parts department. Yes, we're happy to help, but the Privacy Act required that you speak with a manager. We cannot disclose customer identities . . . and so it went.

Suddenly, Dick realized the advantages of investigative credentials in a circumstance such as this, that is, a "case" such as this. He felt like a private investigator, but he was not. And his available information showed it, even when the needle in the haystack appeared.

"Whatayaneed?"

It was Carl, with an ever present toothpick, his single concession to personal hygiene.

Dick explained what he was after.

"Nuthin' like that," drawled Carl.

Dick thanked him and started to leave, when from the shop a young guy in overalls spoke up,

"Hey Carl, what about that guy who bought all the little Blazer parts? He was all worried that everything would fit a Bravada."

"They do, ya' know," he further directed to Dick.

"Oh yeah, I forgot about him. Completely pulled all the outside stuff from that swimmer," added Carl."

Dick remembered. Swimmer. Flood vehicle. Usually an electrical mess but sometimes physically intact. He asked Carl,

"How did he pay? Check, card?"

"Cash, but he was pretty light and used his buddy's card for almost half of it."

"Still got the slip?"

"Should. Blondie's been on vacation and I don't even know shit about the office unless it's cash. I got enough trouble with the DNR and EPA."

Dick walked out with a photocopy of the charge ticket, and with one less twenty dollar bill. Wow.

That was too easy. He wondered how much he could charge for this kind of thing.

Next day he was looking at vacant office and loft space over a defunct furniture liquidator.

ELEVEN

···

. . . Dick's fingers were walking through the piano runs in "Dancing in the Moonlight," eyes closed, swaying left to right, intoning the lead vocals, entertaining the small crowd . . .

The ring of a bell and the bark of a dog. Jung was a wag-fest as Jean Paradise came through the door of the old gas station. Dick lifted his chin off his chest and peered out from behind the Foster Grant Aviators. More sunglasses. Dressed in a pair of faded black jeans, a white t-shirt and matching socks, Dick looked the part of working at this place. An aging pair of black penny loafers graced his feet, which remained on the desk. Every time you get a good nap going . . .

Dick was a proponent of power naps. He thought he slept pretty well, but his ability, and tendency, to nap spoke otherwise. Whatever the cause, he always needed to catch up on the sleep.

Dick had bought the long derelict Conoco gas station while he was still teaching, and he had cleaned up the old place until it had an original 1950's look. The building was one of those porcelain panel stations. The panels were actually baked enamel over steel, and in its day these stations was assembled on site as kits.

Behind it was a concrete block addition that afforded a big storage area and featured updated restrooms. The pumps were long gone, and thankfully the corporate owner had removed the tanks. The canopy remained, and it worried Dick when the winds got steep. He had installed larger windows in the office corner for better visibility of the outside lot.

Two stalls were on the north half of the building, and were laboratory-like. Epoxy floor, modern equipment, well lighted, just a little cramped. This was why he had restored the old warehouse that came with the property, across the back parking area and alley.

Dick ran a used car business out of the station, which for an enthusiast like him allowed a ready supply of interesting rides. The original concept was to fuel and feed and fund his car obsession. So far it was working well, and provided a good income besides.

Renovating the station was an exciting project, and he retained the vintage 1960's signage and artifacts found on the grounds. His favorite was a case of Bayberry Christmas Candles, boxed in sets of four, which, according to the enclosed memo from Conoco Central Headquarters, were intended to be given during the holidays to purchasers of $2.00 or more of fuel.

Each box had a little sticker identifying the donor as "Roth's Woodstock Conoco Service, Reuben Roth, Prop." Today if you filled up the F150, you would go home with forty-five boxes of candles.

Dick added old automotive signs, displays, parts packages, and model cars to capture the 1950's – 1960's mood. All he needed was a jukebox with Elvis 45's on it. Jung had a favorite pillow on a chair strategically placed in the sun.

TWELVE

....

Into this carefully arranged museum came Jean Paradise. Jean was the bookkeeper for a large fireworks store named Life's a Blast, on the south end of town. It was owned by none other than the prominent, by his own standards, Boris Shiraz.

Jean was just about six feet tall with very short dark hair, blue eyes, and an almost skinny physique atop long legs. She tended toward tight jeans, short shorts, strappy t-shirts and tank tops to accent what Dick thought was an outstanding build. And don't forget the cowboy boots.

Add to that a huge smile with perfectly white teeth, a capacity for beer, and her two Harleys. A little too much perfume, but that was excusable considering her other virtues, especially the Harleys.

That was Jean Paradise. Smart beyond her roots, hardworking, and over the top loyal to her husband Giorgio Danto, who worked for Dick at the bookstore. To Dick, Jean and Giorgio were friends, staff, Italian compatriots, and all around good people.

"Hey, Dick! Hey, Jung!"

Jung pawed at Jean's knees and jumped around her on his back legs.

"Jean, what are you doing here on a workday morning? Help yourself to a coffee. It works just like the others."

Dick had Jura Capresso espresso makers in the kitchen, the office, and now the car lot.

"Cool, huh, Jean? Refurbished. Half price. Now you can get one of your own at home."

Dick thought Jura was the Apple of the coffee world. Great for the home and small office, like an iPad. For the Café, however, it was a professional La Marzacco, handmade in Florence since 1927. Over the top, the best.

And Dick always let staff have coffee drinks free for themselves and spouses and significant others. Between stopping to see Giorgio and stopping to see Dick, Jean never had to buy a cappuccino.

"Dick, you know, I do believe I'll help myself. But I have another reason for being here. And the boys are doing inventory at the store, so we're closed for a couple of days."

"So what's up?"

"You know, I just don't get it out at Blast. I've worked for Boris from his start. At first it was just him and me at that firecracker stand. Then he got big. And now he's really making a lot of money, but we really don't have a lot more customers. Oh, you know, it is better with the new store and all, and we're year 'round now, but jeez, Dick, I can't believe how much is coming in."

"But Jean, that's an expensive building on expensive land. Is there any money left at the end of the month?"

"Well, yeah, you know, there is some left."

"So how can there be too much income?"

"Dick, you know, I just have a weird feeling. I know it should be Boris's and Lars's jobs to worry about this stuff, but I'm the only one who sees all the paperwork."

"So why should you worry?"

"Well, I'm the bookkeeper, you know, and I don't want to be accused of anything with all this money floating around."

"Sounds like the opposite problem. Too much money, not disappearing money."

"Yeah, okay, but too much of its goes away every month. I do okay, Terri doesn't get paid too much, and neither do Ricky and Juan. And Lars gets really good money, plus he must get something at the end of the year, they always take an expensive vacation in February and come home with high-priced trinkets."

Dick knew what was worrying Jean. Talk around town had always been, how do Jean and Giorgio do it all on their wages? Harleys, late model four door pickup, Corvette, always upgrading their house.

But Dick knew the story. The couple bought inexpensive houses, renovated them, and either rented them out or sold them. Once they got the first few paid for, it was good money and they had been doing it for twelve or fifteen years.

Jean and Giorgio's cash flow got a little tight now and then, and Dick knew that too. Paying things down, waiting for closings, and the like. This was Dick's piece of the pie. He ran a small off-the-books loan deal for people like Jean and Giorgio. He had done this for many years and the return was way better than the Teachers' Pension Fund.

"Jean, let me think about this. Pay attention to what is coming and going. Protect yourself by doing some extra trial balances, and watch the basics. Vendors, billings, packing lists. The normal things. Schedule what you need to, and let's talk in the next few days about keeping some of your own records off site."

"Got it. Oh, and you know, I need to give you this."

She pulled an envelope out of her purse and counted out forty one-hundred dollar bills.

"Giorgio is just gonna crap when he sees the chrome package on his bike. He gets it back from the shop this weekend. And he thinks it just got tires. Thanks again for the help."

Dick did the math in his head. Thirty-seven hundred dollar loan, three months. Everybody's happy.

Jung hopped off his pillow and stood by Jean, wagging his tail. Jean gave Dick an air kiss and headed out the door.

THIRTEEN

....

. . . Dick sat on a backless stool at the Roland Electronic Keyboard, looking out over the Café patrons gathered for one of his famous "Easy Listening Brunch" events, and using all of the Roland's capability to do a wall-of-sound version of "Easy Like Sunday Morning" . . .

Dick shook awake to the sound of dog toenails dancing on the hardwood floors of The Library's table area.

Sunday morning it was. Dick had gone to early church at the new ELCA Lutheran Church in town. This liberal and humane branch of the Lutherans had restructured in town, and the congregation was meeting in different digs. It was an exciting time for the small but growing group, and he normally did not miss on Sunday mornings.

Jung's toenails heralded the arrival at the table of Jack Bluhm. Jack was mid-fifties and about five foot seven, with straight sandy hair and blue eyes. His fair skin had weathered a bit during a twenty-two year stint on the road with a band performing warm-up for some middle range rock bands. He was square shouldered with good posture, good arm muscles, and skinny legs. The bulging legacy of beer was appearing in his gut.

With a main role as lead singer and rhythm guitar, Jack could also play bass guitar and electric piano, and as a result was Dick's local musical fantasy idol.

Jung had popped out from under Dick's chair and was greeting the visitor as an old friend, his toenails clicking away as his paws scrambled on the oak, then sitting patiently with a furiously wagging tail as Jack sat down.

Dick rose from the table and slapped Jack on the back. The tables, in nicely finished wood, and themselves quite a splurge when the place was being put together, had already acquired a suitable patina in the first year of use.

Jack scratched Jung behind the ears.

"Dick, good morning. I see Jung is happy as usual."

"My karma detector."

"Hey thanks for inviting me for brunch. I've got the notes on what we talked about."

Jack helped Dick with investigations, moving about inconspicuously and questioning in an unassuming way. He was doing the legwork on Trixie's earlier request.

Dick caught Sage's eye and nodded over at Jack, putting him into the brunch loop.

"Well, Dick, I've made some visits to the store and to the farm. First, the store. Have you been there?"

"Never. Living in a loft, I just don't get around to fireworks."

"Well, it's a big place, and full of inventory. Everything you can imagine. Some of it I guess you can own and sell, but you just can't set it off legally. At least not in Woodstock. But it is big. I paced it off, one hundred by two hundred, with two thirds as retail space, one third as offices and stockroom."

"I know it looks big from the road. I guess that's the idea."

"Yes, well, there is kind of a competition with those stores to say whose firecracker is the biggest. Plus, there's a warehouse half that size in back. Anyway, both times I was there I was the only customer. And Terri Moody is the sales staff. She is so bored she runs at the mouth, and, among many other things, she said she used to work here."

"She worked at the bookstore, and in the café just when we needed a hand. But she had to retire early. Kate got cell-phone photos of her putting new releases into her backpack. And we came up short on a digital reader from the display cabinet one day. She had the only display key other than Kate."

"Well, she sure sounds disgruntled."

"Truth hurts. Isn't she over that yet? It's been a year."

"But she made a couple of comments that sound like she may be still planning revenge. The 'I'll get even with her' type of thing."

"Excuse me while I enter 'Beware of Terri' in my calendar."

Jack rolled his eyes skyward and reminded himself of Dick's invincibility streak.

"Anyway, on the second visit, after finishing spouting 'Life of Terri' at me, she went on her lunch break and your friend Jean was watching the store. She speaks well of you. And I did have to tell her that I was on an investigation. No details. She was okay with it, but then I left pretty quickly. I never saw Lars Lundstrom, the store manager, and Jean told me that Boris is not there a lot, but that she assumes he does night work in the office and in the warehouse."

"She was right that Boris is not there a lot, but she was wrong about him working at night. I tailed him for a couple of days, and he mostly drives around and does some errands to the hardware store or the liquor store."

"He's on the cell phone all the time – at least it looks that way. Always talking in the car by himself, and looking down occasionally. Has an odd habit of always being on the brakes when he is looking down, as if that will save him when he runs into something dialing his phone. I'm guessing he is on Bluetooth all the time – either that or he has an imaginary friend he talks to in the car."

Dick played around with his hot tea while Jack spoke. Lapsang souchong tea. A musty, smoky, black oriental. Antonia called it shit-tea to memorialize the aroma, what she called "the odor." He may have been its only repeat consumer.

Jack went on, taking bites of his brunch between sentences.

"Well, I went to the farm, too."

"You mean Feckenmeyer's Mailbox?"

"What?"

"Feckenmeyer's Mailbox. The entrance to their road is near to where Feckenmeyer's Mailbox used to be. That town road up the far side of the hill? The upper half of that used to be Feckenmeyer's driveway. The farmhouse was where the llama ranch is now. This was a while back, of course, but the old timers still refer to that intersection as Feckenmeyer's Mailbox."

"Wow, the things you learn. I wonder if that's the return address on the Christmas cards."

"Ha ha. See if I give you any more valuable local history."

Jack finished his bacon, which he had saved for last.

"Well, they have quite a spread up there. The house is big, with a sort of mock Fallingwater effect. But it's no Prairie house, just a lot of windows and water features. Then there are several out-buildings, all quite new. Plus the cornfields behind the house. And across the road the corn takes both directions beside the back road that eventually goes down the hill toward town."

Dick was looking for more than a crop report.

"So did you talk to Wayne Nelson, the farm manager?"

"Well, he wasn't there either time. Neither was Trixie. It was nine in the morning each day I stopped, and the only person around was Boyd."

"Who's Boyd?"

"Jay Boyd IV, farm hand, handy man, pool boy. Lives in the efficiency over one of the garages at the farm. Long rap sheet for cocaine and marijuana. Disowned and disinherited from the Boyd's family and fortune."

"Boyd's fortune" Teddy bears?" asked Dick, sarcastically.

"No, you idiot. Boyd's footwear. Sweatshop athletic shoes."

"Sorry man, just a little humor for the day."

"Dick, kid all you want. Us independent contractors charge by the hour. I'm at work and I'm eating your food. Ca-ching. Ca-ching."

"Okay, okay, just don't want to overbill the client."

"Well anyway, this Boyd guy. He's a Fabio look-alike, with a long ponytail, prison-built shoulders, skinny legs, big steroid biceps. Smells of patchouli oil over a vaguely pharmaceutical odor."

"Jack, I know this guy. Always hits on Pearl Wisdom in the store, she holds up the back of her hand to him so he can see her rings, and she walks away."

"That's funny. Jean Paradise told me essentially the same story. I don't know how he's faring with Terri Moody, if at all. At the farm, he was very open with me. Talked a lot about the expensive buildings and home, and the new irrigation project. He said with the fields being on the top of the coulee, the wells would have to go four hundred feet for water. Boyd thinks the fireworks store is carrying the farm. Terri Moody thinks it's the other way around."

Dick knew the store itself was not part of Trixie's order for Truth is Strange Investigations. But maybe, he thought, it was becoming so.

"Jack, Jean came to see me, and she thinks something else is going on at Life's a Blast. She sees too much money coming in."

"Well, that's a new angle on things. I believe we have a complicated little set-up here."

"Spoken like a TV detective. Maybe even older, like a radio detective."

"Thanks for the support. 'But wait, there's more!' There's a soap opera angle. Both times when I took the back road to the farm, someone was driving out of the driveway, and really stared me down heavily. And each time, Boyd was standing in the dooryard. The someones were Melissa Schwartz one day, Anna Lundstrom the next."

Dick took a gulp of tea, and leaning over the cup inhaling the aroma, rolled his eyes upward to stare at Jack.

"They own the yoga studio together. Private lessons?"

Jack grinned and held the last scrap of bacon down by his feet. Jung's mouth was open in a smile and his tail was wagging gleefully.

FOURTEEN

···

Dick and Jack lingered over more tea and coffee, and Dick was thinking out loud,

"Melissa and Anna. They have the studio together, they make red wine together. And Melissa always comes on to me, especially after a few wines at gourmet club."

Dick did not realize that Kate had walked up behind him at the table, and was about to sit down. She stood, arms akimbo, frowning. She obviously heard the last of his words. Dick said, for her benefit,

"Dang it, Jack, why didn't you kick me? And you, Jung, where was my early warning?"

By this point the dog was stretching his front paws out on her shin, acting happy.

Kate had on a long, earth mother type dress complimenting her shoes. She collected herself from a blush and pulled out a chair.

"May I join you or is this all business?"

Dick smiled gently, as he felt Kate deserved, and said,

"Of course. We were just updating a case, but we've covered it all."

She gave him a "Yeah, right" smile and sat down.

Dick gazed at Kate, thinking that she wore the earth mother dress well. In fact, the best he could ever remember.

Kate lived in an apartment, actually two apartments opened into one, across Main Street from the Stranger complex. She was thrilled to be so close to the bookstore. She owned her building, and one of the two lower tenants was Melanna Yoga.

She gave Melissa and Anna credit for a mystical sounding name. The mystical effect was heightened by the fact that, ever since moving to Woodstock, Anna pronounced her name "Ahh-na," lending a metro flair and making the Yoga studio sound as if from afar.

In the bookstore new yoga students were always asking for a Melanna Yoga book, as if it existed as a famous yoga discipline.

Kate often sat near the large windows in her apartment facing the street, where she read, took in the passing days on the street, and occasionally played a game of Scrabble with herself on the card table she kept perpetually set up next to the largest window. She kept the game board on a lazy susan and simply rotated it for the turns.

Once in a while she had guests who joined her in the game, or challenged her at playing cards with one of the several decks she kept at hand on the card table.

The sight lines from Kate's apartment to Dick's loft did not quite line up, and Dick liked that, but Kate did not. He did not care to eavesdrop, a tendency curious in a private detective, but she did. Kate now fully understood Dick's intentions, or rather his specific lack thereof, after she had asked him out on a diner date some months earlier.

They had a corner table at The Florentine, a remarkably romantic Italian place, by local standards. They shared small talk, antipasti, and Chianti.

Dick engaged Kate with a game he liked to play in restaurants. He called it "The Restaurant Game," whimsically enough. The plot was to observe couples at other tables and imagine their conversations, the more outrageous the better. Determining the story, and then watching their body language as the story played out, was the fun.

"Now those two, I think he just told her about the other woman, but she already knew, and she's just hoping for new jewelry to fit those chubby fingers after she finishes those giant crab legs."

"Those two are married, and the girl across the booth is their housekeeper. The wife doesn't know the housekeeper is having an affair with the husband, or that the two of them are playing footsie under the table right now."

"This girl is being lied to about the success of his investments and what the real color of his hair is under the dye. If the hair is real, that is. Uh-oh, I think the hair just moved on its own."

"This couple hasn't said a word to each other. Is it a standoff or has it just gotten boring? Or is the FBI coming to his office tomorrow to help the SEC in its investigation?"

"This young lady is telling her parents that the older man at the table will soon be their son-in-law, and that he will not be going back to the merchant marine for several weeks now, and that his probation will be over next year. After all, the weapons charge was dropped."

Two bottles of Chianti into it, she suggested,

"Dick, shouldn't we do this more often? There is so much more to life than what we talk about at work. Maybe we could take a weekend road trip, I know someone with a B & B up in Egg Harbor."

"Kate, I'm just not there yet."

She was visibly deflated.

"But I do like spending time with you."

She was visibly inflated.

"So for the moment let's just do dinner now and then and catch up on things."

At least the wine left some color in her cheeks. This was almost like dating.

"So no nightcap at my place?"

"Sorry. Rain check?"

Kate had remained loyal to Dick and to Stranger Than Fiction. She was working a labor of love in the bookstore, and so far that had to be all. Maybe. She vowed continued pursuit of the prize.

Dick appreciated, maybe too compulsively, a handsome woman such as Kate. It was a mystery to all who knew him, why he was living alone with a Cairn Terrier.

Dick ordered cappuccino for Kate and refills for himself and Jack.

"Kate, Jack tells me that Terri Moody is still grinding her axe for us."

"What? A disgruntled former employee who is disgruntled? No threats?"

"Nothing solid. Yet," added Jack.

"She hasn't been in this building since the day she was dismissed."

"I know, Kate. I just wanted you to be on the lookout," Dick said protectively.

Professionally, Kate changed course.

"So Jack, how is the book buying going this week?"

"Two big estate lots. A few amazing finds. The rest you can decide. I'll have them all Tuesday."

Kate knew that a majority of these would go into the "Free Library" program. She was now completely on board with the plan. Those two years as a Library Science intern were finally doing some good.

In a matter of weeks, "Free Library" had become a regional phenomenon, the complex had steady free book traffic all day, and most stayed to read, write, shop, or sip. Book sales in the store increased, and even The Silent Muse had an up-tick, mostly wine and craft brewed beers. Was there a free lunch after all?

Jack headed out, and Dick and Kate spent the rest of the afternoon flipping through books, with Dick hearing the latest reviews on the new releases, and watching the people fill the store and café – book people, buyers and borrowers.

Jung slept with his head on Kate's foot.

FIFTEEN

....

. . . In tuxedo, Dick was performing at the Civic Center, warming up the crowd for a charity dance concert, in full EJ voice, well into "Tiny Dancer" . . .

"More hot water here?"

Dick's cloud funneled into nothingness as he pulled his gaze away from the café window.

" . . . um, sure. Thank you. No more lemon."

Apart from The Library, The Woodchuck was Dick's favorite breakfast and lunch place. They had the best of what was the defining café food for Dick: BLT's. The best anywhere. Lots of butter on the stone ground toast, mayo on the side, plenty of dripping bacon, thick slices of organic tomato.

Further, the homemade potato chips were real, fried to order, warm. Finally, they had the guts to feature, as their signature dish, "The Woodchuck

Burger," the composition of which was the subject of discussion for countless tourists and other first-timers.

The Woodchuck was on the ground floor of the old Masonic Lodge building. The second floor had been the Lodge, and it enjoyed the tall ceilings and plaster and walnut décor of its 1920's remodel. The long narrow stairwell was losing its appeal to the aging Masonic Lodge membership and, interestingly enough, for about the price of an elevator retrofit, the Lodge had built a brand-new one-level building adjacent to a retirement villa.

At the time of its last sale, Dick did not have real estate on his agenda, and he now realized that an opportunist could have sold all the inlaid paneling and fretwork and joinery for enough to pay for the whole building.

Fortunately, a preservationist bought the edifice, tuck-pointed the brick, and installed Myra's School of Dance in the old Lodge. Every Saturday morning you could enjoy The Woodchuck to the rhythmic clump-clump-clump, pad-pad-pad, stomp-stomp-stomp back and forth across the hardwood floor above, and consequently the dining room ceiling below.

Occasionally, the music piped into The Woodchuck matched the beat of the dancing steps above, and somehow the sympathetic vibrations could be felt deep inside one's breast. Experienced diners would silence their conversations, forks down, to drink in the vibe, as these were considered very special times.

Dick poured one last cup of tea from the inevitably dripping metal pot. Two cups worth, hinged lid with a goofy, sloppy hinge, always running tea water astray. What a design. Didn't they even try it? Dick was sure he could do better at a Swedish department store.

He paid the check directly to the server and walked back to the loft to retrieve Jung. When on foot, Dick usually used the front stairs so he could see what was going on at A Stranger Place. The creaking wooden stairs, the hollow steps on the terrazzo floor echoing through the wide and tall hallway, his key in the door. No barking. Not a sound.

I'd recognize those steps anywhere. Oh, it's just you. Thanks, Jung. Just lying around digesting breakfast, eh? It did look tempting.

The loft was a combination of modern Italian and clean Scandinavian, plus a touch of Bauhaus European. Bright colored area rugs stood out on the refinished maple floor, and lent traction to Jung's romps and laps throughout the loft. The dog delighted in making new racing lanes and agility chutes between chairs and tables, and in working counter-clockwise around the entire living space. Without Woodstock having dog parks, per se, this was his occasional playground.

Medium cherry was the wood of choice for furniture, and much had been purchased on Antonina's and Dick's travels together. It successfully made the transition from the bungalow.

The walnut door and window framing and various moldings had been refinished. The walls were painted in most areas, with no one dominant scheme. Dick had considered just numbering the walls and rotating through ROY.G.BIV, but his cooler mind prevailed. He was disappointed that the paint mixer at the hardware store did not appreciate the joke about the acronym for the colors of the spectrum. Not a science major, he guessed.

In the living space stood an ebony baby grand piano, his and Antonina's gift to each other for their tenth anniversary. She was the family pianist, a position to which Dick aspired and fantasized. The instrument was a Steinway, and was properly maintained with controlled humidity and temperature, both of which suited Dick anyway for the loft's climate. In their bungalow the piano had taken up the entire dining room, as that stood unused anyway. Dick and Antonina were the type to gather around the largest seating kitchen table possible.

The rest of loft was IKEA, Frank Lloyd Wright, and Danish Modern, plus a few historical items like Dick's mother's chrome Oster Beehive Blender. This sat on a small bar supply area. Included there was a small fridge full of Hamm's and Peroni, enough liquor for a few specialty drinks, and fixings for Sazerac Cocktails, of which a successful toss was one of Dick's triumphant life skills.

Bang and Olufsen audio filled the loft. A few half-walls delineated space in the overall area and gave Jung traffic barriers. None were more than chest high, some lower.

A large stone fireplace dominated the north wall, which itself was exposed brick. An efficient wood burning insert had been installed, and the only problem was the volume of wood that Dick had to carry up the stairs to keep up with his need for fire.

Dick was deeply involved in the loft rebuild, and although it had been hard to leave the bungalow, it was cleansing to design his new space.

SIXTEEN

Jung arose, stretched in classic down dog fashion, and stood ready for the day. Dick and the dog exited via the back stairs and headed into the garage. There, along with his MG, stood a 1993 Ford Probe GT, Calypso Green over Grey leather. Dick kept this car around as an everyday driver, and Jung knew the routine. Hop in the passenger door, go between the buckets to the back seat, and get into the soft kennel.

Dick wheeled into the car lot and cut the engine. Looking up to where the letters "CONOCO" had been, Dick smiled to himself reading "Miracle Motors," the name he had chosen long ago for the car venture. Period-looking letters made the new name fit right in.

Jung reversed procedure, hopped out Dick's side of the car, and ran to the front door, stopping to water a small pine on the way. As he pulled open the aluminum framed glass door, Dick looked at the "Sorry We're CLOSED" sign. It was one of those pasteboard office supply store items, red letters on white stock, with the reverse saying "Come In, We're OPEN." It hung on a string from door-mounted clear suction cup with a hook.

The "CLOSED" sign was looking faded and tattered. Almost that time again, thought Dick. With the effects of the morning sun on the cheap pasteboard, Dick was on his fourth sign. None had ever been flipped to "OPEN." Customers somehow thought they were entering a private enclave, an off hours club of sorts, an automotive speakeasy.

The same went for the "Not For Sale" signs he put in the cars before they were ready for the lot. At least half of the cars sold at this stage. Not for sale cars at a closed lot. Forbidden Fruit.

"Hey, boss!"

"Otis, good morning!"

Otis Graves stepped from the shop into the office, wiping his hands on a shop towel. Jung ran circles around him, swiped a dog biscuit from an outstretched palm, and headed for his window seat and pillow.

"Can't 'cha see we're closed?"

Otis loved to ask this of Dick, and he too enjoyed the idea of working at a retail establishment that was never open for business.

Otis wore a dark blue cotton lab coat, which either meant that a service customer was expected, or that an extra special vehicle was being protected. Under this, a creased pair of jeans, a light denim work shirt, and sensible shop boots. He smelled not of petroleum, but of the natural oils in men's toiletries. In fact, the shop itself hardly smelled like an auto repair shop at all.

Otis was in his early sixties, and in his high school days was probably called a greaser. The six foot frame was lanky, the hair still styled but now featuring salt and pepper. Poor Otis: hair oil had become gel; hair tonic had become product. Brown eyes and a big smile were Otis. Smoking was off limits on the grounds and in the shop, but Otis rolled his own for later use. Consumed with cars, he had never married.

When Dick decided to buy the station, Otis was working at a local franchised car dealership, and the two were spending some spare time restoring cars in a shed at Otis's ranch. They had embarked on their first retail job: a 1968 Ferrari 330 GTC was being restored from barn-find condition for a local ultralight aircraft inventor and manufacturer.

Eccentric but apparently quite successful, the inventor encountered money problems in his normally high profile local business when his product crashed. Literally. The well-known scion of a local plumbing family empire lost his life in the crash of one of the firm's ultralights. The manufacturer claimed pilot error, based on toxicology tests and a lack of fuel in the plane's tank. The jury said otherwise, and $4.5 million dollars in damages were awarded.

Unfortunately for the Ferrari owner / ultralight builder, after the court award his insurance certificate to the FAA was revealed to be a forgery, and it became apparent that he was self-insured and over-leveraged. Plans for appeal were cancelled.

By this time Dick and Otis were deeply into the Ferrari project, and payments had already dried up well before the ultralight crash. Thinking that the owner must share their mindless devotion to old vehicles, the boys had blindly soldiered on. Financially upside-down on the project, Dick and Otis finally called a meeting with the ultralight mogul to confront the situation.

With no contract, no work order, a few payments, and only a handshake or two, they recognized that possession of the car was their only defense. At this point the Feds had the car's owner suitably worn down, and he offered Dick and Otis the car in payment for the work.

Otis negotiated the inclusion of two ultralights from a warehouse that remained under cover from the Feds, and after overcoming the not small matter of the car still being titled in the previous owner's name, the account was settled.

Dick and Otis appraised the car as-is, added their costs of material and labor thus far, and Dick bought out Otis's half for cash. Then, on the condition that Otis got to keep both ultralights, they finished the project together.

In turn, Dick offered to put up the money for the station and he and Otis would own Miracle Motors together. Otis would quit the dealership and be on site doing what he loved, fixing cars, and occasionally selling one for the team. Dick would get a rent check, keep no schedule, buy and finance the inventory, and sell cars. At the end of each month they would split the profit. Everyone was happy; Dick had the Ferrari.

"Yah der. When you ever gonna open the place up, yah den?" said Dick, feigning his finest Upper Peninsula Michigan, or The U.P., Yooper accent.

"How about 'Later.' Hey, I thought about making a sign that says 'Open Tomorrow' to put up permanently by the 'CLOSED' sign. Kinda like the tavern sign 'Free Beer Tomorrow.'"

In truth, the State DMV had given them some static about not having business hours posted, per Wisconsin law. They posted a schedule to approximate Otis's work week. The DMV never did admit to appreciating the humor in the "CLOSED" sign.

"So what's going on today?"

"Got the fireworks cars today. One of Boris's BMW's and Lundstrom's Volvo."

Otis's skills included an intuitive ability to diagnose cars engineered abroad. Dick always thought that this had to do more with how Otis was wired than how the cars were wired. He could instinctively duplicate the thought processes that went into complex machinery.

Mechanical aptitude was a given for Otis. He was known in his youth for the ability to drop a Chevy transmission in record time, on the street.

He and his hot rodding buddies always tore them up, and he was the fixer.

Dick first met Otis when Dick's Pontiac Fiero V6 caught fire. Beyond warranty help, the local GM dealer termed this as a "thermal incident," and sent him on his way. Otis ran a moonlight garage and knew how to fix these essentially great driving and handling cars.

And thus here they were today.

"So Otis, what's the Focus doing over by the sidewalk?"

"Oh, come on Dick, give it a rest."

"Hey, just checking."

Dick knew that every day Otis pulled a car over by the sidewalk for the school crossing guard to rest his butt on the fender, doing his little part for humanity.

" . . . So what else is going on?"

"I just got an earful from Marian about Kate's Free Books deal."

"I wondered when that would start. And it's not just Kate's idea, you know."

"Well, she thinks Kate is trying to kill the Public Library. She was in such a lather she forgot to bring me any muffins or cookies."

Marian. Marian Horton, Head Librarian at the Woodstock Free Public Library. Drew quite a crowd each year for her annual story-time reading, in character and costume, of "Horton Hears a Who." She managed the city-owned library, a prairie style beauty funded by Andrew Carnegie during the library boom. Tastefully restored and brought up to date mechanically, it was a jewel in town, and was situated right across Main Street from the car lot.

Marian had the hots for Otis.

She was a very well kept mid-fifties, a ten year widow, prone to long denim jumpers over long sleeved turtlenecks, and sensible library shoes. Good looking and trim, her kids were long grown and she was alone among the many couples that made up her social circle. Her hair was short and layered, and was no longer grayish. To the observer, she was a wardrobe makeover away from the best of her vintage. And as usual, Dick was the observer.

Marian had first noticed Otis in the midst of the Community Work Days during the Library renovation about three years ago. He was a Library regular, always checking out science and physics texts, and requesting obscure journals on engines, propulsion, and flying.

She recognized his interests right away, but observing him investing literal sweat equity in the Library had set other thoughts in motion. With her card catalogue shuffled after all these years, she was a little perplexed with how to sort out her emotions for him.

The Librarian had started getting her car serviced more frequently, even though she walked to work, and she stopped by often to ask car care questions. Then the cookies and muffins began. And continued.

Marian and Otis seemed like two old-timers at the chessboard in the park. Both knew the game but neither was sure of a good first move.

Today was Otis's first peek at Marian's resolve. She was defending her Library against a non-alien, but enemy, threat.

"Otis, I feel bad about your treats. Want me to send Jung up to the bakery with some petty cash?" Dick offered.

"Hey man, she's a great cook. Muffins, at least."

"Any permanent harm?"

"No, but I've never seen her so feisty. I wonder if she was a student radical in her day?"

"A little young, if you ask me. Missed the sixties."

"Anyway, said she'd like to meet up in a dark alley with, quoting now, 'That fake flower child with the red hair.'"

"Wow. Maybe I should talk to Kate about a peace offering. Maybe we could include Woodstock Public Library bookmarks along with our own or something. We'll brainstorm it."

"I'd avoid her today."

"Agreed, but I thought a side effect of our deal was people understanding how a real library works."

"Maybe, but I think she's been miffed ever since you named the café The Library."

"And I suppose she forgot the ten grand I gave as a charter member of the capital campaign for the renovation. What were we called – the Dewey Society, or something like that."

"Oooo . . . all part of your sinister plot to weasel in with your own library."

"Thanks for the support, Otis."

"Sure. And, oh yeah, Dick. I'm quitting smoking. First day."

SEVENTEEN

....

Dick puttered away at some paperwork at the lot, Jung snoozed in the sun, and Otis performed the BMW and Volvo maintenance, informing the owners and moving on to some other jobs. Dick talked to a couple of car customers who thought the place was closed.

About eleven-thirty a big Ford Diesel Dually pulled to the curb out front, with Boris at the wheel. Out bailed Kidd O'Connor and Ian Jackson, two young truck drivers who worked for Boris hauling fireworks, grain, farm machinery, and anything else needed. Obviously they were there to pick up the cars.

Ian Jackson was first through the door,

"Hey, Mister Stranger, whas' goin' on?"

Kidd O'Connor was next,

"Fuck you."

Dick did not flinch, smiling,

"Hello Ian. Hello Kidd. Nice to see you."

You too," from Ian. A glare from Kidd.

They were both about twenty-three, and fancied themselves to be hot shots. Growing up together in Woodstock, the two competed on everything, yet remained best friends. Productively, they raced go-karts, and eventually graduated up through the more challenging steps available at the local speedway. Both had great talent, and with the right backing, they had the potential to move up to ASA and ARCA, then to NASCAR.

This is where Miracle Motors came in. Dick and Otis had once dreamed of being racing drivers themselves, and in fact Otis was an accomplished drag racer. Dick had acquired a skill for fast driving and maneuvers as a hobby on the highway.

Sponsorship was their way to participate at their age, and they always found a couple of promising drivers to help out. This was one of the few ways that Miracle Motors advertised. The speedway was a nice half-mile set-up, very official, about 30 minutes away. Classes included the four-cylinder entry level all the way up to the NASCAR feeder series on occasion. Demo derbies, and school bus and camper and trailer races fueled the racing flame for true amateurs.

Ian and Kidd and their cars formed the current Miracle Motors stable. Otis helped some with the chassis set-ups and engine work, and Dick wrote some checks. But last weekend Kidd's proudly professed Irish temperament got the best of him.

Dick was taking Jung for an early Sunday morning stroll up Main Street, when he noticed a car hauler across the street from the Sand Bar. There was no mistaking the car hauler for anyone's but Ian and Kidd's. It was an old GMC regular cab, a former Schwann's Ice Cream delivery truck, which had the frame extended and a rollback body added. It was still the signature Schwann's medium yellow color.

But this morning, at six AM, someone sat in the driver's seat of the Monte Carlo on the top of the hauler. Kidd O'Connor, passed out in the race car, suffering the after effects of a large evening and a losing bar fight. Giant white letters spelling out "Miracle Motors" covered the side of the dark blue car.

Dick hooked Jung's leash over a parking meter, climbed up the hauler, slapped Kidd awake and fired him on the spot. He called Ian on the cell and told him to get this hauler off Main Street before any more of the early restaurant and church crowd could see it. And he didn't think Kidd was sober enough to drive the hauler.

This must have been the fifth time Dick had to confront Kidd about issues related to benders, fights, and representing Miracle Motors as a paid driver.

Finally, he told Kidd to peel those vinyl letters off the side of the car. It was over.

Today Dick left the conversation stand as it was, and he watched the two cars leave the lot, Kidd at the wheel of the BMW, burning the tires as he pulled away. It was too bad. Kidd was the more talented of the two, but Dick simply had enough of him.

"Otis, I see Kidd still isn't taking the discharge too well."

"Man, that's for sure. He said old man Stranger better watch his back."

"The well-chosen words of a man just sobering up."

"Four days later? Maybe so, but I still don't like his temper."

EIGHTEEN

....

. . . Dick was in the front corner of The Crow-bar, sitting at the old upright, holding court for the Friday night crowd. With one hundred patrons, at ten PM the place was packed. The owner had just walked in, having pulled up out front in his white and black Nash Metropolitan, each side adorned with an oversize crow depicted in full formal rega-lia: top hat, tails, monocle. Dick wrapped up "How Sweet It Is" and launched into "Rock The Boat" with the crowd cheering . . .

Dick stirred slightly as Jung barked excitedly. Swinging his legs down off the desk, Dick yawned and came around. Into the station walked Jack. Jung wagged around and let out a few happy yelps.

"Dick, my man, you looked to be in dreamland."

"Favorite spot."

"Got time for an update?"

"Always time for you, Jack. What's up in the world of home explosives?"

"Well, I've gotta start with a coffee. Mind if I help myself?"

Jack already was an espresso insider, and he made a coffee for himself, and one to help jolt Dick awake.

"Well, I saw Jean again and told her that the information she had for you would help us both with an investigation. No disclosure of the client but she looked fairly knowing. It seems she is a more observant bookkeeper than we thought. She said she had lots more to tell you. Her eyes were pretty big."

"Sounds like I need to talk to her. I need to see the store up close anyway. How about Feckenmeyer's Mailbox?"

"Well, still no Wayne or Boris. Jay is always the welcoming committee. And I saw Melissa sneaking her return to town on the back road again. She really gave me the look."

"Anything new or obvious?"

"Well, I'll find another time of day to wander around those buildings by myself, I guess. I was hoping Jay was in the fields so I could look around a bit. But he's right there when I pull into the yard."

"Like a guard?"

"More like someone who doesn't want a private snoop around."

"Anything else?"

"Well, no, but the Melissa and Anna visits are already on café.com."

Café.com was the small restaurant rumor mill, perpetuated by a group of older guys who met downtown for coffee at one place, breakfast at another, then pie and coffee later at yet another. With them, rumors never truly died.

Stories on café.com worked like sourdough starter. If nothing juicy turned up for a few days, they just scraped up little of the last story and let it grow into a new one. Just a good way to keep the live gossip going.

"Of course, new Top 10."

"Yeah, everybody seems to be talking about it except the two of them. Trixie must know about it.

I have to tail her some morning and see where she goes."

"Jack, I'll take care of following Trixie. If she spots me it's easy to say I'm trying to find her to update her on the case. I need to research Boris and Wayne a little more, and see what Jean has. I hate it when I always have to do something on a case."

"Right. Well, that's all I have."

"You know, Jack, I wonder about Boris. With real estate showing its current, ah . . . malaise . . . his developments are stalled, I'm curious about how he keeps the whole show on the road. The new store, the projects at the farm. Maybe Jean's on to something with the cash. He could have something funny going on somewhere."

"And that makes it a little dangerous if we get too close. After all, this is just a private investigation, not a criminal investigation."

"But the client is paying us to find out. So we'll keep on it. What else is on your mind?"

"Well, in the interest of keeping my day job, I have to make a couple of book runs. I've got a line on a couple of home downsizings. Those are a lot better than when the heirs get their hands on the books and suddenly become rare book experts from the Internet. One of the lots has a bunch of good titles, and if I can make a deal, I need to get the books out of there right away. Mind if I ask Otis to come along?"

"Not at all. I know you'll issue me credit on your bill for his time."

"Well, yeah. As always. Where is the dear boy?"

"Look north."

As Jack took the count of three to read his internal compass, Otis appeared in the shop doorway,

"Hey Bluhm. Look alive. Jeez, another cup of coffee? Doesn't anybody work anymore?"

"Otis. Join us for a hot one."

Jack and Otis were good drinking buddies, and knew enough not to combine that with their ultralight adventures. Otis's ranch had a nice grass runway cut into the back forty, and it was perfect for the little aircraft.

The two had become friends years ago when Jack was nursing an old Fiat through a few years of ownership, frequent repairs, and occasional drives. Otis was a pro with these cars, and had ended up with Dick's 850 model when Dick upgraded to a 124 Spyder.

Otis had accompanied Jack on these book runs before, and always brought a truck from the lot. He thought Dick should just buy a cube van for all the stores to share. He did not realize that Dick needed one too, for the wine pickups, but that Dick preferred the anonymity of renting.

Otis returned with a double espresso, and Jack easily persuaded him to join the book trip. After some normal heckling among the three of them, and another cup of coffee, Jack was restless to hit the road – books beckoned, "Jack . . . Jack . . . Jack . . . buyyyy meee . . . "

"Well, Otis, ready to go?"

"May as well. Can't dance and it's too cold to plow."

NINETEEN

Dick looked at the paperwork on the desk at Miracle Motors, stuffed it into a drawer, and summoned Jung from a sun-soaked nap.

"Okay, buddy, let's hit the road. We're off to talk to some of the big guys."

Jung hopped off the pillow and stretched, then sat staring at Dick, tilting his head first far to the right, then far to the left, wondering who these new people would be.

They locked the lot, zipped back to the loft, and got set for an afternoon as investigators. Nature breaks, a few little household details, and a pocketful of dog biscuits. They headed back down the stairs to the garage.

Always a snappy dresser, Dick sometimes looked like he worked too hard at it. Now he wore sharply ironed stone washed denim jeans, a thick yellow cotton work shirt over a white high-necked t-shirt, European walking shoes, a baseball cap with

a golf logo, and a pair of classic Balorama sunglasses. Jung wore a pattered red bandana to compli-
ment his Indian-weave collar.

"Whattaya think, Jung, nice enough out for the
MG?"

Jung wagged his tail in vigorous assent. The
MG was a favorite ride. Low doorsills meant easy
access to the wind.

Dick coaxed the old rig to life with a deft combination of choke and spark. Someday he would
rebuild the twin carbs. Typical of the breed, the car
ran great but undependably, as the old carbs were
gummy. Dick always knew when the float was
sinking in the forward carb, as Jung would pull his
nose out of the wind and step over to poke at his
master's ribs.

This meant raw fuel was spraying back in the
wind through the hood louvers on the passenger
side.

A screech to the side of the road, idle wildly
fluctuating up and down, a run around to hit the
afflicted carb with a small hammer to unstick the
float, and they would be on their way. This special
service tool, a small ball-peen hammer, was kept
under the seat.

Off they roared to the South End of town where stood Life's A Blast. The building occupied a typically unusable corner of the Interstate highway exit, but signage that would make Lady Bird Johnson roll over in her grave invited one and all to "The Best Fireworks in Wisconsin."

Boris owned this area of property on the slow traffic South End, having bought it at a tax auction. Soon after, the intersection was deemed important by the DOT, exit and entrance ramps appeared, and suddenly Boris's property was choice. Fast food joints vied for a piece; a franchised motel sprang up. Boris built on what turned out to be the poorest spot, but by this time the land was paid for many times over.

The MG rolled onto the blacktop, and with a precautionary hand on the emergency brake, Dick steered into a stall delineated by freshly painted yellow lines. Dick snapped a small reflective lime green "Service Dog" vest onto Jung, and they walked into the store.

Terri Moody turned to them, and realizing Dick's identity, cooled into a glare.

Unspoken, "Hey, girl, you're the one who stole the books and the reader, not me" ran through Dick's mind.

"Hi, Terri. Looks quiet today. We're just going to browse a little."

"Go ahead. But you can't have that animal in here."

"He's a Service Dog."

"Service dog? Right. What does he do?"

Jung stood stock still, mouth closed, staring at her.

"Right now he's serving you by preventing you from being prosecuted for retail theft."

Terri Moody wheeled on her heel and clicked on a mini-TV on the back counter. It looked as if a Jerry Springer rerun, complete with flying chairs, was a more enlightening experience than visiting with Dick and his Service Dog.

Dick wandered up and down the aisles. It was set up with low displays so the store clerk could always keep track of you. Bubble mirrors graced the corners and the ends of each row.

"2 for 1 Everything!" screamed the day-glow letters on black backgrounds, echoing the giant letters atop the roof of the warehouse. Dick pondered the long-term effects on one's "brand" by admitting that everything was 100% overpriced to begin with.

Terri remained focused on the television while Dick discreetly took a few photos of the place with his iPhone. Then, a move to the next level.

"Terri, can I see the boss for a few minutes?"

Slowly turning her head, then raising her eyes in a "don't bother me" way,

"Which one?"

"I'll take whoever is here."

"Let me check, sir," she coolly replied with snide officiousness.

Terri turned and faced the wall as she punched two digits on the overly complex and expensive office phone system.

Dick speculated on the merits of a phone capable of thirty extensions, eight lines, and three receptionists, in this particular canyon.

Terri whispered a short conversation, still facing the wall. Dick watched in a corner mirror and lip-read most of it. She banged down the phone, rotated her head like Linda Blair in The Exorcist, and told him,

"Mr. Lundstrom is here. Double doors, take a left, name on the door."

Dick thanked her and Jung glared as he trotted past. Entering the office area revealed a cheaply finished row of rooms with white sheetrock and faux oak plastic doors. The corner office was Lundstrom's, and with a short knock Dick pushed into the room. Lundstrom had cleared the center of the desk into two gigantic towers of paper, ready to slip over.

"What the hell! Get that animal out of here!"

"Mr. Lundstrom, he's a Service Dog."

Jung stood proudly, head held high, eyes on Lundstrom, motionless. Lundstrom lost the stare-down.

"Need to see his permit?"

"No, dammit. Damn liberals. Everybody's special. I suppose he gets a government check, too."

"Strictly voluntary. But a great idea, sir."

"Lars Lundstrom. Who are you and whattaya want?"

"Dick Stranger. Pleased to meet you. May I call you Lars, Lars?"

"Okay, get on with it, can't you see I'm busy here?"

"Very, sir. Very busy, Lars."

Dick's phone lay on the corner of Lars's desk, recording. Dick found numerous benefits to this practice.

Lars Lundstrom was short and heavy, with chin and jowl rolls. His hair was blond, slicked back with oil, his eyes were a piercing blue, and gold jewelry hung at his neck and wrists and around three fingers, all over very pink skin. He appeared wide-eyed, with an open visage, no facial hair, and ears that stuck out. A Roman nose, formerly broken, interrupted the look. Lundstrom was a Swedish name, but Lars did not have the build of the typical Scandinavian.

He wore black cuffed slacks with pleats, undoubtedly crafted from a stretch fabric. Over this was a casual white short-sleeved shirt with embroidery, pleats on the chest, a large open collar, and a squared hem meant to be worn un-tucked, possibly to disguise some girth. Finishing the ensemble were black tasseled loafers of Italian design, the kind with a very small woven toe, and thin sole, looking like and undoubtedly feeling like slippers. He smelled of Brut and looked like he had just answered the call to dinner on a cruise ship.

"Stranger. Are you a private dick?"

"Yes, Lars, but right now I'm doing some free-lance writing for the newspaper. The story is how professional the retail fireworks industry has become, and how a number of key players have raised the bar."

Lars preened in a small mirror on his desk.

"Ultimately, Lars, we'd like to see a lot of this merchandise legalized in Woodstock, and beyond. The Mayor is just sick that you can't toss a cherry bomb or M-80 on the Fourth of July anymore. Same with the Chamber Board. If we get the right wire to pick up this story, it could be a statewide movement."

"Why us?"

"Lars, it says right outside, 'Best Fireworks in Wisconsin'."

Lars took the bait and ran like salmon headed upstream to spawn. He could think of nothing but more fireworks orders. He showed Dick the store-room in the retail building, which did not hold much more than one of those tents that pops up on the lawn of the fast food restaurants at the summer holidays. The building itself was little more than a pole shed, and the storeroom was primitive except for ground wires attached to every shelf unit, lots of "Danger" and "No Smoking" signs, spark-resistant entry mats, and a few large fire extinguishers.

The prize tour was of the warehouse. A matching pole shed on the outside, the building was spotless and sophisticated inside. All the safety equipment was present, including sprinklers and high tech fire suppression fixtures. A laboratory room took up a good quarter of the space, and Lars said it was for designing and developing their own fireworks. Licensing was not profitable, as the Far East immediately reverse-engineered the designs.

Lars did say that he and Boris had a source in Mexico now that produced most of their fireworks, and that protected their designs. Dick suspected that bribes siphoned off a lot of royalties, but Lars stated that licensing to other vendors last year had netted $25,000 on the "Flying Taco Explosion" alone.

While the storeroom had only a small pad at the garage door for deliveries, Dick was fascinated by the huge, tall garage doors on the non-street end of the warehouse building. The doors were pneumatic, with the compressors outside in secure enclosures. A simple three-valve system disabled the doors by shutting off the air supply in two directions, and bleeding it off in the middle. Then an industrial sized deadbolt locked the door in addition to the air pressure. Anything to keep the electric motors and other spark creating devices out of the gunpowder.

Dick noted the considerable amounts of inventory, all bar-coded and ready to sell. A few pallets of assorted colorful packages sat in the lab. A pair of vault doors stood at the end of the lab, electronic combination locks blinking away.

A pair of offices and an employee break room completed the set-up, accessed through a special neutral spark zone. Passing Boris Shiraz's office, Dick spotted Jean Paradise, and as her eyes brightened he managed to hold his index finger up to his lips. Jung's tail suddenly went crazy as he strained at the retractable leash. Jean put her hand over her mouth and stifled a giggle as she looked down at the "Service Dog" vest, size extra small.

Lars didn't slow down.

"Oh yeah. Jean Paradise, the bookkeeper."

The tour was over, and as they walked out via the warehouse exit, a buzzer started to signal like a truck's backup alarm. Suddenly one of the big overhead doors opened and an eighteen foot cube van backed into the area. No identification, just white with the necessary DOT numbers, "Not For Hire," and the name "BS Holding" in small letters near the bottom edge of the box.

Dick knew when enough was enough, and saying his goodbyes, he and Jung worked their way out to the front door, bidding Terri Moody adieu on the way. Wordlessly, she stood with arms folded and rolled her eyes. Must be a station break, thought Dick. Jung hurried out the door and peed on the plastic flowers lining the front walkway.

TWENTY

....

Jung sat back in the passenger seat of the MG and stared at the building as he and Dick rumbled away. Dick had his eye on a short row of used trucks and SUV's with "For Sale by Owner" signs in the windows. He looked back over to Jung, and they headed to Feckenmeyer's Mailbox.

Turning off the state highway onto a county trunk road, Dick saw Anna Lundstrom zip by, heading back to town. She fixed her eyes on Dick as they passed. Much later than Jack would have predicted.

Moments later, a late model BMW 7-Series rushed up behind the MG and whooshed past, Boris Shiraz at the wheel. Dick followed at a distance, as the MG was no competition for the big BMW. He and Jung pulled into the driveway behind the BMW parked in front of a stall at the garage attached to the house. Jay Boyd was nowhere to be seen.

Dick hopped out to greet Boris, and Jung stayed in the car, as a small pack of herding dogs raced out of the oldest barn, one after the other like cannon shots, or perhaps more appropriately like fireworks mortars. Barking away, the dogs crowded around the side of the MG, gauging the worthiness of the visitors. Glancing up at Dick, Jung took refuge on the floor boards of the passenger side.

Dick took off his sunglasses and greeted Boris,

"Boris, great to see you."

"Hi, Dick, what brings you way out here? Nice car, by the way."

"I just came from a stop at Life's A Blast, and I thought I would take in all your far flung holdings today – or maybe I just came for coffee."

"Might just as soon. Come on in."

The two of them went in through the garage, and Dick ran his gaze over the five vehicles in the main area. Dick had supplied three of the five, including a plum-colored Hummer with a wheel and tire package. This unit had to include a like-new diamond necklace, as long as BS Holdings was writing the check. He had been to the house numerous times for gourmet club, as Boris and Trixie were first string subs, and there always seemed to be an absent couple for them to represent.

Boris was late fifties, about five ten, and had maintained a training regimen to preserve the shape he had sculpted as a young body builder in Poland: trim, broad shouldered, small waist with a flat stomach, and muscular arms. Handsome in a European way, his skin was darker than a typical Pole, and the tan looked original. Topped with black hair that was too black, he had green eyes, and a European nose that turned left from an old break. What's with these guys and their noses, Dick thought.

He wore clean blue jeans, a white dress shirt with sleeves rolled up to display those arms, a black leather belt with a silver oversized Western buckle, and black cowboy boots with no ornamentation. His voice still carried a pronounced accent, though his English was excellent, and he spoke in the pace of a salesman's patter.

Entering the house through the kitchen, Boris nodded to Trixie and Dick greeted her promptly,

"Trixie, good late morning. Boris dragged me all the way out here just for your fine coffee."

"Whenever I see you two together, it usually means some vehicle will appear in the garage in the next few days."

"Sorry, Trixie. No Bentley Continental for you this time, just a social visit. Your new irrigation project is the talk of the town. I had to see for myself, so I drove on out. Hope it's okay."

Boris spoke up as Trixie continued kitchen activities. Dick couldn't help but notice her putting a large box of Trix into the pantry.

"Dick, I'd be happy to show you the project. Take your coffee in a go-cup."

Boris was already on his way out the door. Dick caught up in few yards and they walked past two long machine shed type buildings toward a grassy area adjoining the back forty. There, hidden from view were five big dually trucks from an irrigation firm, complete with overhead racks full of pipe. In the distance men in light green uniforms swarmed in groups of four around pump installations, wrestling with pipe and large square panels.

"This is the latest technology. The pumps are electric with solar panels. Diesel backup. Outfit is from Chicago, best in the U.S. market. This corn is really gonna pop this year. We're using special hybrids to make best use of the moisture. If the next ethanol bill passes, we'll really cash in. It'll be another bonus."

Dick looked over at the trucks. Rain and Sun Irrigation, Chicago, IL. Magnetic signs. Just like the itinerant blacktop sealer and whitewash guys.

"So when will it be on line?"

"This is the fifth week. You can see, we already have a good crop going even without the extra irrigation."

"How did you find these guys?"

"Oh, I knew the owner. We go way back."

"Makes sense. Trust the people you know. So is Wayne the hands-on guy on the project?"

"Yeah, Wayne and Jay. I'm glad they know what they're doing. I'm swamped at the store all the time."

"Hey, I was out there shopping earlier this morning. I met Lars and he showed me around. He seems pretty capable."

"He's been a godsend. Knows the business and the import part of it."

"So what's left for you to do – surf the Net, do your Tweets?"

"Uh huh. I do all the incoming inspections and quality control. With these fireworks makers it's 'Trust but Verify'."

They walked back past the sheds. Dick was curious. There was no way this size farm needed this much space under roof. Boris didn't have a dairy operation. Maybe it was all boats and RV's and ATV's and such.

"So Boris, what about visitors. If this is the first around, and it works, you'll have tons of people wanting to see it. The media will go crazy."

"It'll work just fine. But no visitors, no photos, no press. I paid for a lot of the engineering on this, and I don't want people stealing my ideas."

"Can't people just drive up and look?"

"Not with an eight foot blocking fence around the irrigated property – deer fence, actually. The irrigation guys install it. Next thing happening. Oh -- and Dick, sometime let's get together and talk about that wine thing you've got over in Italy. Some guys are replacing corn and soybeans with grapes. They say Wisconsin is great for the grapes."

"Anytime, Boris. Thanks for the tour."

"Can't you just picture a winery outlet on that lot by Life's A Blast? Shiraz by Shiraz, 2 for 1 on everything!"

Great, thought Dick. America's two great passions side by side. Alcohol and explosives, all two for one.

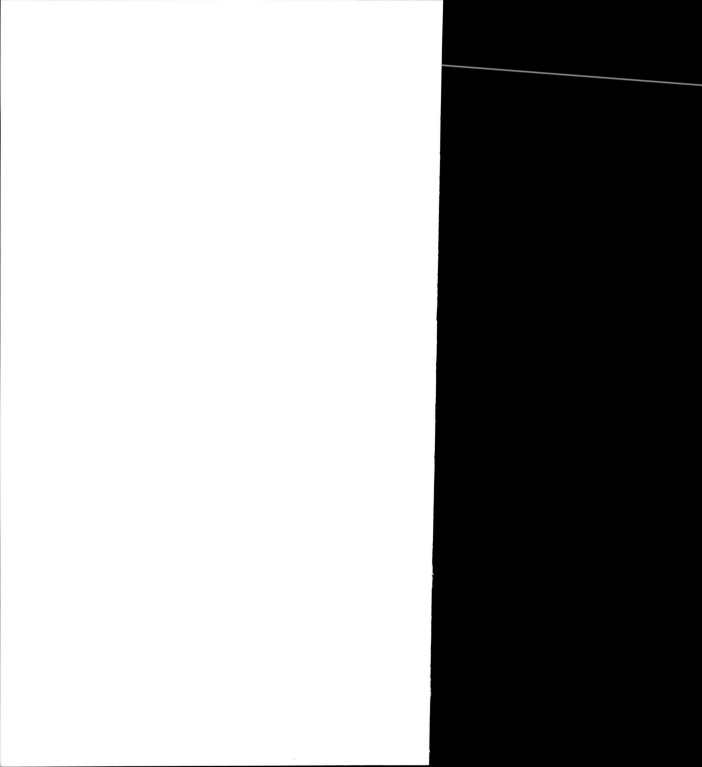

TWENTY-ONE

....

. . . Dick and the woman sat side by side on the piano bench, with Dick singing and gamboling through Private Eyes on the Steinway. On a small table nearby sat a bottle of red wine with two crystal wine glasses. It was a special occasion . . .

Dick's legs slipped off the edge of the desk, and his right foot, then left, slapped the old wooden floor like two Lake Michigan trout hitting the deck on an early morning fishing charter. The sound and the fury of the two feet woke Dick. Creaking the vintage wooden swivel-tilt desk chair to a level position, he took a few deep breaths and came to life.

The old dentist's office was facing Main Street, just on the left as you traversed the wide upper hall to Dick's apartment. It was a time capsule of 1950's dentistry. The former tenant, Dr. Milton Weebles, originally had a financial interest in the building, and after his retirement in 1964 the old family dentist had faithfully come to the office every weekday to open his mail and drink coffee. This routine lasted until his death in 1989. The heirs bailed out as soon as the estate settled, and they did not even check to see what was left in the old man's office.

Dick assumed that after a few years, the only mail was personal, and that the office just became a private coffee shop for old Dr. Weebles. When Dick bought the building, the office still had 1964 magazines on the tables, the dental chairs in the two operatories stood locked in time, with mechanical tools hanging on vintage cables, and the whole place smelled of El-Cre-Sol, the old dental cauterizing agent, plus an overlay of oil soap. Dr. Weebles apparently had his cleaning service continue to keep the place in museum condition.

The décor was consistent with the rest of the upstairs. Walnut, white plaster, terrazzo tile entry coming in from the hall, hardwood strip floors, classic furniture. With the exception of adding some cat-5 cable for a desktop and a Wi-Fi router for the laptop, and some electrical safety issues,

Dick left the suite untouched. Right down to the magazines. He felt that leaving it all intact was just a smart investment.

This was Truth is Strange Investigations' real office, but Dick had the loft set up as a home office for tax purposes. He always kept a mess of Truth is Strange paperwork in a folder on top of the desk in the loft just in case of an undercover visit by the IRS.

Peace and quiet and no visitors were the order of the day in Dr. Weebles' office; no one knew about it except Dick, and it was where the real investigative office work happened. A few employees and friends had asked, but he claimed it now was just a storeroom.

Dick mused about the case of the hit-and-run, and about the start of Truth is Strange. A quick credit card trace, a couple of personal visits, and the buddy coughed up the name of the Bravada driver. Alex Wisdom. Kenny and Pearl's nephew.

At that point, name in hand, Dick went to the parking lot of the muffler plant and looked for a Bravada cobbled up to look like a small Blazer. There it was. Alex hadn't been tipped off by the snitch. Another $100 well spent. To the untrained eye, it looked like Alex Wisdom had traded in his Pewter Bravada for a Pewter Blazer. To the trained eye it was an obvious hermaphrodite. Dick scanned the VIN into his phone and ran the VIN explosion app. Bravada it is. He took several photos and hit the road back to the office.

"Chief Schwartz here, can I hep' ya?"

"Chief, it's Dick Stranger. I have the name of the guy who hit my wife."

"Oh yeah?"

"Yeah."

"Well, sorry Dick, but that's impossible, my guys haven't even finished the skid mark research yet."

"Exactly."

"Look smart ass, what are you trying to prove?"

"That my wife was hit by a Pewter Bravada, and that there was evidence recovered at the scene."

"Look Dick, I feel bad you lost Antonina, but let it go. Let us do our job."

"I didn't say you weren't. But I found the driver."

"Look Dick, off the record. We know each other well enough. Let's say you did, and let's say you're right. It makes my guys look bad."

"That's not my point. I wanted to find out who killed Antonina. Spin it any way you want."

"Interfering with an Official Law Enforcement investigation. Hey, and are you a licensed dick?"

"If you mean Private Investigator, not yet."

"Operating without an investigator's license. That whole thing could be bad for you, Dick."

"And then for you. Take your choice. Want the info or not?"

"Look, Dick . . . well, okay, I guess we should see if there's anything to what you've got. Come see me in an hour."

Dick walked into the Justice Center, and waved to Ofc. P. Justus, who put his hand on the Glock when they exchanged looks.

Dick proceeded through security and revealed all the details to Schwartz. The Chief's animosity about being one-upped did not subside, yet Dick worked through the story. They parted ways with the Chief's promise of an effective investigation, and Dick's promise to stay in the background.

Eventually, the evidence was examined, statements were sworn, and Alex Wisdom was arrested. The hit and run had occurred after an all-night drinking and poker party in the dairy barn of a prominent farm family south of town.

Expensive lawyers were hired, verbal shields were raised, and the case nearly went to trial. Dick's evidence was accused of being fabricated, his actions accused of being vengeful, and he was threatened with questionable charges of practicing private investigation without a license.

On the flip side, on the day of accident Alex Wisdom rashly had driven to work at the muffler plant after the hit and run. There he was sent home for looking and smelling blitzed. He drove home. Finally, he pled guilty to several charges, including involuntary manslaughter. Alex Wisdom got ten years' probation and had to visit the grave once a year with his therapist.

Dick got his private investigator's license.

Kenny and Pearl Wisdom were crushed, as were Kenny's brother and wife, Alex's parents.

Dick knew Kenny and Pearl already, as they were very involved in civic events in the community. Dick had worked side by side with them selling brats or beer or tickets, planting trees, mending and painting fences, rallying committees to make events successful.

At Antonina's funeral visitation, not knowing of their nephew's involvement, Kenny and Pearl had stuck by Dick's side and helped him through the long days thereafter.

These kindnesses formed the start of an enduring friendship that would result in the couple working for Dick at the café and liquor store.

Dick shook off the mantle of Antonina's story, and focused on his desk. Back to reality. There was a paying case to work on. In his laptop were notes from the last few days of Jack and Dick nosing around.

Loose ends were piling up, and suddenly one of the looser ones popped up on his phone: call from . . . Anna Lundstrom.

TWENTY-TWO

....

"Dick Stranger."

"Dick, it's Anna Lundstrom. I need to see you right away."

"What do you need?"

"I just need to see you. Where can we meet."

"Come over to my office. About an hour."

"Okay."

With a beep the line went dead. Dick made a few notes, and left his office for the office.

Dick greeted the elated Jung and popped him a treat. Anything for a treat. Anything. Dick cooked them up himself, in sheet pans, and cut them into tiny pieces. Jung's favorite.

Water was added to the espresso maker, a few magazines picked up, and Dick settled into a teak and green leather chair by the window. He thought about Anna and her situation. Married to Lars. Partner with Melissa in the yoga studio. Alleged paramour to Jay Boyd.   Debtor to Dick Stranger.

Through the open transom Dick heard Anna squeegeeing across the polished hall floor.   Yoga studio shoes, of course. A knock on the door, rattling the glass, slightly loose in its old walnut frame.

Dick swung open the door and Anna stepped in. Jung ran over, sniffed, sat down, and studied the figure before him.   Suddenly, the tail started to wag, but he remained seated.

"Hi Dick," she said through an artificial smile, exposing an excellent set of more-than-white teeth. Straightened, if not capped.

Anna was striking in more than a yoga instructor type of way, and Dick was happy to observe. A slender five foot eight, she had short blond hair with dark roots stylishly exposed, a deep tan, blue eyes, and an athletic build.   Black stretch exercise pants came to mid-calf, and had the sprayed-on look. A pink stretch top covered an exposed white t-shirt, presumably over a sports bra. Professional looking tennis shoes completed the look. A silver necklace and bangle bracelet set off the tan. A citrus scent was undermined by alcohol; the total effect was somewhere between margarita and martini with a strong twist.

"Anna, welcome. Have a seat. Coffee, cappuccino?"

"Double espresso. I've got a water here."

Dick surmised that the bright green stainless steel water bottle carried a custom blend. He glanced down at his favorite Skagen; 11:05 AM. Five o'clock somewhere, he guessed.

After presenting the espresso, he settled back into the chair by the window. A low table sat between Dick and Anna along with Jung.

"What's on your mind, Anna?"

"It's kinda complicated. First I want you to know that I will get you paid."

Anna was frequently delinquent but never a problem account. Dick studied her face. He wondered who paid for her nose job and how much it cost. Was it a summer after eighth grade event, or was it a high school graduation present? Or maybe just a little perk to herself. The tip was a little too pointy and the side contours had a slightly chiseled appearance. A quality job, no doubt, albeit a bit aggressive even for her slim frame.

Dick's moment of pause lent gravity to the lender-debtor dynamic. He was not near so serious as the pause made it seem, but this kind of daydreaming did occasionally work to his advantage.

"Really, Dick. I'm just waiting for the next membership promo to start at Melanna Yoga. We're calling it Transcend Mental Meditation. Cool, eh?"

"I understand, Anna. But you could have texted me that. You know I'm okay with your payments."

Anna owed Dick for diamond jewelry, and for cash. She had a slight casino habit on the side, which regularly ate up her share of the studio proceeds.

"Well, alright. I really wanted to hire you for something else, too. I think Lars is up to something at the store, and I want to find out what it is."

"Have you asked him?"

"Gosh no, Dick. It's too serious for that. See, he's gone a lot and suddenly he has a lot of cash."

"Is that a bad thing, or isn't he sharing it?"

"Not at all. It's like I'm not supposed to notice."

"So what do we want to accomplish here? Spy on outside activities? Other woman? Source of funds?

"Everything. I'm planning on leaving him and I want to know everything before the divorce."

Oh great, a shotgun case. May as well break the bad news.

"Anna. These things take time and money. How do we plan to pay for this?"

"I was kinda hopin' . . . well, I think . . . no, I . . . Dick, I want to see if we can work out a little deal."

Dick's mind wandered, as he scanned back over her total appearance package. Was this the magical client included in the steamier mystery novels? The one who threw herself at the private dick? He doubted that his services qualified. But . . . may as well clarify the situation.

"So . . . how does this pay my bills?"

"You see, once before, he was all like this, with lots of cash and wouldn't talk about it, and then suddenly we had to move up here from Chicago. My god, I don't want to do that again. Anyway, I think maybe whatever he did before wasn't good, and it's the same now. I have reason to think that there may be a reward from before, and from now too. See what I mean?"

Dick stared at her. School: Sleuth U. Course of Study: Private Eye. Class: Conspiracy Theories, Spousal. Level: 101.

Jung slid down into a prone position after a classic yoga "down dog" stretch, and rolled his eyes up toward Dick. We're in for a long one, Dad.

"Really, Dick. Then that could pay off what I owe you already."

"Anna. Let's slow down a little."

Dick settled in for an hour long debriefing session with Anna. Whatever was in the green sports bottle, glugged frequently, kept her tongue liberated, possibly more than she planned.

The short version was that Lars had been in the import-export business in Chicago, and had a lot of Italian friends. On a vacation trip to South Texas he had visited some old buddies who promised to set him up with some new import lines.

Soon thereafter, he was gone from home eighteen hours a day or more, and was flashing a lot of cash. Two new cars arrived in the driveway. New furniture. New clothes. Money seemed no object.

And then one Friday Lars failed to come home, and was gone for three days with no contact. He had warned Anna that if this ever happened he was probably called away suddenly on business and that she should not worry because he would return.

Return he did, looking like he had been awake for three days, at least one of which included a beating. Lars refused to answer any questions, and announced that he and Anna were moving to Woodstock, Wisconsin to help a friend with a fireworks business.

TWENTY-THREE

Dick had a lot of digesting to do. Notes from Jack. Family and marital history from Anna. Boris and the fireworks and the farm. Plus a complete BLT lunch, in a basket, from The Woodchuck.

What to make of Anna's version of the reality of Lars Lundstrom? Dick exited the loft and walked over to the old dental office, the real office, with Jung in tow.

The old office floor had been scrubbed and scrubbed again, and sanitized repeatedly. Dick did not know the half-life of mercury, but he did not doubt that enough had spilled on the floors in there over the years. Jung's proximity to these floors was the issue, so they were ultra clean and the old laboratory was off limits.

Dick's favorite private eye websites and web searches revealed conflicting stories about Lars. Lundstrom was a ghost until about fifteen years ago. Research led to dead ends.

A few phone calls were in order. Upon becoming a private investigator, Dick had soon discovered that non-competing PI's were great gossips, and were willing to share information more readily than he expected. Conversely, Dick received office calls from afar looking for information and favors.

Dick pondered. How could even peaceful Woodstock generate so much interest, both locally and from out of town? Was every small town full of intrigue?

Bottom line for today: As long as you understood that this was the investigators' version of café.com, and that all information begged confirmation, you were okay.

Dick spent the afternoon calling in such favors and touching base with a few of his own contacts in Chicago. One of his old college friends was still there, teaching a course in Intellectual Property at the University of Chicago Law School. The friend knew a friend who knew a friend who knew a friend, etc. Finally contact was made with a fellow investigator who was familiar with the elusive Lundstrom.

"Lars Lundstrom? Is he getting in trouble again?"

"I don't know that he's done anything. To my client, he is acting suspiciously."

"Well, he's not above it. Career 'made guy' who is on a short vacation."

"Uh-oh."

"Yeah. You know, he blew into town about fifteen years ago doing some kind of penance from New York. Real name is Nicola Lombardi. Showed up here with a play on his Mother's maiden name."

"What happened in New York?"

"Zigged when he should have zagged. Pissed off the wrong guys so he got sent to Siberia. Worked for Vito here and was just a good soldier. For a while."

"Repeat offender?"

"Never to the police, but to his employer. Six or seven years ago he started his own gig on the side. Bringing in drugs from Monterrey, packed inside something new – fireworks."

"Ahh."

"Turns out it was an original idea, locally here anyway, and he got rewarded with his life when his boss decided to absorb the action. But, he got deported again. Further than Siberia – Wisconsin. I guess that's where you come in."

"I get it. He lucked out."

"Yeah, you know, the guy who ratted him out didn't fare too well. Owned the fireworks store that Lars sold and had used as a front. Thing burned. Pretty spectacular. He was in it at the time."

"So off to Wisconsin."

"You know, he was ostracized from the outfit here. Only lived because of his dad in New York, and the fact that he introduced a new hustle. He wasn't considered to be a real guy anyway because his mother was Swedish."

"Is that it?"

"It's all I know, man. At least for the price you're payin'."

"Thanks. Call me anytime."

Dick closed the call. He had it recorded on the phone.

TWENTY-FOUR

....

. . . Dick looked around at the loft full of friends. What better time than now for a little entertainment? Sliding onto the bench, he instantly launched the intro to "Lean on Me" as the women drew closer to the piano, and he started the vocals . . .

Suddenly a dog on the lap and a lick on the face. Wow, he'd been sound asleep and, yes, the time had gotten away from him. Time for Jung to make a trip to the back yard. Maybe putting his feet up on the desk while trying to think things through was not the best strategy for someone with sleep deprivation symptoms. But, as his grandfather said, short naps like these and you'll live forever.

Jung led the way out the office door, back to the loft, and to the back stairwell door. Off he went.

Dick called Jack Bluhm to catch up.

"Bluhm."

"Jack, it's Dick."

"I knew that."

"So why didn't you just start the conversation?"

"I thought I'd give you the pleasure of introducing yourself."

"Thanks for the ego boost. Hey, Jack, we need to get together on some new developments."

"Same here."

"How about The Library around six PM?"

"Got it."

Dick realized his mistake as soon as he waked in. It was class night at the "Liquor Lab," as Pearl had dubbed the area in the back of The Liquid Muse.

The "Liquor Lab" hosted beer and wine making classes. Pearl had recently started a class on limoncello, and tonight was merely a monitoring visit, checking on the brittleness of the lemon peels immersed in the grain alcohol, with everyone awaiting the right moment for the addition of the sugary syrup for the concoction to become the pleasurable ending of any great Italian meal.

Knowing that a lot of mental prowess would be unnecessary for class tonight, the participants had convened an hour early to warm up at the Café Bar in The Library.

Dick knew most of the limoncello class. Artsy bottles, blank labels, corks, fancy stoppers, booklets, grain alcohol. Dick saw dollar signs in these classes and had to give Pearl a lot of credit for getting them off the ground. Currently she was working the crowd, showing them a new bottle line that had just arrived.

Jung strained at his lead, tail wagging crazily, ears perked, and feet nearly off the floor. He loved crowds who knew him, and this one did, plus Pearl was one of his favorite people. Good outing.

Kate sat at a table, alone with a glass of white wine, going over some paperwork for Stranger Than Fiction. This was her night off.

Jung had his paws on her chair already, and she was stroking the top of his head. Kenny Wisdom was already on his way over with a large Peroni tap beer for Dick.

"Thanks, Sage."

"Anytime, Boss."

"I told you not to call me that."

"That's why I did."

Dick asked to join Kate, and her glow was not from the wine. She tried to act all business, and Dick played along. Jung scanned the crowd from a sitting position beside her chair. Dick warned her that Jack was coming for a private meeting.

"Sorry we'll have to split off, Kate, but we're working on a couple of investigations."

"Couple? That sounds like too much work."

"Crazy, eh? But it keeps me out of the bars during the day."

"Right. And away from the bookstore."

"Touché. Sorry. But hey, you're looking great. Still going to the yoga studio?"

"Why yes. And you know they're getting to have more and more pure exercise options beyond yoga. I like it."

"How are Anna and Melissa getting along?"

"I'm not sure. Right now they must be having a tiff. They're never there together, and if they are by mistake, it's mighty frosty between them."

"Well . . . ,"

"I know. It's all over café.com."

"How about the business?"

"Seems busy, but it's tough getting the rent from them right now. So I think they may be ducking me. I already did the "Lifetime Membership" thing with them in exchange for the free first three month's rent, just to help them get going. Plus I'm not charging them enough as it is. I don't need the money, and I like them, but still. I've talked to them, and Anna got a little snippy. Something about a new promotion coming up that will bring in some more money."

Dick nodded knowingly, and a little small talk ensued. Presently, Jack arrived and joined them at the table, with Jung happily greeting him.

"Sorry, Kate, you'll have to excuse Jack and me. Work time."

"See you later?"

"We'll see how late this goes."

Dick turned to Jack.

"So did you and Otis have fun with the books?"

"Looks like a haul. A few great ones, a pile of discounters, and a whole mess of free ones. It was fun."

Sage dropped off a pair of Peronis. Jack was more of a Miller Lite kind of guy, and also liked his wines, but when the boss or a client was buying, he went with the flow. He pulled a big notebook and a small laptop out of his shoulder bag.

"I've got some more updates."

"Alright. I just got the others logged into the cases today. Let's start with Jay Boyd, but before that I just gotta tell you about my day as a detective. . ."

Dick filled him in on Anna's story and Lars' background. Finally, they worked back to Boyd. Jack began:

"I've talked to him a couple of times. I'm using the newspaper story deal – important fireworks mogul with innovative irrigation system at his farm."

"Good, Jack. We'll stick with it. Maybe later we could actually sell the story to the wire."

"Right, Mr. Pollyanna Stranger. Anyhow, Boyd seems to front the security detail on the place, protecting their mysterious irrigation project. And, he seems to have the time on his hands for guests."

"Melissa and Anna?"

"Yeah. But there's something else going on up there. With all my comings and goings and watching, I've caught Trixie in the truck with Wayne

Nelson three times. By the way, thanks for letting me swap out the undercover car over and over. Those old Cutlass Cieras you use for service loaners have come in handy. Worn out, so they look right at home cruising the coulees."

"Where do Wayne and Trixie go?"

"Get this – I've got the photos. I followed them the other day. Jesse's Well-Rested over in Wellville. Wayne must be tight with Jesse. He parks in back. Has his own key. Never stops at the office."

Dick toyed with his beer glass, twirling the chalice around until the logo pointed toward him.

"What is it with this farm? Doesn't anybody work anymore?"

"Looks like Wayne and Jay have the 'work hard, play hard' thing down pat."

"Where is Boris all this time? Isn't it a little risky for Wayne and Trixie to be riding around together?"

"Out of town each time."

Dick sat back and took a long pull on the Peroni, and took a deep thought on the activities at Feckenmeyer's Mailbox. Why was he hired by Trixie to look into the farm and Boris if she was already on the inside track with the farm manager?

"Jack, what do you think is going on out there? Just an opportunity to play?"

"Maybe, but I don't get all the secrecy on this irrigation thing. How exotic can it be?"

"Jack, I guess that's ours to find out. Private Investigators, and all, you know. Anything else?"

"All for tonight. I gotta run. Some of the old rockers are jamming over at Otis's hangar. I'll email any other tidbits that come up."

Jung got up for a quick treat and a big scratch down the back as Jack readied to leave. Dick was already drifting off into piano land.

Dick studied the notes on his laptop. Wayne Nelson. Six-foot-four, a body builder, like Boyd. He was mid-thirties, and lean but very muscular in a competitive way. His coloring was a dark Spanish, and he shaved his head, keeping a very trim and narrow beard of three day's growth. Tattoos highlighted the major muscle groups. His face looked like a young Walter Matthau, with length and a square jaw. How did someone with this exotic look land in Western Wisconsin carrying a name like Wayne Nelson?

Kate returned as Dick was closing the laptop after a background check on Wayne Nelson. Wisconsin boy. Must take after his mother because the Nelson name was real. One minor setback: sixty months at the Federal Camp at Leavenworth for manufacturing crack cocaine. Got out early on the drug program. Something sounded familiar about this.

"Hi, Kate."

Jung was eyeing up her lap and thought better of jumping up, settling instead on top of the Earth Shoes. Dick's mind was still racing around the loose connection.

"Sorry, I've got to look up something. Order a wine. On the house, of course."

He re-opened the laptop and consulted case notes, then cut and pasted "Jay Boyd IV" into SENTRY, the law enforcement, prison, and probation program. There it was: "Five years, Leavenworth Federal Prison Camp. Manufacture, possession, and delivery of marijuana. Successfully completed RDAP Residential Drug and Alcohol Program for twelve months early release."

Dick and Kate finished their drinks at The Library and walked up the street to The Sand Bar for burgers. Not really structured for dining, the place had a good food trade nonetheless. Mostly a long bar plus a dozen tables adjoining the pool table and a small parquet dance floor, The Sand Bar had a grille and two deep fryers that together cooked all the food.

The burgers were the best in town, notably with meat ground fresh daily at the tiny neighborhood grocery at the west end of town by the lake. Berg's Store was a family owned throwback to the forties. The original west side grocery, it stood about one hundred and fifty years and was grandfathered into the zoning in the residential area that grew up around it.

The original homestead lay just behind it, with a gigantic garden that once supplied all the retail produce. For the meat market, a live chicken chopping block and a ham smokehouse occupied the back yard, where a small barn completed the scene.

Fortunately, money was not a huge issue for the current generation of Bergs, and the entertainment of the fresh meat counter was the only thing keeping the store open.

The owner of The Sand Bar attended the meat grinding each morning, ostensibly just another customer present for a cup of coffee.

The Sand Bar had acquired a nautical theme some ten years before, when it transitioned from Bob's Never Inn. Dick and Kate eased up onto stools with captain's chair backs and notched their heels on mooring ropes. Each table was routed to look like a ship's wheel, but unfortunate graffiti carved in the spaces between the spokes broke the jolly helmsman mood.

Three bartenders and a waitress all sported nautical attire, which devolved to pirate outfits on truly special occasions. Management had dispensed with eye patches upon discovering that temporary and sudden one-eyed depth perception, for drink pourers in a dimly lit saloon, was less than optimal.

Flocks of wooden and plastic pelicans, yards of netting spiked with corks, coils of rope, sawn off pilings, "gulls and buoys" restrooms, and a huge fish tank highlighted the décor. Mid-winter beach parties required a few wheelbarrows of sandbox fill, and the remains gritted underfoot.

Dick and Kate finished dinner and drinks by eleven, and strolled back down Main Street. He offered to walk her across the street to her door, and chose the corner of Main and Central to cross, controlled by a stoplight and adjacent to their buildings.

As they started to cross, a black Silverado pickup, straight pipes roaring, blew the light and brushed back Dick and Kate. Purple neon glowed beneath the chrome side tubes, smoked plastic shields covered the head and tail lamps, and the rear bumper carried an unreadable paper license plate. A graphic reading "Like A Rock" covered the rear window.

TWENTY-FIVE

The following day, Dick sat in the loft sipping a coffee and thinking about the black Silverado. A minor moment of danger the previous night, but he was certain he had seen the truck somewhere around town.

Jean Paradise was due any minute, and Dick had straightened up the sitting area a little. Hearing a Harley come to a stop, Dick looked down from the windows to see Jean parking her bike. His mind was still on the truck when her knock came on the door. Jung started the alert bark.

Dick let her in, and Jung hopped on his back feet until she bent over to give him a scratch. Happy dog. Happy owner.

Jean was a pleasing sight as usual. This time in a pair of blue jean shorts. Dick got her a coffee.

"Dick, I can't stay long, I'm on the morning bank run for work."

"Jack told me you had noticed a few things at the store that looked irregular."

"You betcha. First of all, the cash. It looks like most of it, and there is a lot, comes from wholesaling fireworks to other outlets, mostly in the Midwest. But I can't find these places in my normal industry directories. A few have websites, but they look fairly cheesy. When I ask Boris or Lars they say that the stores are all new places setting up."

"Sounds good and fake. Go on."

"No kidding. The other is that we are paying big money to vendors I've never heard of before. No history, just websites."

"Sounds like some creative cash flow. And creative products."

"Dick, I just wanted you guys to know. I can get documents and names if you need them."

"Not yet Jean, but we may at some point. By the way, have you seen much of Trixie lately?"

"Not much at all. But she isn't around a lot anyway. Now that you mention it, it's been quite a while. Mostly haven't seen her much since Lars arrived."

"Anything else I should know?"

"Just that Terri Moody is still talking smack about Kate. And about you and Jung, too, after your visit. I guess she doesn't know we're friends. How smart can she be? She worked with Giorgio at the store and couldn't put two and two together. Duh."

"Sounds like she needs a little drama in her life."

"Maybe so. After she washed out as a big time model, life must seem pretty tame around here."

"Model?"

"Yeah. Dick, didn't you ever do one of your private eye background checks on her? About three years ago she answered one of those modeling ads and was talked into launching her career in Minneapolis. Turns out it was as a lingerie model, and the career was her photos all over a biker magazine one month, and that was it. The next gig had something to do with cheese curds and she bailed. Left the bohemian lifestyle of the Twin Cities and drove home. Her parents were mortified; her friends still think it's hilarious. But Dick, what I really want to know is how your big date went last night."

"Big date? Burgers with Kate at The Sand Bar?"

"Yeah baby. You're all over café.com this morning."

"Well, small town living. Anything about our near death experience?"

"Was there one? Can you talk about it in public, Dick my dear? Did it happen before or after you took her home? Were the lights on?"

"Oh, come on, Jean. It was pretty far from romantic."

Dick proceeded to explain about the black Silverado. He went into detail; Jean was a cycle, car, and truck junkie, and she might see it around.

"Of course I know the truck. I see it every day at the shop. It belongs to Ricky and Juan. They have some kind of used car license in Mexico, and they sell mostly trucks and SUV's and some boy-racer cars. You know, slammed and neon."

"License from Mexico? The vehicles at your place all say 'For Sale By Owner.' I thought it was becoming one of those private party lots."

"No, everything is theirs. Got five more yesterday. They must lease part of our lot from Boris."

"Wow. Probably on a test drive last night."

"Juan likes that truck, he's always using it. Was probably him. But, Dick, I've gotta go so Lars doesn't miss me too long."

"Jean, you've been a sweetheart. Thanks so much for the info. I'll buy you and Giorgio some drinks at The Library one of these nights."

Dick escorted her to the door, where she bent down and gave Jung a big kiss on the nose.

TWENTY-SIX

....

Dick knew the auto sales deal at Life's A Blast was fishy. Wisconsin was well-known as a consumer friendly state, and car sales were no exception. Inspections, licenses, rules, stickers, disclosures. Play by the rules and everybody prospers, and the buying public is better off.

Dick called Miracle Motors and the call clicked over to Otis's cell.

"Otis here."

"It's Dick."

"Jeez, can't I even go outside to pee without the boss tracking me down?"

"Pee? Outside? You better be camping somewhere because I just sunk a bundle into new indoor outhouses at that place. Honestly, how far away from the lot are you?"

"About six blocks. Need something?"

"Just want to pick your auto sales brain a bit."

"Where at?"

"My place. Just park in the back drive."

Dick heard him at the door as well as Jung's advance alert. Following Jung's festive greeting, Dick and Otis settled in, with coffees, near the windows in the loft.

"Am I keeping you from anything, Otis?"

"Just a few errands and then home for lunch. 'Closed' sign is in the window at the lot anyway."

"As it should be."

Dick explained to Otis the near miss with the Silverado last night, and what Jean Paradise had told him about Ricky and Juan.

"Sounds like a professional curbstoning operation, Dick."

"Exactly, Otis. They sell off the curb, appearing like a private party. But they really meet the definition of dealers. Or, they really are dealers, avoiding regulation. I just wanted to see how close to the law they are. I know you read all the bulletins."

"Right. After you give them to me. Come on, the license is in your name."

"Okay, okay. It looks to me like this. They buy vehicles at the auctions, under a supposed Mexican license. Then they sell the vehicles directly from the Mexican lot, bypassing state and federal law, taxes, consumer disclosures, all with no investment in a facility. If things heat up, they grab their briefcase and drive elsewhere to do the same thing."

"And people think the vehicles are private-party."

"And the license is probably mail order. They don't have dealer plates or anything."

"Dick, there was talk of stamping titles with 'Export Only,' but I suppose everything can be worked around. So the buyer does his own paperwork and takes the title to the registration office himself."

"Think of it, Otis, the ultimate low overhead operation. Jean says two or three a week. Cash only. I think I'd like to ride out and see what's really going on. Want to come along? I'll buy lunch downstairs."

"Why not. Too wet to plant and the dog's in heat."

Dick and Otis wheeled into the parking lot of Life's A Blast and cut the engine. They walked over to the side edge of the lot where seven vehicles were lined up for sale. Dick quickly took photos of each VIN with his iPhone, and noted the miles for each.

Indeed, the black Silverado sat on the end of the row, unlocked and with shades and a baseball cap on the seat, along with a carton of cigarettes, torn open at the end and along the side. Executive driven vehicle, no doubt. Paper license plates reading Libre Autos, Monterrey, Mexico adorned the front and rear of each vehicle, and large red and white "For Sale By Owner" signs were in each windshield.

Not exactly a high traffic area for the locals, but Dick knew that these below the radar operations prospered with their own word of mouth. They were also ripe for fraud: understated sale prices, structuring to avoid cash reporting, mileage rollbacks, disregard for branded titles, failure to maintain facilities and provide repairs, to think of a few. The branded titles alone – salvage, flood-damaged, and so on, directly stamped on the titles. They retitle the cars in a state with few regulations – "wash the titles" – and it makes us all look bad, thought Dick.

Presently Ricky walked over from the back of the warehouse. Seeing the dealer plates on Otis's

Taurus SHO, Ricky was on the defensive immediately.

"Hey, we don't wholesale our cars."

"Sorry, just looking at the merchandise. Hi, I'm Dick and this is Otis."

"Ricky. Whattaya want, anyway? Hey weren't you in the warehouse with Lars the other day? Guy with a dog?"

"We don't want anything. Just heard you were opening a lot out here and we came to see for ourselves."

"No lot. We ship all our cars to Mexico. We just park them here.

This was totally false, of course, as Jean had explained.

"I suppose they gotta go somewhere."

Dick stared at a "For Sale By Owner" sign and the hand written price and description on the front passenger window.

By this time Terri Moody was on the prowl, taking a cigarette break outside the building, and whispering to Juan Rios, used car co-dealer. She glared at Dick and Otis. Especially at Dick.

As Terri ducked back into the building, Lars stepped out, or rather careened out, waving his arms and yelling at Juan. Lars's head looked like a fresh radish stuck on the end of a young stalk of celery.

Dick watched as Ricky raced back to defend Juan from the tirade.

"Well, Otis, shall we go?"

"May as well. Fish aren't bitin' and the cooler's empty."

Dick asked Otis to drop him off at Miracle Motors. He sat at the desk and pondered the day's events, as an Amish buggy clip-clopped down Main Street with a new mattress tied to the roof. He supposed that walking behind an ox and plow all day would make one appreciate the latest orthopedic memory foam upgrade.

Time stood still, or maybe even rolled back a bit, as Dick looked out the big plate glass windows. Across the side street an ice cream stand once stood. Dick had seen the photos. Four angled parking places at the curb qualified it as a drive-in; bicycles could roll right over to the walk-up window for ice cream. Burgers, fries, root bear, popcorn. Easy menu to memorize. Family owned and run, and no one cared that a Cities Service gas station shared the property. No one feared a gas spill on the concrete drive. Legend had it that in the mid-sixties a quartet of teenage girls had set up lawn chairs on the roof and set a new world's record for continuously singing the Herman's Hermits classically misspelled "I'm Henery the Eighth I Am."

The stand moved to a new building with year 'round indoor seating. The old site was now the back stalls of a muffler shop.

Jethro Tull's "Living in the Past" whirled through Dick's head as he drifted over to an imaginary piano. He snapped out of it.

Dick got to work on the iPhone, running the AutoCheck app on the vehicle information from Ricky's lot. He printed out the results on the wireless printer. Comparing the vehicle histories with the mileage being currently represented, it was obvious that the two trucks which had been on the lot for a few days had "lost" mileage. About one hundred thousand miles each. The ones that arrived yesterday were consistent with the records.

Yikes. All he needed was more work. Dick decided instantly that this deserved a referral to the DMV Odometer Fraud Section. He also knew this wouldn't' win over any new friends.

A few emails to his acquaintances at the DMV, and soon Dick was sauntering back to the loft.

TWENTY-SEVEN

....

. . . Dick sat under a thatched roof at the keyboard of the smallest piano bar in Cabo. He wore a floral shirt and white shorts and a great tan. The indoor-outdoor pool allowed swimmers to glide right up onto underwater barstools. Having just finished a tropical set, he was delivering oldies, and ignited the group with "Don't Pull Your Love Out on Me Baby," followed by "You're The One That I Love," and the crowd started popping bills into the oversized brandy snifter with the tropical drink umbrella taped to the rim . . .

Jung's barking interrupted Dick's well-deserved nap. He had spent the morning sitting in The Library meeting with each of his managers. Pearl first, since The Liquid Muse opened at nine AM, then Kenny "Sage" and Kate as early morning traffic allowed. The stores were all doing well, Dick was upbeat, and the conferences were short.

His mood shifted somewhat upon seeing Marian Horton, City Librarian, sitting in the bookstore, then the Café, taking notes on a yellow legal pad. She wasn't there to buy scones for Otis. She stared, alternating between Dick and Kate, and then at the whole scene.

Then along came Melissa Schwartz, looking for Dick. She was late thirties, about five six, and like Anna, sported the fitness center build. Her dark hair was straight, jaw length and swingy, and her dark brown eyes were large, focused intensely on whomever was the current comrade in conversation.

Some took this as flirtatious, and her body language never denied it. Today she wore white exercise shorts that showed off her tan, and high-top sneakers, plus a red t-shirt over an athletic top. Her aroma was beyond yoga studio fare. Dick was happy to note all of this for the memory banks. You never know when there might be an investigation.

Spotting Dick's table, she pulled her chair just a little too close for his comfort, and leaned in to talk in hushed tones.

"Hey Dick, I've got to talk to you. But let me get a coffee first."

She bounced over to the counter and returned with a large house blend. Dick had no chance to play host.

"I've got something I need you to do."

"As detective, auto purveyor, or red wine friend?

"Oh Dick, you are so funny."

This was the closest Dick had been to her face in a while, and concentrating on the nose a mere eight inches away, he wondered if it, too, had come under the knife. Too perfect.

"So here's the deal. I've heard that Anna has been seeing this, like, friend of mine, and I, um, don't want to see him get hurt. So I'd like some info on her, you know?"

"You mean pay me to follow her and take photos?"

"What a great idea! Dick, you are so smart."

Up close, a mild hangover scent under-toned the garden of floral essences.

"You know what, I think that witch took a case of the Merlot we made. I can't find a whole box of it."

"Melissa, you know I have to charge you to do this. It's my business."

She put her hand on his forearm, squeezing it as if testing his muscle tone, and leaned closer to him.

"Dick, I've always paid you for the diamonds, haven't I? I won't stop now."

In the midst of this confab, Kate walked back in from the bookstore and stopped in her tracks to survey the scene at Table #4. She strode over to the table, slammed down a small binder, and intoned icily,

"The sales reports you requested. Sir."

She spun on an Earth Shoe toe and marched back into the store.

Jung was at the door as Dick opened it, and Jean walked right in.

"Dick, big things at work today."

Dick tried to slow her down.

"Coffee, cappuccino, espresso, or can we just speed you up with some Red Bull? Anyhow, hello and welcome to Truth Is Strange Investigations."

"Oh, sorry, Dick. Hi, Jung."

They settled into the green chairs.

"Well these two guys from the state were there just before lunch, to see Ricky and Juan. Terri freaked out when they showed ID's, and she sent them right to the warehouse. They questioned the guys for a while and then one went outside and took pictures of the dash of a truck and then left with an old banker's box full of papers that Ricky had in his locker. They asked me to take photocopies of Ricky's and Juan's ID's and to enlarge them on the copier. They offered to pay me but I did it for free. Then the state guys left and the boys were shouting at each other. I don't remember a lot of high school Spanish after all these years, but they used 'Dick Stranger' a lot and the rest didn't sound too good."

She took a breath.

TWENTY-EIGHT

....

Dick hopped out of the Ferrari and grabbed the bottle of Cabernet spirited inside of a brown plastic bag, and reached over to the footwell for the large ceramic bowl. A special night deserving a special car: card club at Boris and Trixie's.

Most of the regulars' cars were already there. Everyone brought an hors d'oeuvre, and Dick's was his famous hot artichoke dip and wheat crackers. The walk to the door was a delicate balancing act as he also had a small hard-sided cooler with a six-pack of a local craft brew.

The card club was made up mostly of members of the Gourmet Club, where it all started. Always after a big meal and lots of wine pairings, the cards would come out and the night extended. Soon it was just another excuse for the group to get together.

The schedule was always the same. Everyone spends about forty-five minutes on the hors d'oeuvres, then to the tables for euchre. Eight rounds of eight hands, with a refreshment break after each round, and the winners advanced tables, the losers sat still. Things usually got a little unfocused after the fifth or sixth round, and someone usually had cigars to light up outside on the deck, just to reduce the oxygen level further.

Boris and Trixie had a perfect family room for such a get-together, and it held four card tables easily. Plus it had the audio equipment, HD TV's, a fireplace, and a big built-in cabinet full of games, cards, poker chips, and all the necessary items to entertain. Just a few steps through French doors, a spa awaited on a deck overlooking the corn beyond the lawn to the west. Occasionally, this was the final gathering place of the night.

Trixie met Dick at the door.

"Well, Dickie, it is just great to see you! Artichoke dip? Just put the beer on the porch. I'll take the wine."

"Trixie, will I ever see it again?"

"Oh, Dickie, it's in good hands – I'll just keep it away from Melissa."

Soon, the first course of snacks and drinks was under their belts and the draw was held for competitive seeding of the tables. If you got the first table, the challenge was simply to stay there by winning. Score cards were inscribed, the small souvenir change bags from the banks were pulled out, and the antes were made.

Everything stopped when the first hands were dealt. Evidently, there was some mix up with pinochle decks, or some other game with a different card count. There were not enough cards to go around.

"Hey, we're short of cards here. Are they all up your sleeves Boris?"

"Yeah, we're missing lots of cards from this deck. I thought it looked a little thin."

"Same here. Whatcha' doin' Trixie? Hidin' the cards?"

"You guys must be sitting on some cards. I got them all out of the cabinet this afternoon. I didn't really look at them, though."

Sure enough, all the decks were short of cards. Boris and Trixie jumped up and started to tear through the game cabinet. Maybe someone had dropped them last time and there was an assorted pile somewhere. Things did get a little foggy late in the games some nights.

"Sorry gang. We've looked at where we store the cards. Are you sure you don't have them under the score cards or on the floor or something?"

"Boris, it's early in the evening. I think we can see the cards."

"Okay, okay, I've got a box of old ones in the basement. I'll grab them and be right back."

Knowing to stay out of the way, Dick grabbed another beer and walked out on the deck. What a beautiful evening, he thought, as a new structure caught his eye. It looked like a large version of those backyard storage buildings you see for sale on the side of the road. It looked very well-built, generously sized, cedar material all around, plus a fresh trench in the yard where the power must have been buried.

Melissa Schwartz had walked out after him, Cabernet in hand, and was standing a little too close for comfort. Chief Bill was inside, after all.

Dick turned, managing to back step three paces in the process.

"So Melissa, what is that little cedar building there? Is that new?"

"Oh, that? Boris has gotten into ceramics after that night class they took last winter. He and Trixie just had it built so they can throw the clay right here. He calls it his pottery barn. Cute, eh? I hear he's even teaching Jay Boyd how to do ceramics."

Bill walked out onto the deck and put his arm around Melissa.

"Hey, time to play inside here Boris found some more decks. May have to find a detective to solve the mystery. Whattaya think, Dick? Get it? Detective?"

Dick suppressed the rolling eyes response and held up his beer in a toast.

"Game on."

TWENTY-NINE

Dick's days were filling up, and the next two included briefing Jack, warning Otis, tailing Lars, tailing Boris, tailing Anna, soothing Kate, and generally keeping in touch with his other businesses. Jung rode shotgun on most of the drives, proudly wearing the Service Dog vest when in public, while Dick flaunted a new pair of Oakley's that Kenny and Pearl had given him as a birthday gift. Evidently they were buying into his habit.

Dick pulled the Ford Probe into the garage behind the apartment and he and Jung ascended the stairs to the loft. The early afternoon sun poured through the windows, and while Dick settled in with the laptop, Jung settled in with the pillow.

Email messages included one from the air freight office notifying Dick of a shipment to pick up. Right on schedule. The cube van was already reserved. One hundred cases of red wine from Strangere Vineyards arrived as the final delivery of ten from a private charter. The airport was an easy drive, seventy-five miles away on the Interstate.

The afternoon was consumed with emails and phone calls. Finally,

"Jung. Car ride?"

The dog did the full body wag, with his back half twisting from side to side and tail fluttering. Four-thirty, and time to pick up the cube van before the rental agency closed. Dick affixed a black bandana to Jung's neck, and they headed to the garage where the MG awaited the trip. After about an hour getting parked, signing the rental agreement, and checking out the vehicle, Dick and Jung were on their way in the cube van.

The airport was situated on the far west side of a city of sixty thousand, the next town of any size beyond Woodstock. There, the regional airport included some freight storage areas, and the one for tonight was private.

First things first. Pulling into town, Dick worked his way down some side streets to his favorite taco place. Realizing that the drive-thru was not a good idea in the cube van, he parked at the curb, and looking back on his way into the restaurant he could see Jung standing on the driver's seat, front paws on the steering wheel, mouth open in a smile with his tongue hanging out. Jung knew where he was.

Dick used his phone to snap a few photos of the little guy, thinking of the Christmas card collage, or maybe even a canine greeting card cover. Maybe he could sell it to some big greeting card company for their writers to dream up something worth $5.95. What kind of great job did those guys have, sitting around making up jokes and cute things and sentimental sentiments to put in the cards.

Coming back to the task at hand, Dick ordered for take-out, including a plato para ninos for Jung: two mini-tacos and a small tub of potato puffs. The dog waited patiently while Dick put a small towel on the floor of the van, and broke up the ta-cos into bite sized pieces. Can't work on an empty stomach, you know.

At the airport, Dick pulled through the security gate and to the storage hangar. There, it was a simple matter of proving ownership with a freight bill and signing the manifest for the prepaid ship-ment.

Jung stood guard in the front of the cab, and peered through the safety screen into the cargo area, while Dick loaded the cases. At the exit, Dick turned on the interior lights and handed the freight manifest to the guard, who looked into the back of the cube van through the front cab. Their conversation was mostly about the dog.

Dick worked his way back across town, avoiding the freeway, and headed back east on the state and county roads. He knew that a flat tire or break-down or burned-out headlight would fare better with a county policeman than with the State Patrol.

To his dismay, about two-thirds of the way home, a black Crown Victoria fell in behind them. Even in the late dusk, it was obviously a police cruiser. Four antennae, embankment of lights in the rear window, blackwall tires, the reflection of a quartet of lenses behind the grille, and a pillar mounted spotlight. A municipal plate, city owned, and not county or state.

Five miles short of Woodstock, the Crown Vic lit up with red and blue flashing lights, and Dick pulled to the shoulder. He saw that the spotlight was trained on the windowless rear roll-up door of the cube van.

A large figure crunched up the gravel towards Dick's window. Jung started barking and Dick turned on the cab lights. He pulled out his license and the rental agreement, lowered the window, and put his hands in plain sight on the top of the steering wheel. Might as well make it easy for the guy.

"Sir, do you know why I pulled you over tonight?"

It was Bill Schwartz.

"Bill, no I don't, but I'm guessing it was something endangering the entire driving public, like a flickering license plate light."

"Cut the sarcasm, Stranger. Let me see your license and registration."

"Stranger? Call me Dick, Bill."

"Just give me the license and registration."

Dick handed it over, including the rental agreement to prove he had not stolen the cube van. Schwartz worked back to the cruiser with all the information. Dick watched in the side mirror. No radio calls, no time on the laptop. He was back in less than five minutes.

"Get out of the truck."

"Bill, you haven't told me why you stopped me."

"Open up the back."

Dick obliged. With the door rolled up half-way, Bill told him the reason for the stop.

"We received word that you were bringing in a shipment of undocumented imports today."

Dick froze. Of course, that was the shipment, and that was the purpose of the charter arrangement.

"What's in the boxes?"

"Wine. My own. From my own Strangere Vineyard and Winery. For my own use.

"Right, Stranger."

Jung resumed barking, and stared to growl at Schwartz when the Chief started opening the cartons.

"Shut your dog up."

"Sorry, man. He's just very protective of my personal property. Jung – quiet, quiet, buddy."

Dick resisted the urge to slam down the door on the truck and take off with Jung in the police cruiser. He knew that was useless in the long run. But how would Schwartz explain why he was in the cargo area of a cube van full of wine and his squad car was missing?

"Let's see your paperwork for this stuff."

"Right here. One shipping receipt from Italy. And the manifest."

"It says glass bottles."

"Indeed."

Schwartz pulled down the door, and Dick latched it.

"Stranger, come back to the car with me."

Dick thought this did not bode well. But he had no choice. He squeezed in the front passenger seat between the dash-mounted laptop, the local radio, and a number of electronic devices, including a credit-card terminal. Once in the squad car, Chief Bill Schwartz leafed through a file folder full of official looking ATFE and U.S. Customs documents.

"Look, Dick, you know you don't got the tax and Customs paid on this, don't 'cha?"

"I'm not prepared to answer that without my attorney present." Or an English grammar book, he thought.

"Hey look, Dick. I'm willing to work something out on this deal. Huh? Do ya' want to work with me on it? Huh?"

"What did you have in mind?"

"Let's say I found that all it was is glass bottles. Ten boxes. A personal collection shipped from Italy. Then you and me we split the shipment. I gotta guy who prints the right paperwork. I know it'll fly."

Thoughts spiraled in and out of Dick's head. Can this be happening? Shaken down by a small-town Police Chief? And gourmet club and card club partner? So this is why only the single officer for a so-called major bust. At least it's not a full hijack. And where will the Chief go with fifty cases of wine. Aside from a few for his wife.

"C'mon Dick. I've got you with your pants down. Take the deal or I get the cuffs out. And the dog goes to the pound."

"Where do I need to take your wine, sir?"

THIRTY

Dick got back into the cube van and Jung jumped onto his lap to give him a big lick on the ear.

"I'm doing this for you, buddy. I can't think of you going to the joint."

He followed Chief Schwartz into town and over to a residential neighborhood on the west side. They drove down an alley and up to a barn behind a small store and large house. Berg's Store.

Schwartz unlocked a large padlock on an old logging chain, and slid open the barn door. He waved in Dick with the truck, and pointed out where the cases should be piled. The barn was amazingly clean and modern inside, with a concrete floor, and included most of the stock for the store, plus a small workshop flanked by half a dozen classic cars under covers. Dick really wanted to wander over and look under the covers, but he also wanted this night to be over.

He pulled out the ramp and started to carry the cases to the designated area. Next to the wine were cases of cigarettes, extending to and filling the end of the barn. He counted the tiers and rows. Four hundred cases, easily. Curious.

Dick rolled the door down and hopped back into the cab to pull out of the barn. Jung looked at him intently, and then turned to look out the window at the squad car, letting out two angry growls. Dick nodded,

"You got it, fella."

Jumping out of the cube van, Dick wanted to wrap up the evening and get out of there. Schwartz re-chained the barn and turned to Dick.

"Bergs sure keep a lotta stuff in there, eh? Now Dick. Two things and we'll keep this quiet."

Dick pondered the Chief. Product in hand, re-open the negotiations? Crafty.

"We need to use some undercover cars at the PD. A couple would do and we'll change them out every month or so."

"I guess I can help with that. What's number two."

"Same deal on the next shipment. You know I'll have advance notice."

The ride across town to Dick's little warehouse was quiet, with Jung lying on the passenger seat eyeing Dick sympathetically.

"Well, Jung. It looks like old Schwartz should have had the black bandana on tonight, not you. Maybe pulled up over his nose. And with an eye mask, too."

Dick backed the cube van from the alley into the driveway of the warehouse. He went through the remote security disarming procedure and opened the electric overhead door. Pulling out the loading ramp and raising the van's rear door, Dick proceeded to unload and stock the fifty cases.

Suddenly, Jung started barking from the other side of the warehouse. Dick guessed the mighty guard dog had sighted a mouse in a trap, and he walked around the van to take a look. Jung continued to bark, facing an empty stall.

The breath evaporated from Dick's lungs. The Ferrari was missing, cover and all.

THIRTY-ONE

Dick called Otis quickly to verify that no surprises were in the works with the car. The two of them were the only people with access to the warehouse, and occasionally Otis had some small item to fix or improve on the vehicle restorations. No such luck.

This had the makings of an expensive night. The fifty cases of wine were worth about ten thousand dollars retail or to restaurants. Dick self-insured the wine.

The car was worth hundreds of thousands, and it was insured by a classic car coverage company. Making a claim would require a police report. That meant publicity, and Dick did not want people snooping around to see what else might be expensive in his warehouse. Like undocumented wine, for instance.

Not a scrap of evidence where the Ferrari had stood. The shop was spotless, so no tracks in dust, just the faint rubber smudges where the tires rolled out. The battery tender had been carefully disconnected, and the cables were coiled neatly on the workbench. There was no way to know about the security system. Someone knew how to disarm it, and how to get into the building.

Dick and Jung were less than buoyant on the trip back to the rental agency, and then home. As a final insult for the evening, the lights on the MG failed entirely, so Dick was confined to puttering along at a bicycle pace and parking whenever another car approached. For a multitude of reasons, it was a long trip across town.

Once home, Dick tried to make sense of the events careening through his head, while Jung relaxed. A nice glass of Strangere was in order, if for nothing else than to commemorate the lost cases.

Schwartz, to believe local legend, had surfaced in Woodstock a number of years ago from a Lieutenant's job in suburban Chicago. No wonder Melissa and Anna and their noses went together.

At that time, the outgoing Woodstock Chief had been nabbed in a gambling ring raid along with

Carlo Pignatelli, who traveled back to Chicago for a weekend and never returned. Jumping bail, Mr. Pignatelli was pursued but disappeared from any public records thereafter.

Schwartz had interviewed forcefully on a platform of eradicating these types of hustlers and con men from Woodstock. Bowled over by his presentation, the Police and Fire Commission recommended him unanimously without a background check.

Dick knew he had to meet with this champion of justice in the morning to discuss the Ferrari's disappearance. He poured another glass of Strangere, put an old Simply Red CD in the audio system, and propped his feet up on a footstool. Jung jumped into his lap and curled up into a ball.

THIRTY-TWO

The Justice Center loomed in an early morning fog the next day. How very Holmesian, thought Dick. After a brief encounter with Ofc. P. Justus, who appeared to be stuck with the receptionist's job, Dick was escorted into Schwartz's office.

"Stranger. What do you want?"

"I want to report a little criminal activity."

"Hey, that deal last night was just between you and me, and it saves you catchin' a case."

"It's not about that. This was under my office door this morning."

Schwartz carefully picked up the piece of paper, handling it by the corners, and unfolded it.

"Don't worry. It's a photo copy. The original is in the safe."

Newsprint cutouts graced the page:

$200,000 for the Car

Stop snooping

"What car?"

"My Ferrari. It's missing."

"The one you had at card club the other night? What's that worth and where was it stored??

"Market is in six figures. I had it in the warehouse behind Miracle Motors. I was putting the remains of my wine shipment in there last night and saw it was gone."

"Wine shipment?"

"Schwartz, you snake. I have a secure stockroom there. Otis says he was in there earlier in the day and everything was in order. Whoever took it knew I'd be gone, or at least delayed, last night. Anyone you know – other than you, that is?"

"Stranger – get this straight once. I saved your ass last night. End of discussion."

"Let's find my car. I've had no other contact from the kidnappers, phone or otherwise. They're letting me stew for a while. I talked to my insurance company, and the jury is out on whether or not they will pay ransom just like a reward. No email back yet.

"Two hundred grand. That's a lotta jack. Anything else from the, um, carnappers?"

"Bill, take this seriously, would you? I need a police report for the insurance company, but I want to keep this quiet for now, out of the news. Professional courtesy, right?"

"I'll give you a few days, Dick, but I recall a certain someone once raking the department for failure to investigate. I won't get into that again."

Dick proceeded to give Schwartz the details on the theft, and he received a copy of a sketchy police report. He left the Justice Center for the office, stopping by his downstairs enterprises for a checkup. Settling in for a quick coffee, Dick heard Pearl's voice across the café.

"Dick. I was looking for you. Lots of barking upstairs, but no you."

"Well, that wasn't me barking. Here I am."

"Very funny, boss. Anyway, I wanted to tell you about yesterday. That Jay Boyd guy, you know the one who always comes on to me in the store? Well, he said he just had to talk to me. I was sure it was another line. So I listened, but kept my distance. He said he was representing a new distributor, selling hard liquor and cigarettes. Dick, I know you let me make these decisions, but the prices are too good to be true. Twenty to fifty percent less than our current guys."

"Nobody has that kind of margin to play around with. What's the catch? Freight, taxes, fuel surcharges, all of the above?"

"F.O.B. The Liquid Muse loading door, Woodstock, WI. Meaning he picks up the freight, complete, to here. So he claims. And he was pushy, like it was urgent."

"Put him off until I can find out a few things. Too suspicious for me."

"That's why we're having this conversation, hon."

Dick sat erect in his desk chair while Jung rattled a plastic kibble-dispensing ball around the office suite. This was another amazing invention. A football-shaped plastic ball screws apart into two pieces, with holes on each end. Put the dry dog food in the ball and screw it together. The dog has to roll the ball around, end-over-end particularly, to get the food to come out past some interior baffles. Ben Franklin would be amazed. It was like Jung taking an additional walk.

But on Dick's mind: Schwartz, Boyd, and the Ferrari. On top of everything else. Sometimes life is a full-time job.

He picked up his cell and called Trixie Shiraz.

"This is Trixie."

"Hi Trixie, this is Dick. Got a minute?"

"Oh, hi Dick. What's up?"

"Just thought we should do an update. Can you drop by the office, say, late morning?"

"I'll be there."

Dick thought he should find out a little more about Chief Bill Schwartz. All his background information was blank before coming to Woodstock. What is it about this place?

His credit bureau did show his previous job, but otherwise no credit cards, auto loans, or mortgages before landing in Woodstock. Dick was dying for the same system that the FBI had, as this guy had all the earmarks of a relocated witness.

Dick decided to call his PI contact in Chicago again.

"Hey, it's Dick Stranger from Woodstock, Wisconsin."

"You again."

"Thanks for the warm welcome."

"Anytime."

"I'm looking for background on another guy. Local PD Chief, Bill Schwartz. Supposedly was a Lieutenant out in the burbs."

"That's no secret. He was next in line for Chief. Ratted out a bunch of Officers and the guy who is now the former Chief. They went to jail and he went to Wisconsin. Word is, the others were in the pockets of a street gang, but Schwartz was in with the Mob and it saved his butt. Didn't sing a note about the Outfit, so he got an escort out of town and protection. Kind of like witness protection, but privately funded. I remember the gig, and I know for sure he'll never be bothered by that gang."

"That explains a lot. Or at least a little. Anything else on him?"

"The Feds thought he was a hero, too."

"Got it. Put it on my tab, please."

"With customers like you, who needs competitors?"

Dick and Jung went back to the loft to await Trixie. Dick made a quick call to Otis and explained that Chief Schwartz would need the use of one of the Cieras for a couple of weeks. New community service donation and write-off.

Otis chafed at the idea of being short a loaner car, but Dick promised to add another car if shortage became an everyday event. Regardless, Schwartz would pick up the car today for some undercover work tonight.

Trixie rolled in about eleven-thirty armed with two foot-long Italian subs and chips. Jung advanced barking and wagging his tail, fell back a few feet, regrouped, and made another run at the guest, hopping up on his back legs and scoring a small dog treat from the visitor.

"Dickie, I knew I was running close to lunchtime, plus it's my turn to cook. Got anything to drink?"

"Coffee drinks, iced tea, cola, plus a full line of cocktails."

"A well-made Sidecar sounds perfect this time of the morning, but the good little angel on my other shoulder says iced tea, so I guess that's it. Light lemon."

"All right. It's a fresh batch of sun tea from the roof. For two."

Dick pulled over a small table and he and Trixie enjoyed their lunch. He had to focus, as his mind kept wandering to the concept of a Wayne and Trixie relationship. While appreciating the strictly physical aspect, Dick was at a loss to mentally embrace the idea of Trixie and Wayne sharing real life together. It was not just a class difference, or poise and manners; it was just that, that . . . she could do so much better. Dick chastised himself, thinking maybe he was selling Wayne short.

"So Trixie, it looks like we're pasting together a picture of the comings and goings of the cash at the store. Most of it comes from, and goes to, some dubious companies. At the farm, we still don't understand all the security over an irrigation system. And we don't know where Boris is going all the time. When we follow him he usually ends up at the airport or on the Interstate to Chicago."

"Follow? Like are you following people?"

"As needed."

"Oh. I see."

"The only other thing we've uncovered is that Boris recently took out a jumbo life insurance policy. Two point five million."

"I know about that. Six months ago. I'm like the beneficiary but the bank has a like hook on it because we have kind of a, um, big mortgage on everything. Nobody knows it, but we still have the houses from when Boris was doing all that building. We're like renting them out at a loss. We had a good system, owned all the companies. Excavation, concrete, building, electrical, security, landscaping. Like everything except plumbing and HVAC. We took a little profit at each stage. But we shuttered it all in the real estate crash a few years ago. Now it's just, like, fireworks and the farm."

"I understand. Well, that's the highlights from me. Just wanted to keep the client up to date."

"Dickie, you're the best. Let me know when you need some money."

"You can be sure of it."

Dick thought carefully about Boris and his construction related companies. Jung ambled over and nosed out a small piece of Italian salami that had hit the floor.

THIRTY-THREE

....

Dick pulled open the old wooden screen door at the entrance to Stage Door Pizza. Housed in the old town movie theatre building, the pizza place occupied what originally was an oversized lobby, concession, and lounge area. After the original cinema closed due to the popularity of the mega-plexes in a few nearby towns, the fully art deco building somehow had been adapted very tastefully for the new food venture.

The concept was to have diners stay for com-munity theatre productions in the auditorium por-tion of the place. As both a freestanding restaurant and a community gathering locale, Stage Door Piz-za was a success.

Dick had called Boris for a lunch date, and a chance to catch up on things. Boris was already seated and a bottle of wine was breathing on the table.

"Boris, I see you have my best interests at heart. I haven't had my prescribed two glasses of red wine yet today."

"Anything for you, Dick. So what are you doing for fun these days?"

"Oh, you know, a little car business, a little book and café and liquor business, a little investigation business. All in all, it normally keeps me out of the bars and out of the wine at mid-day."

"Same here. The fireworks thing has really been good lately. Lars brought a lot of revenue generating ideas with him. We made the right move with the new building."

"So tell me more about this this big fence."

"Well first of all, I want to keep people from crossing my land and getting over to the federal property next door. I never know what some idiot is planning to do, and I don't want to be the launch pad for some survivalist's assault on the US Government."

"But I thought the idea was to hide the irrigation system."

"Well, sort of. I just don't want people wandering in and copying all the patented ideas we have on that system. So we keep the weirdos out, the freeloaders out, and as a bonus the deer don't get into the corn."

The waitress came over to the table and conversation stopped. She was late teens, but had a look of self-sufficiency about her. She brought the plain paper menus, simply printed with no logos and no restaurant name on them. A home computer job.

Her uniform consisted of faded bell-bottomed jeans riding a little too low at the hips, a tee shirt revealing tattoos on both biceps, and black tennis shoes with no socks, also showing off an ankle tattoo. The t-shirt proudly said Angie on the front, and Sven's Roofing and Siding on the back. Maybe it was a low cost softball team jersey, maybe it was her dad's business, maybe it was her pajamas, or maybe it was a joke. Details, details.

Dick addressed her as Angie, and received no correction. Boris and he ordered a pizza from the time saving "no waiting" menu of four prepared pies. Angie left to retrieve the main course.

"So Boris, I don't see you around town much. Are you doing some traveling for business?"

"I do some on-site vendor inspections and negotiations. So I do have to fly away now and then. But it keeps the old blood flowing."

"How are the troops doing managing the farm? I hear you're giving pottery lessons to Jay Boyd the Fourth."

"You know, he and Wayne are doing a good job out there. Jay just seemed so curious and has kind of a creative streak. So I've been showing him how to get his hands on the clay. I don't question them too much on what they're doing. They are on budget and the crops are looking good."

The pizza arrived and was placed on two large tomato juice cans in the center of the table, almost at eye level. Boris and Dick finished it off promptly along with the wine.

Angie returned with the bill, and Dick made some small talk.

"So Angie, you did a great job today. How long have you been doing this?"

"About three weeks now. I used to work at Dairy Whippers. This is heaven."

THIRTY-FOUR

....

. . . Dick was back at the piano after a break at The Crowbar. His mind was racing over the propositioning he had endured while working through the crowd to the restroom. 'It's all about the piano, Dick,' he thought to himself as he started to slam "Reeling in the Years" on the keyboard. The crowd started to dance and the club owner set up a rack of Jell-O shots, free for the taking, first come, first served . . .

The door of Miracle Motors slammed and Jung began barking. Dick awoke to see Marian Horton coming into the office, red in the face and mouth open.

"Mr. Stranger, you and that Kaul woman are ruining our library. I've been to your store and those free books are a dirty trick. You're just . . . you're just . . . well . . . selling people coffee."

"Marian, calm down. You and I go back too far to be arguing. Now, sit down and I'll get you a cappuccino then let's sort this out. Plus, call me Dick. Like you used to."

"Well . . . all right. Dick."

She sat down with her back to the door. Jung stared at her, and she glared back at him. Might be a cat person, he thought. Never been friendly since Dick pulled the Service Dog routine with her in the History Reading Room of the Library.

"Look, Marian. You know we have to buy a lot of titles that aren't too popular for sale anymore. That's what we're lending out. I don't know if many of them are even competing with your books."

"Nobody asked me in the first place. It's that Kaul woman's fault."

Otis walked into this hornet's nest unaware. Marian was never in conversation with Dick unless she was soliciting a contribution.

"Hi Marian. What's happening?"

"Nothing good, Otis."

At that moment Jack walked in, addressing Otis with enthusiasm.

"Otis. I was just at The Library. Kate said that last batch of books we got is flying off the shelves. Great job, eh?"

Time for a break. Dick walked back over to The Library and ordered an espresso from Sage. The room was bustling, and Dick left Jung to guard a table while he went over to see Kate. She joined him at the table and Dick elaborated on the conversation with Marian.

"Blame it all on timing, but it didn't finish well. She still thinks you and I are the Frito Banditos."

"Oh, Dick. Won't she get over it?"

"I don't know. It's as if she owns the library books and gets commission on each one she lends out. It was just in the paper that visits to the Public Library are up. Maybe it's the stress of the added traffic."

"So should we pull back on our program? I'd hate to do that after a good launch. And that new batch of 'unsalables' is going like hotcakes. Apparently there is a price at which any book is desirable – free."

"Keep it going. It's good for the Public Library too. She just can't see it right now. Let's get this off our minds and take a little drive this evening. It's rib night at The Bogside up in Cranberry Point. What do you think?"

"Great. What time?"

"Walk over at six and we'll leave from the loft."

Jung lay on the floor, wagging his tail. He got up to stretch and got a good ear rub from Kate before she airily walked back into the book store.

Dick and Kate backed the Probe out of the garage and headed northeast out of town. Dick looked over at Kate. Date Kate, not Work Kate. Fresh citrus and floral aroma surrounded her. A thin Kelly green top over tight jeans with boot cut legs, a wide black belt with a silver and turquoise western style buckle, black boots, and a short lightweight black leather jacket. Dangly earrings and a pendant matched the belt buckle and strikingly highlighted her coloring.

Dick appreciated the effort and the results, but did not have the heart to comment on the clash between Kelly green and the Caribbean-hued Calypso Green of the Probe. A bit too much of a car guy?

Dick, for his part, was also making a fashion effort. The khakis set kind of a preppie tone, with a light beige leather weave and brass buckle. Add a brilliant blue windowpane plaid shirt with a black undershirt, plus soft beige driving shoes with no socks. His shirt cuffs turned up once and two buttons were open on the front of the shirt. A light windbreaker in yellow completed the look. All was couched in a tasteful dose of Polo cologne. Dick felt like it was a date, and Kate approved.

They took the shortcut to Cranberry Point, a scenic trip through cranberry country. Reservoirs, flowages, and planted cranberry bogs flanked Cranberry Boulevard for nearly fifteen miles. The roadbed, originally built over the aged peat bogs, deteriorated and sank a bit every year, just like an old cranberry bed. The washboard effect was graded out and re-graveled annually. Still, the narrow two lane lacked shoulders of any merit, and faced submersion when reservoir water was high. Nevertheless, it was a classic drive through the cranberries, and the bar food at The Bogside was worth the trip.

The Probe GT, with its handling suspension further tweaked by Dick, was possibly not the best riding car for this road, but Dick did not push the limits of adhesion, and a pleasant getaway progressed.

The Bogside overlooked an operating cranberry marsh, owned by the restaurant proprietors. The food was a labor of love, and the packed house was testimony to its quality. After a short stay at the bar, Dick and Kate were shown to a window table in the single bar-pool-dining-banquet room. A salad bar topped the pool table during dining hours. A beautiful sunset capped off barbecued ribs and baked potatoes for two. The best for miles, at that.

As the driver, Dick stuck to NA beer, and their return trip down Cranberry Boulevard was slow, with lots of deer crossings and other animal sightings. As dusk turned to dark, Dick noticed a car quickly coming up behind them with its bright lights on. He tapped the brake a few times and flashed his own high beams into the trees to signal the other driver.

Suddenly, the other car pulled out to pass the Probe, and pulled in directly across the front, almost brushing the front bumper. Dick slowed immediately to avoid contact since the two cars were passing a reservoir. The water's surface loomed a foot or less below the roadway. The passing car slowed to a crawl, and Dick slowed more, and the other car nearly stopped. Dick powered by, only to have the game resume.

He realized after the first exchange that the other car was a Cutlass Ciera, and it looked familiar. He would recognize it anywhere. His own loaner car, just borrowed that very day by the police for undercover work. The PD had put on another set of plates but it clearly was his own car. Who was at the wheel? The cat and mouse game continued, as Kate's frightened gasps descended to silence.

Dick decided to take action. He knew the Probe could easily outrun the Ciera, but a long series of tight turns lay ahead on the gravel road. And this was not a good area to exit the roadway. He couldn't get a good distance ahead, if any, yet it was worth a try.

The Probe hunkered down and took off on the straightaway, leaving the Ciera to fade in the dust.

But the first turn was tight, there was no room for error, and Dick had to slow down. The Ciera had finally gained speed on the straight stretch, and now it was sliding recklessly through the turn, catching up.

Impossible, thought Dick. He knew these cars, and the other could never keep up with this one. Unless you didn't care about where you landed when you slid off a curve. Dick pulled away again on the next stretch. But going into the next curve, the Ciera didn't slow at all, and slammed the Probe in the rear bumper. Amazingly, Dick maintained control, straightening the wheel just at impact.

Half-way through the next bend they were not so lucky. The Ciera punted the Probe, already scrambling for traction in the gravel, across the road toward the reservoir. Skidding at a forty-five degree angle to the intended path, Dick hollered to Kate "Hang on!" and simultaneously floored the throttle, cranked the wheel, and pulled back full bore on the parking brake lever.

Given the correct ratio of pavement length to speed, this maneuver actually could work, resulting in a reversal of direction. But Dick and Kate and the Probe ran out of road surface as the car spun backwards in the marbles toward the water.

As the Probe slowed in its slide, the Ciera skidded past, barely under control. Time slowed in the Probe, with every human motion seeming to move through honey. Dick felt the rear of the car start to drop off the edge of the road toward the water and he reached for the power window switches. Abruptly, the back end popped up with a sickening crushing sound, and the whole car went airborne for a few feet before landing with a giant thud in a whirl of dust.

The front drive wheels hung spinning out over the water and the floor pan of the car was planted sideways on a sand dike road that crossed the reservoir. The rear suspension collapsed on liftoff, so the car sat flat on the dirt. The Ciera skidded back into the curve and turned with its headlights playing directly on the Probe.

Dick guessed this was not an offer of a ride home. The other driver hopped out of the car, a shadow in the dark. A flash, a zing, and Dick knew for sure.

"Kate, get down!"

Another bullet whizzed past, this one directly above their heads through the window opening of the Probe, whose windows Dick had lowered instinctively, expecting a water landing.

"Dick, what do we do?"

"Kate, I'm not sure. Here I am the only PI in the country who doesn't believe in carrying a gun. Keep your head down for now."

Another car approached on Cranberry Boulevard, scaring off the Ciera driver, but not noticing the car parked sideways on the dike with its headlights shining over the rippled water. Probably a few too many Bogwaters at The Bogside. At least they had their eyes on the road.

Dick and Kate sat staring out the windshield. "Take The Long Way Home" played on the radio.

Dick shut off the lights and ignition and he and Kate both unbuckled their seat belts. He leaned over and put his arms around her shaking shoulders. A few minutes of tears, and Kate was back to normal. Dick grabbed his phone out of his jacket pocket and tapped on "call Otis."

"Otis, its Dick. What are you doing?"

"Jack and I are putting the ultralights away. It was a beautiful night for flying."

"No kidding. Could I bother you to grab the rollback and take a little ride up Cranberry Boulevard?"

"Why not? Steaks are cold and it's too dark to hoe."

Within the hour, Otis pulled in driving a shiny black Ford F550 Super Duty with a gleaming aluminum rollback body. An indispensable item in the auto sales and repair business, the truck was purchased by Dick as a bank repossession.

Ironically, the former owner was Buddy's Recovery Service, a nascent car repossession firm. Buddy's lack of respect for the importance of proper paperwork had resulted in an equal number of grand theft auto charges as there were paid recovery orders.

When the heat rose, Buddy went underground. Acting on a tip, the Police found the Super Duty in a storage unit rented by Buddy and owned by Boris. A late model Escalade still sat on the rollback, and Dick made an offer on it too. But the SUV now sat behind Miracle Motors in paid storage awaiting its legal fate. The permanence of Buddy's company was telegraphed by his use of stick-on mailbox letters in place of custom vinyl or painted lettering on the truck and rollback.

Otis winched the car off the dike in a delicate balancing act, and dragged it up onto the rollback. Dick regaled Otis with the story of the cat and mouse action that nearly landed Kate and him in the drink.

"Otis, I found out that our chassis setup on the Probe is better for blacktop than dirt tracks. And my last minute try at a power braking j-turn didn't do a lot of good, either."

"Who was in the other car?"

"I couldn't tell, and it's too late to call Schwartz at home to see if he really knows who had the car tonight. Oh, maybe it isn't too late, but I'll let him off his police hook tonight. If it was any other kind of accident, I'd just call 911 and talk to dispatch, but I don't trust them to keep a secret, if there is one."

"Well, someone wanted your attention, and then some. It sounds like a little more than road rage."

"Absolutely. Whoever was driving that car was no upset commuter. What he did driving that old V-6 Cutlass took guts and skill. Firepower isn't your common commuter trait, either."

"Dick, this is serious stuff. Wake up Schwartz and make him be a cop."

"Give me overnight to collect my thoughts."

The trio babbled all the way back to town, as Dick and Kate verbally worked off their nerves. Otis dropped them off on the corner of Kate's block and headed back to Miracle Motors to park the evidence inside the warehouse.

Dick walked Kate down to her sidewalk entrance door, gave her a reassuring hug and kiss goodnight, and jaywalked Main Street to his building. Their plan was to meet at the Café for early breakfast and a debriefing.

He was halfway up his stairwell when his phone lit up. Kate.

"Dick, someone broke into my apartment. It's a mess. And I can't find Gerald and Doug anywhere."

Dick's mind raced. Routine burglary? Or catnappers?

THIRTY-FIVE

....

"Kate, I'm sure they're around here somewhere."

"But they never go outside. Never."

"That's with you here. With some burglar turning the place upside-down, don't you think they must have slipped out the door?"

"Heeeeere Gerald. Heeeeere Doug. Suppertime!"

"Let's look around again. But don't touch anything. What else is missing?"

"My new iPad, a couple of watches, some other jewelry. And get this – the Scrabble board, with pieces, and all the playing cards from the card table. Nothing else I can tell. Oh, and of course, the boys."

"Not a real theft burglary. Most of your big stuff would be a little hard to fence around here. Too classic. But they sure did make a mess of things. Better call the PD."

A young officer arrived to take photos and statements, and repeated Dick and Kate's own line of questions. They discussed tracking the iPad, but it was not transmitting. He was critical of Kate not having the building security system activated, and he rolled his eyes at the story about Gerald and Doug. Obviously not a cat person.

Kate was indeed a cat person, but most importantly an animal person, as Jung could attest. The officer neglected to obtain a physical description of the two fugitive felines.

Meanwhile, Kate talked to her older sister in town, who offered to put her up while the apartment was being put back together. Dick was pretty sure Kate was going to ask him for lodgings first.

Dick spent the following early morning hours in thought. The chase, the break-in, and worst of all the gunfire. That was just one night. And now another insurance claim. What ever happened to the peace and quiet life of small loans and large diamonds?

He stopped downstairs at the bookstore to pick up Kate for the appointment with Chief Bill Schwartz.

Back with the Chief after the Ofc. P. Justus routine. Dick flinched extra this morning as Justus fingered his Glock

Now he and Kate sat across from Chief Schwartz.

"Stranger, you mean to tell me that you were chased by your own car? We had that car out undercover all evening."

"It certainly was. My car, your plates, Cranberry Boulevard."

"You can't be sure it was your car. Did you get the plate number?"

"Of course not. They're your plates, not mine."

"You still can't be sure it was your car."

"I can be sure. Not only did it have the Miracle Motors tag on the trunk lid, the rear bumper cover gave it away. In the headlights it was obvious, when he slowed to a crawl. I put a used rear bumper cover on that old car, but I found one close to the color from a different year. A mismatch, but not enough to need paint. Cheap solution for a loaner car. You should be able to verify the car when it comes back from undercover. It will have a little damage on the front. So who was driving it? They tried to kill us."

"I can't disclose our undercover people. You know that."

"Except when they are the source of the criminal activity. My lord, Schwartz, you can't protect that."

"You still can't prove it was your car."

"I can prove enough to make the front page of the paper."

"Stranger, I did you a big favor."

"Schwartz, who has the wine-stained hands?"

Blustering for a few minutes more, Bill Schwartz agreed to meet again with Dick after lunch, giving the Chief a little time to "look into things."

"Okay Kate, your turn. Tell the good Chief here about your episode. I'm sure he has read the reports already.

Kate recapped the burglary report and confirmed a few items for Schwartz.

"Has anyone seen Gerald and Doug? If all they did was flee the intruder, they're still in danger. They're house cats and with all the traffic and all. Well, I'm just sick."

"Nothing yet. We've got an ACB out on 'em – All Cats Bulletin – ha, ha, ha . . ."

"Mr. Schwartz, Chief Schwartz, I'm being serious. I called all the shelters and clinics this morning already. What if they were stolen? Who do you think broke in?"

"No, who do you think? The door wasn't damaged. Did you leave it unlocked?"

"Absolutely not. I keep it locked even when I'm there."

"Sorry, no clues yet."

The lack of clues sounded familiar.

Dick walked up the stairs to Kate's apartment. Observing the disarray in the cold light of day, he told Kate to take off as long as she needed to get her life in order.

"Kate, Giorgio will do a great job."

"You know I'll check in anyway. It's not like I'm a world away. Plus, I'll eat a few meals in the Café."

Dick found a table at The Library Café, planning to decompress a bit, and to make some plans, but café.com was raging, and at least ten people stopped by the table to get "the real story."

Among the current headlines:

> Dick was drunk and lost control of the car.
> Kate was driving because Dick was drunk.
> The car rolled twice. I saw it myself.
> They refused help at the scene from the police.
> Dick already entered a treatment program.
> Kate was dead.
> Dick was shooting at the police.
> Kate's apartment was emptied. And burned.
> The cats were executed. Mafia style.
> Kate had the Probe on a date with another guy and Dick ransacked the apartment in a jealous rage.
> Marian Horton helped. Aided by Terri Moody.

Well, Ollie, this is a fine kettle of fish you've gotten us into now. Dick's public version of events was hastily arranged and highly abridged. Yes, there was an accident, he was driving and sober. Yes, unknown person or persons broke into Kate's apartment.

Maybe this was a good thing, an opportunity to douse the flames flaring from the gas jets of café.com. It took the rest of the morning.

Giorgio was briefed on Kate's schedule. He was excited to help, and he was concerned to contribute to a solution. He told Dick that he had heard about the undercover car last night already, at a meeting of a local motorcycle club, which was finalizing plans for a charity pancake breakfast and horseshoe tournament.

Miraculously, the PD had the information about the time that Dick and Kate and Otis rolled back into town the previous night, and one of the off-duty officers at the meeting kept his PD radio on at all times.

Giorgio moonlighted doing high level stainless steel fabricating for the racing crowd, and one of his clients was also at the biker's meeting. The biker client had inquired,

"Hey G, I heard that O'Connor was doing some undercover work for Schwartz, working off some disorderly conduct rap. Isn't he the one who pissed off your boss, Stranger?"

"I don't know, but sounds normal for Kidd."

Dick sat in silence. That part made sense, and would explain the Ciera driver's skill. Dick knew Kidd was a more talented driver than Ian, but he also knew Kidd couldn't contain his temper and his alcohol.

Further, Giorgio told Dick that his wife Jean was worried. While working at Life's A Blast, Ricky and Juan had been making some wild comments about Dick in the wake of their legal heat. No police charges floating around yet, but the boys were already mad.

Giorgio got back to work, and Dick got back to thinking. Plausible, but none of it could explain the gun. Shooting out tires would have been one thing. A bullet at head level through the open window was quite another.

Dick migrated upstairs to the loft, and was greeted as royalty by Jung. First a long stretch sneaking into a yawn, then a few spins, then hopping around on the back legs. Did he forget to feed the little guy? Missed the trip outdoors? No, just a welcome. The royal subject was rewarded with a dog treat and time in the back yard.

Dick sat in one of the green leather chairs with yet another cup of coffee – this time a double espresso topped with hot water.

Paging through the calendar on his phone, Dick remembered Pearl's cigarette and whiskey vendor question. Letting Jung in from outside, he clipped a leash on him and went downstairs to The Liquid Muse.

Jung was all over Pearl when they got into the store. Dick noted once again Pearl's ever present smile and infectious mood.

"Pearl, what did you decide on your new vendor?"

"I decided I needed to talk to you some more. What do you really think?"

"Go ahead and buy the stuff. Make sure his paperwork is in order – if he has any. Make copies and notes of everything. Record your calls if your cell can do it. Meanwhile I have someone to call for a little CYA"

Dick and his chief investigative canine walked through the complex and out onto the sidewalk.

Dick had a plan. They ran upstairs and put the Service Dog vest on Jung and Oakley's on Dick. This situation called for only one thing.

A Woodchuck Burger.

THIRTY-SIX

....

Dick and Jung settled into one of the twosome booths at The Woodchuck and Dick declined a menu, ordering a Woodchuck Burger for himself and a Woodie Jr. child's meal for Jung, substituting apple slices for the fries.

The locals responded to Dick and Jung with either amusement or disgust, and tried either to catch his eye for a wink or tried to remember the name of the chair of the health department. Tourists – The Woodchuck was a destination in itself – observed with a cautious combination of enthusiasm and detachment.

Comfort food on board, the pair set out for Miracle Motors. Otis was glad to see them, and Dick wanted to inspect the Probe. The body damage was visibly minimal, but upon close inspection the car exhibited a slight twist to the body which resulted in a cracked windshield and a door that would not close correctly. Dick was surprised he hadn't noticed the crack last night, but it may have taken a while for the stress to exact its toll.

The undercarriage had absorbed a major hit, with the rear suspension twisted and collapsed. The unit-body frame did not like the launch angle off the ditch bank, and was twisted front and rear. Clearly, at its age, the car was a total loss. To Dick's and Otis's dismay, their hours modifying the suspension, upsizing the brakes, and hot-rodding the engine would not improve the insurance settlement. With a commercial collision deductible of $1500, they decided to pass on filing a claim while the Ferrari remained absent.

Dick and Jung walked the lot selecting a new demo to join the fun, if impractical, MG in the garage. Jung approached each car and gave an opinion, making the first cut among the candidates. First criterion was tires, and in the case of new tires, the best aroma was from the sidewalls, where the vegetable oils in the tire shine proved attractive. The best tires had a few miles on them, however, and Jung sniffed the face of the tread, savoring the remains of the road's Amish horse droppings, food waste tossed out a car window, rotting grass clippings, the occasional squirrel, and the rare coon, rabbit, or skunk.

Of Scottish extraction, the Cairn favored vehicles from the British Isles, wagging his tail at both a Land Rover and a Jaguar XJ on the lot. Dick admired and enjoyed the better German brands, but they drew no wags from Jung. This no doubt went back to an earlier skirmish over a dog toy with a wire-haired miniature Dachshund, which had left Jung with three stitches over his right ear and an aversion to things German.

The two finally settled on a barely used Chrysler 300C in the newest body style. It was gorgeous in Black Diamond Metallic with Oatmeal leather. The car was a newly introduced model that sustained hail damage sitting on a rail car in Kansas City. With big chrome wheels, dark glass, and a hunky body style, the car invited Dick to lean back with a pair of ebony Ray-Ban Clubmasters. But it would be a stretch to call shotgun-riding Jung "gangsta" regardless of scarf design or color.

Dick walked back to the shop and pulled his dealer plate off the damaged Probe, and Otis waved him over on the way back through the shop.

"Here. Close your eyes and hold out your hand."

"Oh great, Otis. What else. Overdrawn notice? Sugar in the gas tanks? Dead mice in all the air conditioning ducts?"

"Just shut up and do it, Mr. Optimism."

Two items clinked into Dick's outstretched palm with a familiar brass tone. Shell casings.

"I didn't even think of them last night, so I went out this morning with the metal detector. If anyone saw me, I'll probably be on the prime suspect short list."

"Prints?"

"Our friend Jack was able to get a couple. Smudgy but readable.

"I'll save them for my next meeting with the Chief. Otis, you're amazing. Thank you."

Dick and Jung hopped into the car and cruised out west of town for a road test of the Hemi V8. Dick cracked the front passenger window and Jung nosed the fresh country air, his weight just enough for the front cushion sensor to disable the right front airbags.

Dick knew the performance of the car was all about the air. He immediately formulated plans for a cold air induction kit and a tuned free flowing exhaust. Freely inhale the air; freely exhale the air.

Jung's nose also knew it was all about the air.

They swung off the state highway and up the town road that once was Feckenmeyer's driveway. About a hundred yards short of the Shiraz farm driveway, Dick spotted the original Feckenmeyer's Mailbox, situated where the driveway used to intersect the road. Slowing the car, he pulled onto the ditch edge and came to a stop. One tire's width worth of grass was worn down through the gravel edging the ditch, and there was a faint trail through the undergrowth to the mailbox, maybe from some wild blackberry pickers. There was enough of a path to avoid the prickly vines, so he took Jung along to inspect.

The mailbox, unused since the sixties, was a rusty hulk enclosed by boards whose traces of white paint were nearly gone. The whole affair was fixed to an oak stump two feet in diameter, and the shoots from the base had risen to envelop and protect the installation from the weather. Mother Nature takes back.

Yet the mailbox door's tab-like handle and its hinge were exposed, and shiny with use. An oval had been freshly pruned into the oak shoots to reveal the door. Jung approached with curiosity, madly sniffing the ground as if a possum had just waddled past, and then barking crazily when he neared the box. Dick took pictures, and then grabbed his handkerchief to use on the mailbox door pull. Briefly thinking improvised explosive device, Dick opened the mailbox.

Inside rested a King of Spades from a fresh poker deck of blue-backed Bicycle Cards.

Back in the car, Dick and Jung passed the Shiraz farm, Dick noting the fabric sight barriers stretched across the new fence. Also new were the insulators for electric fence. Hands off. Top secret irrigation. At this rate, it must create its own water and pick the corn for you.

Dick took the south route to town on a winding road skirting sandstone bluffs and shallow streams. Passing Life's A Blast, on the edge of town, the inventory of Libre Autos stood nosed into a corner of the real storage lot at the fireworks store. A break in the case, no doubt, for the state and federal

odometer guys. Jung gazed over and emitted a low
growl, before curling up on the warm leather seat.

THIRTY-SEVEN

....

. . . B . . . B . . . B . . . Benny and the Jets . . . Dick was at the helm of the baby grand in the middle of an all Elton set and sailing through one of his favorites. The small club in one of the better hotels in Chicago was packed with delegates to a cosmetics conference. His pink oxford cloth shirt, worn in camaraderie, was soaking through as he repeated the chorus . . .

Jung barked as the pile of mail slipped off Dick's lap and onto the floor, startling him awake. Dick looked around and realized he had dozed off once again in the office chair. The mail had scattered, but the important one was already on the desk in copy form, the original safely locked away.

The note spelled it out:

>Wire Cash to:
>
>Acct: 41718006142A
>
>BancInternationale
>
>Grand Cayman
>
>Deadline: 3 days, 2 pm U.S. Eastern

The note was made to look like a telegram, with strips of text prepared on a computer, cut out, pasted on construction paper stock, and delivered under the loft door.

Dick used a Post Office box, and he had stopped for the regular mail on the way home from Feckenmeyer's Mailbox.   Today he opened the whole batch in the dental office, after preserving the original telegram.

Jung sniffed around at the mail which had spiraled to the floor, and finally circled and lay down next to the current issue of Cairn Terrier Rescue News, providing moral support to his little buddies. Dick was a subscriber and benefactor.

Dick imagined his Ferrari sitting in a building waiting to be loaded into a shipping container headed to the Middle East, a cheap toy for an oil sheik, maybe a gift for his young son. Or, it could be in a garage locally, but how did some amateur

get a private offshore bank account. He understood you could arrange to use a black market account for a commission, but you would still need a
good connection to pull that off.

He speed-dialed Jack's cell.

"Jack, what's going on?"

"Out at Otis's horsing around with the ultralights. Looks like the weather will be nice again
this evening."

"Got a few minutes late today? More developments."

"So I heard from Otis."

"Meet me at The Library at five?"

"Yes, kemosabe."

Dick punched another key on the phone.

"Kate Kaul."

"My favorite Kate. How's the apartment looking?"

"I'm fine, thank you for asking. And yes, the
apartment is returning to normal."

"Anything on the boys?"

"Nothing. You think they would be so out of
place roaming around. Two pampered CEO's from
Cats Inc., tagged, chipped, and de-clawed, collared
with bells, groomed up and Fancy-fed. They'd stick

out like Ralph Lauren and Hugo Boss at a hobo convention."

Kate was serious, but Dick stifled a snicker. Indeed, he pictured the two of them like hobos, huddled around a fire pit, stationed by the tracks and eating tuna out of tin cans with a bunch of stray tomcats. One big old striped tabby sat on a log with a miniature guitar in his paws and a tiny harmonica holder around his neck, singing the cat's blues.

"Dick? Dick? Hellooo Dick . . . ?"

"Oh yeah. Well, if I can do anything, just give a call. I'm meeting on some business with Jack around five at The Library, so I'll be tied up for a while."

"Maybe later. Thanks for the, ah . . . um . . . concern."

"Anytime. Talk to you soon."

Dick and Jung walked back to the loft, where Dick freshened up and Jung took a look at the back yard. Shortly, Dick was seated in the Café at The Library, laptop case on a shoulder strap.

Five PM until seven PM at the Café was a typical two-for-one happy hour with hors d'oeuvres. Dick ordered a wine and waited for Jack, who rushed in and ordered iced tea. Driving, you know. Dick already had snacks on the way to complement the free ones.

"Sorry to be late. Dick. I was just having fun with the ultralight. We're going to work on the edge of the airspace tonight."

"The airspace" was the no-fly zone surrounding the Army Fort sitting ten miles to the west of Woodstock. A good neighbor and employer, the Fort had secure airspace up to the edge of the city, roughly along a north-south line that bisected the Feckenmeyer's Mailbox property.

Otis and Jack liked to fly along the edge or maybe a little bit over, because it was always quiet despite the potential threat of military aircraft. They understood how invisible the ultralights could be, and had occasionally been surprised by a crop duster roaring up out of a coulee like a whale suddenly breaching in front of an eighty-mile-per-hour cigarette boat.

One nearly federal incident involved Otis and Jack flying along and across the boundary just

north of town. Their exhilarating flight was interrupted by a huge military helicopter bearing down
on them.

The big tandem-rotor craft chasing the ultralights was like a hawk swooping down after two
butterflies. The soldiers first signaled orders to
land, but Otis held up his hands, feigning igno-
rance, prompting the giant to wave them off, turn,
and disappear over the bluffs. This, of course, em-
boldened Otis and Jack for future flights.

Back to business, Dick explained to Jack the
chase, the break-in, Trixie, the mailbox, Jean, and
the ransom notes, and he simply fleshed out the
file which he had already forwarded to Jack.

In turn, Jack told Dick about his surveillance, the
Mexican car dealers, and most importantly, all the
local gossip supplied by the snitches, wannabe in-
formants, bar-talkers, and various other rumor
mongers and flame fanners.

THIRTY-EIGHT

....

Primed with Chianti and snacks, Dick walked upstairs while it was still quite light out. Jung expected him this time, and skittered over to the back door after the greeting.

Dick let Jung down the back stairs to the dog's private park, and sized up the tasks at hand. Looking from desk to phone to laptop to napkin notes from tonight's happy hour, Dick understood what was needed to process and to prioritize all this diverse information: a trip to the roof.

Inside the second floor storeroom, which now occupied an apartment sized space across from the dental office, was a wooden staircase to the roof, culminating in a full height exit door in a chicken coop structure.

Dick had contracted a restructuring of the flat roof, and it now had a drop of several degrees from front to back, leading to two huge downspouts that joined halfway down the back wall to exit in the alley.

The roof membrane was black in color, to promote thawing, and was durable enough for walking. Despite the claims of walkability, Dick had a complex of cedar walkways and deck areas built, creating a gigantic figure eight, intended to make the area habitable and inviting.

Dick imagined a rooftop haven as found in all the best architectural magazines, and installed a pergola, along with some built-in seating and cedar planters. In truth, the old two story high roof was just three stories aloft by today's standards, and did not provide the romantic aerie and panorama that Dick envisioned. Maybe it takes a seven or eight story minimum to really pull off the remote effect in a small downtown of similar rooftops.

Nonetheless, Dick did on occasion retreat to the roof to think or to entertain guests. Tonight was a thinking opportunity, and more snacks and Chianti came upstairs with Dick to stimulate his imagination.

A bark from downstairs signaled that Jung was bored with the backyard scene, and Dick made his way down to retrieve the little guy for a rooftop visit. Jung thought that running the cedar race-course was a riot, and the side wall ledge was safely human chest high to contain him. Tempting though the black sea of roof membrane was, Jung merely extended a front paw, as in testing a puddle or stream, and he never took the plunge off the planks.

The Ferrari issue, the ransom, the gunshots, and Jack's findings on Boris topped his list of concerns. How in the world did a single investigative request blossom into all this? A simple "what about Boris?" job ticket was now a full schedule, and the only other paying customer thought that maybe a reward was in the offing. Maybe. Right.

Jack had pursued the drugs in the fireworks angle inspired by Dick's PI friend in Chicago. Boris and Lars had all the elements in place to accomplish this ploy, but more evidence was needed. Dick dreaded getting the police involved, in no small part because of his lack of faith in Chief Bill Schwartz. And the errant wine shipment didn't help. It would be up to Dick and Jack to unravel this.

The concept of gunshots having been fired from his own car by a supposed undercover police person was a dilemma similarly mind-boggling. At least Otis had come to the rescue with the shell casings.

Doubts about Schwartz also clouded the solution to this phase of the ongoing amazing case of Mr. Dick Stranger, Detective. Better dig a little into Giorgio's thoughts on Kidd O'Connor.

The Ferrari. Not only was this another non-paying case, but potentially most costly on a cash basis. Speaking of cash, time was wasting on the ransom. The insurance company was still waffling on payment of the ransom, so Dick determined to arrange the funds.

He knew a name that could help, Giovanni Corazzini. Giovanni was Antonina's older cousin, and he had done well for himself and the family. From Siena, he had huge political contacts, and indeed ties, yet he had managed to survive the many scandals and frivolous investigations and exposes of Italian politics. Particularly in Siena.

Giovanni was a realtor and notary by trade, plus an olive oil business operated in the background.

Naturally, the Strangere Vineyard's olive crop went to Giovanni.

His office was in a small building just a few doors from the Palazzo Pubblico, the Public Palace and Mangia Tower, facing the Piazza del Campo in Siena. Giovanni's two-story apartment above the office was a perfect vantage point for the Corsa del Palio, the medieval horse race run twice yearly in the Piazza. The entire course could be seen from his balconies, and his building was situated at about the half-way point in the course, as the riders and their mounts negotiated the slightly uphill portion of the dirt track.

Naturally, Dick and Antonina viewed many a Palio from this property, as their own apartment was deep in the narrow and winding neighborhood streets of Siena. Giovanni was a favorite cousin, and not just because of Palio viewing. He had helped Antonina and Dick negotiate several legal matters regarding property in Italy, and he knew the right amount for, and targets of, useful bribes.

Giovanni had become very well off as his business and family fortunes prospered, and he eventually became an investor and director of a Swiss and Italian owned bank, headquartered in Zurich, but operating a major branch in a British overseas territory, Grand Cayman. This example of practical financial détente furthered the confusion with a French-sounding name: BancInternationale.

Dick's plan of action from an evening of rooftop contemplation: call Giovanni tomorrow during the Italian business day.

....

THIRTY-NINE

. . . The city was rousing for the morning, and Dick was enjoying an excellent daydream of Venice while he sat gazing out the loft windows at the Bank's jumbotron, flipping the time and temperature and low loan rates and the Woodstock All-City Garage Sale promo. As his mind wandered, he thought what better place to be than Piazza San Marco . . .

Ah Venice. I am fortunate to be an early riser, and I know it. The pleasant security of the morning serenity is not lost on me. Here I am, ears and eyes tuned to the awakening community. Sitting casually splayed in my café chair, coffee before me, I absorb the sounds and sights as Venice casts off its Chianti soaked sleep and joins my table for a blinking glimpse of the new day.

Gazing across the café's swarm of small tables, the history overwhelms. Dirty glazing in the side-walls of the patio, the stains of centuries, dust playing in the amber and horizontal early sunbeams. Was this dirt shared by the Medici and Marco Polo? Was it out of respect for Renaissance artisans that the mortar was allowed to crumble, and the plaster left to erode, peel, and fall in small shards that crack underfoot? Is every patched and mismatched wall a fresco?

I hear the shoes in the still post-dawn air, clipping down the worn stair-treads, punctuated by the metallic click of one extruded steel step edge, recently installed and appropriately loose. What forebears trod these stairs, and on these steps how did the sound of their hard and soft leather shoes compare to that of the dense and formed rubber of today's ubiquitous cross-trainers?

Oh, but these footsteps are Italian, handmade, with the hard click of solid leather heels, stepping around puddles and across the small streams flowing from the gardens and across the heaved pavement, carefully picking a path around water standing in ancient, sinking walkways.

Water is everywhere, seeking sea level, trickling down alleys and out shop side doors, working the heavy sea-side dew down through leaky roofs, preserving the elegance of enduring facades. The damp air soaks your shirt by seven AM, steam rising off the cobbled surface of the piazza.

Behind, from a hidden courtyard, surrounded by the true fronts of the inward-facing palazzos, comes the thump on sodden clay and click and chit-chat of bocce balls, the first game of the day, played by old men with small coffees and more generous grappas.

There is an ancient aura, fed by the expectant sun and the resultant indirect and shadowy light. It is a walled city, of a sort, walled by water. The large and outlining canals already want to reflect blue, while the narrow inner canals remain dark with remains of night, as the twinkling lights of the prior evening have given way to the moonlight which now merged with dawn.

The morning veil of the city lifts, like the veil of a hesitant but determined young widow about to venture back into society, like the rising veil of a nun finally resolved to leave the convent behind.

Indeed, it is the lifting of a veil of a vow of silence, as the city's birds awaken.

I savor the sweet aroma of pastries, and the earthy, yeasty, musty fragrance of the day's pizza dough being mixed and kneaded, even at this early hour. The sound of daily deliveries begins to shout down the canals from the cargo punts, supplying the above-and-under ground economies. Corrupt officials, paramilitary police, entrenched and enriched church leaders, the hands are out everywhere, silently clutching envelopes of cash, beyond the rattle of the shopkeepers' keys. Do you reveal all, or keep silent, or in fact do you risk your all following either path?

Young men pass by, heading to work, flexing muscles in Italian t-shirts before donning the uniform of the day. They will arrive at their shops to the rhythmic "stamp-stamp-stamp" of the bureaucrats' inked pads, of the regulators certification "paid" seals, and of the machine that will drum the beat of their day.

Oh, to dream and one day be a glass guildsman on Murano. That night they will carry man's bags and they will stroll these same streets, in casual, tourist shuffles, late into the moonlight.

Now come the schoolchildren past, all dressed in uniforms, some simply adrift, many with a purpose in their step and noisy chatter floating above their heads and into the café, enveloping my chair . . .

Blipbleep, blipbleep, blipbleep . . .

"Oops . . . hey, uh . . . Dick Stranger here. Oh, hi Otis."

"Sorry, did I interrupt something?"

"Feeding the pigeons in the square, sipping an espresso."

"Where the heck are you?"

"Uh . . . right here, Otis. Thank you for your concern."

"Well, anyway boss, I was goofing around on the special laptop a little after flying last night, and I think I found something useful. For your line of work, that is."

"Where are you and the laptop?"

"Miracle."

"We'll be over shortly."

Dick slipped on a pair of dark blue chinos, a white knit polo shirt with a "Woodstock Golf Club" logo, and his all black Reebok Classics. Sort of a business casual Friday look in his world. Jung's black leather collar with silver studs was accented with a plain blue denim bandana to complete his biker look.

They swung into Miracle Motors and stepped inside, where Otis had his laptop set up on the sales desk.

"Have a coffee. My apologies for interrupting your 'trip'."

"Thanks, Otis. Yeah, I had sort of drifted off."

"Well, I guarantee this will wake you up."

"I'm fully Americano'd and ready."

Jung finished greeting Otis and hopped up onto a pillow in the morning sun.

"So remember how I got us into SENTRY, the system for the police and probation people? I have something new for you."

A few months ago, Otis had procured a laptop from a security contractor at Fort Woodstock. He also acquired an air card from a detective supply agency that shared owners with a small wireless company.

Otis was adept at hacking, and spent a few evenings on the SENTRY project. The laptop had an unregistered and ever-changing IP address and the encrypted air card was registered anonymously with an offshore company that guaranteed privacy.

Together, any trail was faint at best. For SEN-TRY, he had managed to obtain a management log-on that put him and Dick on an information level with Chief Schwartz, or better.

"Remember how you mentioned to Jack and me the other day about the prison records of the guys out at Feckenmeyer's Mailbox? Well, I looked around a little, and with some advice from an old friend who used to work at the Bureau of Prisons, I got further into the Bureau's system."

"Holy crap, Otis. That could really help with the investigation business. How far in?"

"Well, I went in through personnel and set up a mythical employee who is a general consultant. No departmental reporting or charges required. Then we gave him Associate Warden access."

"Let's try him out."

"I'm already in, so let's just choose someone. Any suggestions?"

"Yeah. Wayne Nelson. Mystery to me. I've still got the other background on my phone. Do we need his Social?"

"We could search with it, but this system is name and B.O.P. – Bureau of Prisons – Federal ID number driven. So let's just search by name, and sort it out."

"Wow. Look at that. Lots of them. Who'd a thunk?"

"Let's throw in an initial."

"There he is. Otis . . . again – you're the best."

"That's what they tell me. Let's take a closer look. Okay, worked in the Garden. Horticulture Apprentice Program. Completed Career Planning and Job Fair, twice. And the Ten-Hour OSHA class. Pre-Release classes. Took Victim's Impact class. I guess he was trying. Or faking it."

"Let's look at the incarceration record."

"Okay. Let me change screens. Self-surrendered to Leavenworth Camp. Was on an ankle bracelet from sentencing to surrender. So not a serious flight risk."

"Anything juicy?"

"Look at this. Six months into a sixty month bit. Got a triple shot for contraband, theft, and possession of B.O.P. property. Sent to SHU – Segregated Housing Unit, known as 'The Hole.' Here's the sanitized story: he was random searched on

his way back from the Garden, found to have tobacco, green peppers, and a cat."

"What? A cat? In prison?"

"Let's read on. Somebody was looking to give
this guy some crap. One cigarette, bag of vegeta-
bles, and he claimed one of the kittens at the Garden because no one else was feeding it. B.O.P.
property, you know."

"What else?"

"Three shots at one time and to the Hole?"

"Looks it from here. But hey. One day into it,
'Productive contact with staff,' and 'returned to in-
mate population.'"

"So he turned into a rat for the officers?"

"My guess. Let's see what else. Admitted to
RDAP Program first of the following month. Fulfilled in nine months, was released on the tenth
month. Served sixteen of sixty months. Something is very special about this guy."

"Can we call your buddy to ask about this stuff?"

Otis walked over to this toolbox and opened a
small drawer that normally held tiny special tools
and loose items. Ignoring the new smartphone on
his belt, Otis pulled a battered flip-phone, at least
five years old, out of the drawer.

"Sorry, I gotta go outside, Dick. I bought this from the air card place. Old case, prototype inside. Untraceable signal, encrypted too."

Dick sat with his mouth open. It was enough to have Otis hacking the police and prisons. Now he had a spy phone. Too much Popular Science magazine?

"Richie, it's Otis. Can you talk? Okay. Look, we're on SENTRY, and have some questions."

Otis ran through the incarceration history, especially regarding the short stay. First off, the RDAP Program. Residential Drug and Alcohol Program. Nine month course, with one year early out as a reward. Daily rally, breakout groups. Lots of self-examination.

Most inmates are onto it – the motto is "Fake It to Make It." So he should have served, including good time and six months for half-way house, thirty-four months out of sixty if he completed RDAP.

"Richie, does that make sense?"

"Otis, it's the B.O.P. It doesn't have to make sense."

"Oh yeah. You told me that before."

"I can tell you the story, though. That 'Productive Contact with Staff' was a lot more than a local rat agreement. Look down to the very end for 'Status.'"

"Says: Released."

"Any letters after it?"

"Yes: TFW / D."

"You hit the jackpot, Otis. 'TFW stands for 'Turned Federal Witness.' This guy had some heavy duty information for the cops."

"What about the 'D'?"

"Well, that's kind of a joke. We call it 'Systeme D' for 'Debrouiller.' Means to muddle through, or to manage somehow. You know, the French method of managing life, like the French trains."

"So what does it really mean?"

"Category D. Works for the Government. Your boy Wayne here is a Fed."

FORTY

Dick sat in silent amazement in the office of Miracle Motors. Jung relaxed on his pillow, staring at Otis's cell phone, ears perked in curiosity. The buzzing of the air wrenches, from the open doors of the muffler shop across the side street, shot like arrows to puncture the dialog bubbles that floated as clouds through Dick's head.

"Wayne Nelson. Holy cats."

. . . Brrrrapp . . .

"Wayne Nelson. What about the drug thing."

. . .Brzzp. Brzzp. Brzzp . . .

"Wayne Nelson. Con to Fed. How it works."

. . . Zizzzz. Zizzzz. Zizzzz . . .

"Wayne Nelson. What is really going on at the farm?"

. . . Brzip. Brzip.

"Wayne Nelson. More news and weather at Ten PM."

. . . Brrrrapp. Zzip.

Otis wrapped up his call with some niceties and looked at Dick.

"Happy I quit smoking? This is what I do with my spare time now."

"Otis, we gotta talk."

Between Jack's friendship and Dick's business partner connection, Otis was already working the fringes of Dick's investigations. Now was the time to anoint him a Stranger, First Degree.

Dick spent the next two hours bringing Otis into the inner circle, finally springing for delivery lunch salads from The Woodchuck, and reaching deep into the back of the Miracle Motors refrigerator for a pair of Hamm's.

Otis added his perspective on the various characters in the cast, and on how the drama was unfolding. His quiet demeanor not to be mistaken for lack of observation, Otis's mind certainly had been working on Dick's various situations these past days. He was now proud to be on the A-Team of Truth is Strange Investigations.

Dick, for his part, knew that Otis was a lot like Jack, inconspicuous in the investigative role, a good thinker, and now with extra time on his hands.

Dick and Jung headed back to the loft and checked for any under-the-door updates before initiating the call to Giovanni.

The Italian answered in his perfectly trained English, apparently with some form of international caller ID.

"Giovanni here.

"Greetings, Giovanni, it is Dick Stranger."

"Little brother."

"Giovanni, Giovanni, how is Siena?"

"All is well. Olive oil is, shall we say, very good. Recent news is Strangere is very good also this year."

The two went on to discuss family, health, politics, American tourists, and in due time Dick's situation with the Ferrari. Anything within reason for a family member, said Giovanni, and he proposed a workable solution.

"Dick, the account will indicate '14 day funds availability, subject to instrument certification.' The Bank has such a category for certain classes of instruments, some wire transfers as well. Two weeks is the longest we have. Most clear electronically immediately or overnight at the longest."

"Giovanni, thank you. What is the Bank fee for this and where do I send it?"

"For you, my friend, there is no fee. Keep the olives coming."

The pleasantries continued until Giovanni was summoned by a family member. Dick repeated his thanks, and disconnected.

Dick stopped in at Stranger Than Fiction, finding Kate busy with new books. This was relaxation for her compared to more hours dealing with the apartment.

"Hey Kate. What's the Woodstock Review of Books best seller this week?"

"Today's Full Shade-Grown Fair Trade Brazilian, Espresso Roast and Ground, in a Recyclable Cup. Hands down."

"Well, at least the guy growing it is making some money."

"Actually, we net about the same as a good trade paperback. And no one tries to return it with soiled pages and a cracked spine."

"On the basis of that bullish economic news, I propose an evening out."

"I'm in. Tonight is Manicure Martini Mania at The Library, so that will be packed. Where to?"

Manicure Martini Mania was Sage's and Pearl's idea to fill The Library on a quiet weekday night. At eight PM, the local salon closing time, the community nail operators came and did mini manicures at fifteen minute intervals at the tables. For $7.95 the customer got the nail treatment plus a martini, and the stylist got $5.00 of it.

After word spread – remember café.com – the center section of Dick's building started to fill at six o'clock, and it was always booked. Significant others drifted in throughout the evening. Food and drink sales were through the roof, with Sage and Pearl acting as the perfect hosts.

Far be it from Dick and Kate to stand in the way of paying customers, so Dick had another plan already in place.

"Let's do The Sand Bar for burgers around 7 p.m. Jack and Otis's band is playing at eight. We can make a night of it. I mean an evening."

Kate rolled her eyes, folded her arms, and tapped an Earth Shoe.

"Sounds good to me. Just don't try to get me run over by a truck on the way home this time."

275

The Sand Bar was standing room only, and Dick noted that these must be the people who did not need manicures.

Originally a livery stable, The Sand Bar, as a building, had character beyond the wharf makeover. The exposed brick walls were cleaned and sealed, and the wide plank oak floor still showed marks from its use as a hardware store after the stable days. Fairly wide for a downtown storefront, the building extended to about forty feet short of the alley, and a modern storage room had been built to occupy the additional area. The nautical décor accented the brick, but was clearly non-authentic, and was more like mock Provincetown. The crowd did not seem to care.

Otis had agreed to pile their microphone cases and drinks on a table, in effect reserving one for Dick and Kate, and Dick let any guilty feelings pass.

As usual, the burgers were great, and the beer tasted equal to the task. Jack and Otis's garage band was a rhythm and blues tribute outfit, with a Seventies undertow. They performed at The Sand Bar because the drummer owned The Sand Bar, whose sponsorship included needed musical and audio equipment. Fair exchange for what was essentially a practice session with witnesses.

The playlist was entirely old favorites, and Dick's mind was zig-zagging from memory to memory as he recounted playing trumpet and flugelhorn in his own band, Stranger Yet, many years earlier.

It too was a blues and R & B band. The piano fantasy began back then, when he had the hots for their female electric keyboard player. She had a Fender Rhodes Electric Piano and was funky beyond Stranger Yet, more in the Prince mode, and visually far beyond the rest of the band.

Well into the second set, Otis's band finished Van Morrison's "Domino" and slid into The Commodore's "Brick House," and Dick was mentally on the one-step riser stage with Otis and Jack and the rest of the band, blasting out the horn parts he knew so well.

His fingers pushing imaginary trumpet valves on the table and on Kate's arm, Dick was interrupted by their server.

"The lady at the end of the bar wants to buy the two of you a drink. What'll ya' have?"

Dick glanced over, in that subtle tavern "what the hell" way, and saw Marian Horton give a faint wave. Her other hand was clutching an oversized beer glass, one third full.

From this distance and angle, the giant pelican mounted on the end of the bar appeared to perch on her shoulder in a bizarre pirate motif. Arrrgh. Aye matey. Buy 'ya a rum?

After quietly conferring with Kate, Dick placed the order and requested that Marian join them. The band went on break and they could talk.

"Dick. Kate. Olive branch?"

"Marian, we weren't at war. But we'll always take a tall, cool olive branch."

"Well, I'm sorry I acted so . . . so . . . like a jilted librarian. I've been hoping to run into the two of you together. I think I only have the guts to say this once. I was wrong, and the staff reminded me the other day at our meeting. Memberships are up, and we've been surveying the new patrons. Most got the idea to use the Library from your Library, not mine."

Dick stared at her. No pelican, tight blue jeans, white tank top over a nice tan, high-heeled sandals, hair ruffled, big jewelry, red-red lips, and no eyeglasses on a chain. He had to get his own stereotyping lenses adjusted.

"Apologies accepted, but not needed. All square. Maybe we can brainstorm a few joint promotions some time. Hey, does Otis know you're here?"

"I think so. I'm usually at their gigs, but normally in the background. He's with the band, not me. I go home when the last set wraps."

The conversation, music, and drinks wore on. Kate reminisced about the music she liked, much of which was on deck tonight. Dick babbled on about Stranger Yet. Marian fondly remembered that, incredibly, she was the lead singer in a regional rock band in the late seventies.

"Yeah. You know, I was into Janis Joplin, did a Phoebe Snow phase, Carol King, Aretha. All the big ones."

"Does Otis know this?"

"We've never been on an official date to talk about our pasts. It just doesn't come up over muffins and coffee at a used car lot. Especially one named Miracle Motors. Who came up with that, anyway?"

"Er . . . I did."

"Sorry, no offense intended, Dick. It just sounds so, so . . . shticky."

"Understood. Tell us, how did your band start, and why did you quit."

"We were in college and loved music and partying, and I was engaged to the lead guitarist. We had a lot of fun on our mini-tours of the Midwest. Even an occasional overnighter. Then I was diagnosed with twins."

"That'll do it."

"And here we are today."

Eleven o'clock tolled and the third and final set was over. The crowd, or at least the alcohol in them, wanted more. But few realized that the time displayed by the clock was about, if not past, the band members' bedtimes.

Otis and Jack joined the table, hailed with merriment. After a couple of cool-down rounds, Dick and Kate left. Jack headed home. And Marian stayed behind.

"Don't mind me. Otis and I are going to visit for a while."

FORTY-ONE

....

Dick and Jung rose early, and spent the first two hours of a beautiful morning on a long walk and on an observation period settled in on the favorite park bench, watching Woodstock wake up and drive through downtown.

Without completely reverting to Venice, Dick sat, drinking a coffee, Jung lying at his feet eyeing traffic. Dick took in the rising sun's color play on the Main Street buildings facing east, the birds' welcoming, and the smell of the damp grass clinging to his shoes from strolling through the freshly mown Park.

Jung watched with interest a small team of ants moving a piece of lint across the sidewalk, presumably headed for a small fortification they had constructed in a wide spot in the seam between the sections of walk, mimicking the daily toil, possibly fruitless, that was the destination of most of the passing cars.

Jung stood and crept over to the ant fort, holding his nose near for a close-up. Suddenly, being the crawling sort, the ants formed an ant pyramid in order to, cheerleader-like, vault their bravest to Jung's nose, where two ants got the wildest ride of their life, Jung sneezing and spinning and pulling Dick to attention.

The two ants froze, and Dick could see the little fellows clinging to hairs just above Jung's moist black nose, as the dog crossed his eyes trying to focus on the tickle bothering his snout. Dick swept the ants off and Jung surged toward the ant hill in retaliation.

Dick stood up, grabbed his cup, and tugged on the leash. Back to business, back to the loft. He waved to a few friends on the trip back to the building, and he soon was in one of the green leather chairs, planning his day.

First stop was The Library Cafe for croissants and hot tea and café.com. Pearl was getting The Liquid Muse ready for the retail day, and she spotted Dick flipping through The Milwaukee Journal-Sentinel. Almost at a run, she delivered herself to Dick's table. Jung leapt up and almost did a backflip, hopping gaily on his hind legs and getting slightly over center.

"Dick. Tomorrow's the day."

"You're announcing you've won the lottery?"

"Dick, stop it. I'm serious. Tomorrow morning we get our first delivery from ACME Wholesale, LLC. Liquor and cigarettes. I've got my paper trail all covered."

"Good work, Pearl. Have a coffee on me."

Man and dog exited the Café through the back door, slid into the MG, and took the short ride to Miracle Motors. Otis and Marian were sharing muffins and specialty coffees at the desk, imagining they were at a sidewalk café table. Jung went straight to Otis for a scratch, and then tentatively approached Marian. Obviously, her appeal was greatly enhanced by blueberry muffin crumbs and butter residue on her fingers. Jung sized her up, wagged, and licked some fingers. Dick took another chair at the desk and added a coffee.

"So this is what really goes on at Miracle Motors first thing in the morning."

Otis smiled, and Marian looked flustered. She was once again in her librarian uniform and demeanor, but then blurted,

"Dick, I came to see you. And of course Otis. Hey – wasn't last night a kick in the pants? Good outing for a school night."

Dick sat with his jaw open, yet in a silent smile. The new old Marian.

"Anyway, when I was at the bar, that O'Connor kid – Kidd O'Connor – sat down next to me with that other kid he hangs around with, Ian Jackson. I know them both because I had to suspend their Library cards for attempting to view and download porn sites on the Library computers. So Kidd is telling Ian about doing undercover work for the Police Department, and your name came up a couple of times. About then is when I invited myself over to your table. I hope you didn't mind. That's all, but I thought you should know."

"Marian, thank you. I'll look into it. I appreciate it a lot."

Marian was truly making peace and Dick acknowledged it. Otis sat back enjoying the interaction and a muffin. Marian put her hand on his, said her goodbyes, and walked across Main Street to the Woodstock Free Public Library.

Dick was on the cell instantly.

"Hey Ian, it's Dick. We've got some chassis set-ups on the stock car to show you and get your thoughts. Any time today? Noon hour? Great. I'll cater it."

Dick and Jung took off in the MG to see what Boyd's activities were the day prior to delivery to The Liquid Muse. They rode west of town and made a spot check on the Mailbox, which had a pile of cards in it. Dick snapped photos and continued past the farm. There, pulling out of the driveway, was Jay Boyd IV at the wheel of the one and only rental cube van in town.

Realizing the MG was not the most inconspicuous surveillance unit, Dick hung back so far as to keep the van just in sight, which was not really so hard, with a big white box truck standing out prominently in traffic.

Being more conspicuous, however, was a late model Cadillac DTS, Black with very dark windows, and Illinois plates. The car followed the cube van, turn for turn. At his distance, Dick could not get the plate number, although he was sure it would reveal nothing factual. This was a professional tail.

Finally, the truck turned into a residential area and down the alley behind Berg's Store. The Cadillac slowed but continued past.

Boyd backed up to the door, unlocked and slid it open, and parked inside. Dick parked a few blocks away, but the elevation afforded him a view of the proceedings.

An hour elapsed, far too long for Pearl's order alone to be filled, and the barn door was closed the entire time. Dick was left to speculation. Jung was bored. New local smells were good for a while, but grew stale.

The black DTS repeatedly made a large loop around the neighborhood, and Dick was able to get a license plate number, for whatever it was worth.

Dick followed Boyd as he made stops at the two remaining locally owned convenience stores in town. Boyd carried cases of liquor and cigarettes out of the truck into their storerooms. Dick wanted to complete the delivery route behind Boyd, but knew he had to get back to Miracle Motors to meet with Ian. He called Jack, who gladly picked up the trail for the rest of the day, along with the DTS.

Dick, Otis, and Ian tore into bags of patty melts and fries from the Café.

"So Dick, what about the stock car? Is it in the back shop?"

"Yeah. Let's go back there."

They adjourned to the warehouse where the Miracle Motors – Ian Jackson stock car stood in the shop area. Otis explained the plan and set-up for this weekend's racing, and Ian and he examined the car.

"Dick, where's Kidd's car?"

"Oh, behind that wall, a spare, but I'm sure you won't need it."

"He misses the racing, but he's so busy now he'd never have time to do any of the work. He went full time with Chief Schwartz about a week ago, hauling liquor and cigarettes."

"I can't imagine him leaving Boris. Seemed like an easy gig. Where is he trucking? And it's Schwartz?"

"Said the liquor is from outside Chicago, and the butts are from Virginia. They leased a semi. Schwartz is involved somehow."

"Virginia? How does that work?"

"Get 800 cases of cigarettes in one full load. Something about taxes, but you didn't hear that from me."

"Café.com says he's doing undercover for Schwartz, too. Think there's anything to it?"

"Jeez Dick. Put me on the spot. Well, yeah, he is doing some of that at night. Some deal to keep his CDL. Says he's supposed to keep an eye on Dick Stranger. That's all he says. I shouldn't be telling you all this stuff."

"Ian, thanks. It helps with some things I'm working on. One last thing. Have you heard anything around town about a stolen classic car?"

"Word is some high end street rod went missing. No one seems to know who had it, though. Supposed to belong to some high roller."

Dick and Otis looked at each other, and then both turned to the Ferrari's empty spot. Ian looked over, taking three beats to think and register what was gone.

"No. No, Dick. Not your car. How did they get it? How did they get in?"

"With a magic wand. No security alert, locked door. And vintage Italian sports car, not a high end street rod. No high roller, either."

"Wow, I'll have to listen for a big mouth. Sorry, Dick.

"Ian, you and I are pretty close, right? Keep this quiet. Just listen, okay?"

"Got it, boss."

FORTY-TWO

....

Dick collected Jung, left the Miracle Motors office, and settled into the MG. He dialed Pearl on his cell.

"The Liquid Muse, Pearl Wisdom."

"Hi Pearl, it's Dick. There's a little twist on that order from ACME. I need you to hold it in storage."

"And not sell it?"

"Exactly."

"But the inventory computer will go crazy. Low cost, no sales, high days' supply, you name it, every exception report will pop up."

"Pearl, I hold you blameless. It's just something we have to do."

"Okay, hon, it's your rodeo. I should be recording this. Leave it to me to have a boss who doesn't want to sell things. This will make the rep from Dairystate Wet Goods happy. He said ACME was sweeping through his accounts for hard liquor and cigarettes."

"You'll get the customer of the week award."

"I may be the only contestant. Oh, hey, the counter guy from the car rental place was just in getting beer and said to tell you the cube van is on a long term rental and they don't know if they're getting another one right away. Just FYI."

"Thanks, Pearl. Sorry about storing the order."

"Gotta go. Customers."

Dick sat in his office searching for the owner of the license plates on the car from Illinois. Recently he had managed to get a log-on from an old friend at the DVM for the National database for vehicles, NMVITIS. He ran the plate number, and the plates turned up as stolen. Last registered in Chicago to an aging Toyota Camry, Silver. Definitely not the black DTS. So the plates were stolen, if not the car. He wouldn't know about the car unless he could get close enough, with sufficient time, to obtain the VIN number. Just a quick cellphone photo would do. But for now, a dead end.

Clearing sunny, the day begged for a ride in the country. Dick put on the Clubmasters sunglasses and a cap, and dabbed Jung's nose with sunscreen. A couple of dog biscuits, a bottle of water and a bowl, and the co-pilot was set.

The roads south and west of town followed the jagged property lines through the coulees, and the more geometric patterns of the farms on the flatter ridge tops, few as those were.

The scents of Amish buggy droppings, fresh hay, dairy barns, and of corn and soybeans in the early afternoon sun, engulfed the MG occupants, delighting one with memories, and crazing the nose of the other.

The aroma of sun on vinyl, the woody hot ash body framing, a slightly rich exhaust, and one Cairn Terrier, all contributed to the roadside olfactory assault.

For Dick, avoiding the road apples from the Amish horses was a sporting challenge. Don't get the stuff all over the bottom of the fenders, don't slip off the road.

Inevitably, the road would wind over to Feckenmeyer's Mailbox. The draw of the old mailbox was too much, and Dick and Jung inspected it for the second time that day. Cards. Different cards. A game? A scavenger hunt? Lovers' private message system? A local kid's fantasy tale? Or something sinister?

Jung stared at the mailbox, squinting in a shaft of sunlight, contributing a low growl to the conversation. Whatever it was, he didn't like it. CSP (Cairn sensory perception)? Or merely the trail of a passing varmint?

Knowing that lingering in thought raised the odds of detection, Dick and Jung jumped back into the MG and motored off toward the farm entrance. Perfect timing, as a black Tahoe with dark windows and a set of black-finished twenty-two inch wheels roared up the town Road and pulled over at the path to the mailbox. A white male, mid-twenties, bolted out, left the motor running and music blasting, and rushed to the mailbox. He pulled a card from his jeans pocket and left it in the box. Reversing the process, he roared off, passing them just beyond the intersection. He was preceded slightly by the musical shockwave. Dick snapped a shot of the plate.

Dick and Jung returned to the loft and Dick settled in with a hot Lapsang souchong to collect his thoughts and to make notes for the case files. Time to add Jack to the loop.

"Hi Dick."

"Don't do that."

"Part of the delight of caller ID."

"Easily amused, eh? Hey, any news on Life's A Blast and the loaded fireworks theory?"

"I definitely think they ship the drugs with the fireworks. I've staked it out based on Jean's info on Lars and Boris's schedules. They work late in the back warehouse. After they leave, Juan and Ricky go in. I think I know how they get around that secure door. Let me germinate that a little first."

"On the drugs – a small siphon program by Juan & Co.?"

"Definitely. Plus, I'm not the only one watching them. That DTS that was tailing Jay? Keeps appearing in the evenings near Life's A Blast."

"You'll have to fill me in. I've got news, too, from Ian about Kidd. A few missing pieces. Want to meet me tonight and we can sync files?"

"Have to make it in the AM. Otis promised we'd fly tonight. It's just too gorgeous out to miss. Okay by you?"

"How about seven thirty at the Café for breakfast.

"Done."

Dressed in black chinos, black t-shirt, and the black Reeboks, Dick took the 300C for a ride at dusk to check on Schwartz's barn and Jay Boyd. Dressed for a stealth mission, he parked at his distant vantage point and observed Boyd backing the cube van into Berg's barn.

The black Cadillac DTS crawled into his peripheral vision and across his distant focus. It was driving down the side street again, and it would do so about every five minutes.

In an hour, the cube van emerged and parked out front, leaving the door open, and Dick caught a glimpse of the cars under cover in the barn. Being a car guy, he was curious what classics the Berg boys liked to drive.

The DTS's appearance had taken on a rhythm of its own. Interrupting the evening solitude was the blatting of a diesel Jake brake slowing a semi coming into town. Dick started to walk to the barn. He was just being a car idiot at the moment. To avoid both the DTS and Jay Boyd, he would keep a sensible distance and speculate what was under the car covers.

Dick was a block from the barn when a semi wheeled down the dark residential street toward Berg's. A big black long nose Peterbilt, tricked out like a cowboy rig. Visor, chrome stack shields, double sleeper, lots of lights. Intimidating, cool.

The truck pulled into the alley and in one smooth motion did a tight maneuver to end up backing toward the barn door.

Unless Schwartz graduated to hijacking semis, it must be Kidd O'Connor with a shipment. Sure enough. A magnetic sign over the lettering on the sleeper read: "Leased to: ACME Wholesale, LLC – Not For Hire." Obviously some down on his luck cattle hauler was getting some revenue from a formerly parked truck.

The trailer looked battle scarred and had a couple of clearance lights out. What a ridiculous risk to take, of getting pulled over, for someone like this. Trucks and trailers like these were readily available on a flooded big rig market, and this wheelman just got in and drove, taking his chances with the law. Sure enough, Kidd O'Connor climbed down out of the cab.

Dick altered his route to take in some back yards, and fortunately there was enough light left to avoid the sand boxes, lawn darts, unfenced rose bushes, mole traps, and the rest of normal city estate backyard living.

Still, he felt a pang of guilt walking through these innocent properties, like the feeling he had as a kid stealing apples and watermelons from Mr. Miller's side yard orchard and garden. Only years later did he realize that Mr. Miller would gladly have given him the produce had he just asked. But what thrill in that?

What business did the DTS driver have now, with both Jay's and Kidd's loads arriving? Concerned that he might be interrupting an unpleasant scene, Dick crept near and watched from a not too safe distance as Jay and Kidd unloaded cases of cigarettes and liquor. Looked to be a fifty-fifty split of product on the load.

Craning around a tree, he could see into the barn and have a direct look at the covered cars.

Suddenly he was captured in the glare of high-intensity headlamps. The DTS kept coming toward him as he froze with his head half way around the tree, an awkward position but one that exposed him the least.

Dick could hear the car's tires crunching in the small gravel accumulated in the nearby intersection, and he could see the shadow of a tree with a body clenched to its side playing off a white garage wall. The shadow swiftly went sideways and he could hear the tires rolling down the side street. If he had been seen, he was not the prey.

He looked back over at the barn and the unloading process. It hit him over the head like a case of whiskey.

One of the cars was parked slightly out of line and had a different cover than the others. The adjacent covers were the traditional type, fitted for shape and with an elastic gathered hem. The mirror flaps stuck out like circus clown ears.

The odd car had a cover carelessly thrown over it, and the cover drooped toward the floor. Behind the car was a folded pile to match.

Dick knew instantly. It was the body bag. Put the first flat part on the floor, pull the car onto it, throw on the cover and zip together. Anti-dust, moisture, rust, mold, mildew. He knew of only a few in town, and this one looked familiar.

Then he could see it. One wheel was half re-vealed by the askew car cover. A vintage alloy wheel with the knock-off splined hub. No wheel studs and no lug nuts.

The Ferrari.

FORTY-THREE

....

. . . Dick sat at the baby grand in the ballroom at The Woodstock Golf Club. It was just after the midnight festivities at the annual Golf Ball, the formal New Year's Eve party that packed the ballroom to overflowing. The rest of the band would filter back from break and join in, as Dick began the opening measures of "American Pie." And the crowd flooded the dance floor . . .

Dog paws on his legs and a whine pulled Dick back from this bravura performance, to his lounge chair.

"Oh, Jung, hi. Whoa. One AM. I guess I dozed off, buddy. Ready to go out?"

Of course. Since eleven o'clock. The dog had gone through all the rituals. Run to the door and look back. Sit and stare at Dick. Whimper and lie down, staring. Finally, physical contact was need-ed.

Jung made the short trip, and they retired for the night.

Otis was on the phone at seven AM.

"Hey boss, ya' up?"

"Uh . . . now."

"Oh, sorry. But I've got some interesting news. Can I drop over?"

"Give me half an hour. I'm meeting Jack at the Café, and you can join us."

Dick threw on blue jeans and a grey "Still Plays with Cars" sweatshirt, slipped into some loafers with no socks, and went downstairs.

There, he ordered the European for four, the breakfast comprising meats, cheeses, fruit, and breads. He was settling back into a generous supply of Havarti, when Otis rushed in. Jack walked at a normal pace, a ways behind him.

Seated, with coffees ordered, Otis told of his news.

"Dick, we were flying last night and saw what's going on at the farm, why all this security. We were riding the edge, across Boris's property, and looked down at his irrigation fields. On the entire west half they're growing marijuana between the rows of corn."

"How could you tell?"

"Well, we can fly fairly low, so I looped back and went down for a closer look. It's marijuana alright. And they're watching it. Somebody ran out of one of the barns, and aimed a rifle at me, so I know they're serious."

"Anybody we know?"

"What do you think, Jack? I wasn't sure."

"I was flying a little further away, but it looked like Boris to me. I don't think he recognized us with helmets on in the ultralights. I don't even think he knows Otis owns them."

"What do you think, Dick?"

"Dick, excuse Otis. It's his first 'break in the case' since he became a card-carrying member of Truth is Strange."

Dick paused for more cheese, which gave Otis a chance to catch his breath and serve himself. Maybe this was too public a place for this. Dick looked around, and thought there was a safe buffer of empty tables around them. Jack picked up the story.

"Dick, they do have a great place for grass in the corn. The Restricted Air Space extends over half their property, but the unrestricted half is untillable – little bluffs of sandstone and stone mounds and sand outcroppings and the like. He should sell that all to the sand and gravel guys and have real dirt brought in. Anyway, no aerial surveillance by the people who look for marijuana operations. I know these grass in the corn deals have become common, but with irrigation, no planes, and a fenced yard, it's a good climate for kilos."

"Jack, where is Wayne in this whole thing. Shouldn't he have been the rifle man, not Boris?"

"He supervises, mostly. Of course, they're not milking cows, so he could be sitting in a bar somewhere at night. Plus, we kind of know something of his employer, so . . ."

"You know, I follow him during the day, mostly. My fault. I need to see where he is and why, and how that jives with the federal thing."

"But what about Boris with a gun? That's a commitment."

"And what about the day and night watchman, Jay Boyd?"

"Oh, Jack. Stay tuned for news. Kidd's driving for Schwartz now. Last night I watched Boyd and Kidd empty a semi-load of cigarettes and liquor into Berg's barn, with my Ferrari sitting there. Plus, there is a car full of tourists from Chicago tailing Boyd who watched the whole scene. I just hope they didn't see me playing like bark on a tree."

"Oh my. Schwartz, Boyd, and O'Connor together in the cigarettes and liquor? And a little grass operation on the side. And some friends from Chicago here for their share?"

"So I assume Boris knows nothing about Boyd moonlighting?"

"We'll have to find out. The DA would have a field day with conspiracy charges. Assuming a doubtful provenance on the merchandise, of course. Then add the special crop."

"And I still need to find out if Kidd was really the driver and trigger man out on Cranberry Boulevard. I think I scared Ian yesterday, so maybe something will leak."

The trio made plans for further surveillance and research. Poor Otis had a full-time job, though liberally scheduled, and now he was miffed that he could not do investigating all day long. Dick's marching orders involved finding more details about the drug and fireworks connection, as Jack was running out of information.

Alone back in the office, Dick punched a number into his cell.

"Boris Shiraz here."

"Hey Boris, it's Dick."

"Dick, my friend, what's going on?"

"The other night I spotted your pottery barn, and I'm fascinated, and wondered if I could get the tour sometime."

"Of course. What are you doing right now?"

"Other than talking to you, I'm available. Okay if I drive on out?"

"See you soon. Stay for cocktails?"

Dick pulled into the Shiraz farm, parked in a paved area beside the garage, and cut the engine.

The pottery barn was directly ahead, just a few yards from the blacktopped drive that looped through the barnyard. He hopped out of the Chrysler and headed for the front door of Boris and Trixie's house. Boris was already at the door.

"That was fast."

"Always in a hurry to see you, Boris."

"Even when I'm not in the buying mood?"

"Like I said . . . always."

"Well let's take a little walk, it's right around the corner, but I usually go out the back of the house, off the deck."

"It looks like a great place, Boris. How do you have time to do pottery?"

"I've been doing so much running for the store that I decided I needed another hobby to give me an excuse to be home. I've been helping unpack fireworks at night for Lars, but that's getting old. I told him no more night work. The pottery is my new night work. Here, step inside."

The cedar outside was mirrored inside, and the place looked constructed like a luxury cabin. Boris had the workmen who could do this sort of thing on payroll, or at least on call, but it still had to be an expense. With windows on all four sides plus skylights, the shop was bright and open.

Shelves lined two walls, containing pottery in various states of creation. In one corner stood a machine that had a large hopper on it for clay, and another corner had the kiln. Even though it appeared to have forced air heat, there was a free-standing woodstove, and Dick commented on the apparent surplus of available warmth.

Various bins held raw material, workbenches circled the room, and the very center had two electric powered variable speed potter's wheels. Boris went off explaining all the equipment and the process.

"This extruding machine is called a pug mill. Don't get your hand in that. And these electric wheels. No ties or scarves, no long hair that isn't pulled back. It's like any shop. I still like the old style kiln though. The electric ones just take the element of chance out of things. I had to put an afterburner on the chimney though – some sort of air quality thing. You know those California types."

Boris went on and on about the several states of fired pottery, glazes, and styles – he preferred the

Romanesque look that influenced the pottery of his homeland. Dick was getting the world history of pottery, and it was actually kind of fascinating.

"Boris, they told me at card club that you're even teaching pottery to Jay Boyd. How does he have time for that? Isn't he busy with the crops?"

"Remember, Dick, we don't have dairy cows, so the schedule is more flexible. You know, in the few places I have done the kernel count, things look good, so I'm letting Wayne and him do their things out there. They both seem to have a little time left over, and I'm okay with it. Plus Jay seems like a nice young man, sort of artistically inclined. Got the feel for the wheel right away."

"Seems like I've seen him in town a lot lately."

"Oh yeah, he's doing some favors for some friends. Delivering some stuff, taking a few nights to do that. And during a few other downtimes. He's still putting in more than a full week for me"

"So tell me about the fireworks business. You know I got the tour. Looks like a lot going on."

"I pretty much let Lars do his thing there. Once he got on board, he had so many ideas. I never knew the markup you could get repackaging the fireworks for wholesale. He's got some accounts he brought with him that ante right up. It's amazing. We've got that big showroom building but most of the money comes in from the outside sales and shipping. So I'm doing some quality control and watching the books. And making pottery."

"What about your man Wayne. I never see him around."

"Seems to do his job and that's about it. Not interested in pottery, but he likes firearms. He's always going to the rod and gun club to shoot clay and the like. Plus he fools around with pistols on a little range he set up out back. He says Jay has been a real help, and that the kid has some good crop ideas. Wayne just says 'it's in the corn, it's in the corn,' whatever that means. He says just wait for the crop when it comes in. It'll be a bonus crop this year."

"Oh yeah. Well, Boris, that's sounds great. And thanks for the tour. I'll have to come out and throw a little myself. Seems like a harmless enough hobby."

"Cocktails?"

"Boris, it's only two o'clock. I guess maybe one."

Dick returned to the loft, coming up the back stairs and in the back door. Jung greeted him at the door, but then scurried through the loft to the hall door, where he stood ground, growling.

On the floor, clearly having been slid under the wide-gapped door, were several playing cards. Dick picked them up. Five cards. Ace of diamonds, eight of hearts, ace of clubs, eight of spades, queen of hearts. Aces and eights.

FORTY-FOUR

....

"Jean Paradise."

"Jean, hi, it's Dick. Can we meet to talk?"

"I'm paid up, aren't I?"

"Of course, plus I wouldn't have to harass you guys anyway."

"I was kidding, Dick. You are so serious. When and where?"

"How about noon at my place. I'll invite Giorgio and order sandwiches. My treat. Park in my driveway."

"We'll be there."

Giorgio arrived a few minutes early with chicken croissant sandwiches and salads. Today this was his normal lunch hour. The potato-potato-potato sound of Jean's Harley was met by Jung barking his head off until she got off the bike and called him by name. Dick had unlocked the gate, and Jean brought Jung upstairs with her.

Striking as usual in jeans, black motorcycle boots, and a purple cotton shirt with cap sleeves, Jean came in the back door and greeted Giorgio and Dick, giving her husband a big hug.

"Hey guys, what's happenin'?"

"Lunch, Jean. Grab some iced tea and have a seat."

"Great. But why are we here, Dick? It sounded like business."

"After lunch."

Three sandwiches and salads and six iced teas later, they moved to the loft's sunspace, Dick's guests settling into the green leather chairs with him pulling up a side chair.

"Jean, I know we can talk in front of Giorgio; you two must talk at home. Plus, you've both already contributed to this case. First, Jean, can you tell me exactly how the process works at Life's A Blast for receiving and selling the drugs. Jack already told me you and he talked about the bogus fireworks shipments."

"Dick, I've been wandering around a little more. Always an excuse to carry a file and appear to check on something. It looks like all the shipments from Chicago already have 'the load,' as they refer to it. Ricky and Juan are the drivers for that.

"Lars comes in at night and opens the fireworks, removes the drugs, and repackages. Some cases get sold as-is, I presume to other 'distributors'.

"On the product from Mexico, same drivers, but they use the enclosed car hauler. Sometimes they take cars down there, but mostly I think that is all just on paper. Especially since our DMV visit. I don't know if any fireworks from Mexico are 'loaded'."

"Jean, it seems like too much risk. The borders, I mean."

"But, shipments from established firms? I don't know, Dick."

"I think Jack and I need to get in there at night. Possible?"

"It must be. Juan and Ricky are always there after Lars. Juan leaves the overhead door active, even after he has disabled the air system. They just leave the deadbolt off, then throw the valves and use a handheld opener when they return. And the security system? You could guess this one. Good old Boris. Password: trixie123."

Dick explained to Giorgio his questions about Kidd O'Connor.

"You know my Ferrari is, sort of, missing."

"Oh, no, Dick. It can't be. Not that car."

"Giorgio. Stay calm. I already know where it is being hidden. I just need to find out anything you know, or can find out, about Kidd."

And then the stunner.

"And Giorgio, remember the undercover car conversation? Whoever was driving that car took a couple of shots at Kate and me that night."

Knowing that this was the real thing, Jean and Giorgio got very quiet. They interrupted each other trying to speak first:

"Dick, I'll find out . . . "

"Dick, I'll talk to . . . "

Dick updated his notes and emailed the files to Jack and Otis. Feeling a need to check on the downstairs, he installed a blue bandana on Jung and made his rounds. Liquor, Café, Bookstore.

The ACME Wholesale LLC shipment had arrived safely, and Pearl said her regular suppliers were pleased to get their business back.

"Yeah, Dick. I might have stirred up something, though. Dairy State Wet Goods thanked me for telling them who the new supplier is. Said they are contacting their distributors because they supposedly had exclusive territories for a couple of the brands we're buying. Probably why Don Juan Jay Boyd swore me to secrecy on my new source. Man must not believe in word of mouth advertising."

"Pearl, you're doing the right thing. Don't get too far onto Boyd's bad side, though. I don't think he is as charming as he portrays himself to be."

"Newsflash, Dick. 'Us Women' already knew that. On the bright side, we're having a big day. A retirement party, a surprise fiftieth birthday, plus the motorcycle club night."

She punched a dollar number into a pocket calculator and held it up to Dick. He smiled and Jung wagged.

"So Sage, looked busy this morning. And the croissants were outstanding. Can you set up a tea and a cappuccino at one of the tables for me?"

"Sure enough, Dick. Here's today's numbers so far. Good day."

"Kate, Giorgio's back, take a coffee break next door. I'll be there but your cappuccino will be getting cold."

"Okay, okay. I'll bring the numbers. Order a salad, okay?"

Jung was having a wild time. Favorite people and places, then a plate of dog biscuits at the table. Too good to be true. Kate joined Dick at the table and slipped a biscuit to Jung.

She had just begun to toy with her salad when Giorgio rushed into the Café.

"Kate. Policeman to see you. Where do you want him? Your office or here?"

"Right here is perfect. My legal advisor is already at the table."

Walking away, for an instant Giorgio thought, 'is that Dick or Jung?' and smiled to himself.

In seconds an officer appeared at the doorway and Kate motioned to him. Ofc. P. Justus. Dick snickered as the officer strode over, file in one hand, the other on his Glock. He looked at his shoulder speaker and turned down his radio.

"Ms. Kaul, I'm Officer Justus. I have some information on your burglary."

"Call me Kate. And your name?"

"Paul. Paul Justus."

"Born to be in law enforcement."

"I guess so. Ms. Kaul – er, Kate. Is it okay if we speak in front of Mr. Stranger here?"

"Yes. In fact, he is advising me in this matter."

Dick and Kate both grinned at the pseudo-formality this lent to the proceedings. This was likely Ofc. P. Justus's first time off the reception and dispatch window.

"We have a pretty solid lead on your burglar. I know you gave us the serial number on your stolen iPad, but can you produce a receipt if we need it?"

"Of course. Did you find it?"

"Yes. Last night Kidd O'Con – I mean, our undercover operative bought it as a fenced item for a hundred dollars cash. The guy joked that it had a bunch of Celtic tunes in the music files, and he said he replaced them with rap. Our man verified that."

"Is the seller our burglar?"

"If you verify that number, we'll question him."

"I'll do it right now. I scan all my receipts into the computer at the store, so I can get at it with my phone."

A few finger slides on the touchscreen, and Kate had it on display. She zeroed in on the number, certifying the match.

"We'll try to talk to him today. Has a prior for stalking. Charge was cut down to disorderly conduct on a plea deal. Thank you, ma'am . . . Kate. Here's my card with my phone numbers on it. Feel welcome to text me also if I'm on patrol. I'll respond when I can. Thank you."

Dick thought this probably was the inaugural presentation of one of his cards, except to the family of Mr. and Mrs. Justus Senior. Other than slipping the identity of their "undercover operative," he had learned to comport himself well. They silently watched as Ofc. P. Justus walked out, his radio garbling something out of the epaulet-mounted handset.

FORTY-FIVE

....

Dick's cell phone jolted him awake.   One AM.

"Dick, it's Trixie. You better get out here. There's been a shooting!"

"Trixie, did you call the police?"

"Yeah, they're on the way, but you're our guy. Come out right away!"

"Is everybody OK?"

"I think so, but come out now!"

Dick threw on some clothes and ran down the stairs to the Chrysler 300C. Ripping out of the alleyway, he thought about the odds of him getting stopped by the police. After all, it was bar time, and he was roaring his dual exhausts around town, a big black car with chrome wheels and blue high-intensity discharge headlights. Not exactly inconspicuous.

Feathering the throttle a bit in a nod to blending in, Dick managed to get to the west side of town and onto the county and town roads.   He could see the colored strobes of two squad cars far ahead of him, and the reflective back of an ambulance.

Coming toward him, though, was another squad car, emergency lights ablaze. When the car passed him on its way toward Woodstock, Dick could see in the lighted interior the face of one of the force's newest and youngest officers. On a mission.

Dick's car was held at the gates to the farm. After some finagling, Dick was able to join the scene at the pottery barn, following just behind the police and paramedics.

Inside was a messy scene. The potter's wheel was a red mess, and bent over onto it was a man with a pony tail, Jay Boyd. Boris seemed calm, but Trixie was hysterical. She was sure he was dead.

And from the looks of the scene, she had good reason. Blood was splattered around the barn in a circular pattern from the wheel, and clay was thrown in a line around as well. Jay Boyd was slumped over the wheel.

The paramedics pulled him away from the wheel, and verified that he was alive. He appeared to have two or three bullet wounds, and as he had fallen against the wheel, his arm had hit the variable speed control for the wheel and his head had come down on the blob of clay that was once a future work of art. Boris had turned off the wheel.

It became apparent that there was plenty of blood loss, but that the wounds themselves were not life-threatening. A graze to the neck was the single item closest to being fatal, but the other wounds just produced a lot of blood as he fell against the wheel.

With Boyd on the gurney, and vital signs stable, one of the paramedics directed a statement to Boris and Trixie.

"This guy is lucky as hell. His head fell onto the clay, and not the wheel itself. And the clay that was flying all over piled into the wounds. It's like a compress. It held the bleeding. He'd be done otherwise. He's unconscious, it's really bad, but I think he'll make it. Who was shooting into this place at one AM, anyway?"

One of the officers interrupted this lecture,

"We'll take it from here. Just get him to the hospital."

The north wall of the pottery barn was riddled with bullet holes, and the window was gone. A number of the rounds were embedded in the cedar, both outside and on the inside of the far south wall. Officers were milling around outside the building when Trixie grabbed the one who appeared in charge by the collar.

"I saw it happen. I saw the car. It was big and black and had dark windows and big wheels. The gunfire came from the car. I saw it!"

"Ma'am, calm down. How did you happen to see the gunfire?"

"I heard a car in the driveway and I thought maybe it was Wayne's truck coming for an emergency or something. Boris and Jay had been in the pottery barn all evening, so I was pretty sure Jay was still there. Boris was with me. I looked out and this car was going fast into the barnyard, and went around the circle by the barn. Then they stopped and the gunfire started. Then they squealed out. It was a big black car."

"Ma'am, this gentleman just arrived in a big black car. Guys, please hold that gentleman. Is that the car you saw?"

Dick cringed as the officers grabbed his arms and held them behind his back. Holy crap, don't they do a little more questioning?

"Officer sir, I called Mr. Stranger to come out here. I called him right after I called 911. But yes, the car was a lot like that."

The officers loosened their grip on Dick, but kept him warily in sight. Two of them went over to examine the Chrysler.

"Hey guys, check the car for a weapon, check me for powder. I am an invited guest here. Trixie, Boris, I'll help in any way I can."

Trixie latched onto Boris and dragged him over to Dick, where she clung to Dick with the other arm.

"Dick, what if that was Boris in there. Do you think they were looking for Boris? Why would they do that?"

"Trixie, we don't know very much about anything yet. We'll let the police do their job, and we'll look at everything. Boris, I think you should have some protection here after this. Or, you're welcome to stay with me."

"Sir, we'll assign someone to stay here tonight if you wish. One of our late night shift officers should be returning from town immediately."

"Was that the guy I saw heading back into town when I was coming out?"

"Yes, he was partway out and we realized we needed some tactical supplies. He went back for them."

"Wow. It looks like everybody and everything is here. What is the missing ingredient?"

"I can't say sir, it's a police matter."

"Oh come on, I'm on your side. What did we forget?"

"I can't say sir, it's a police matter."

"But we'll all know in a few minutes anyway."

"Well . . . well, we realized we were out of caution tape and we wanted to secure the area. I had to send him to the Wal-Mart."

"Fair enough. We all have details to look after. Let me know if I can help in any way. Meantime, I'm going to talk to Boris and Trixie for a little while."

"Tell them I'll be back with them shortly. I'm still getting some measurements and the like."

Dick led Boris and Trixie over to a patio table sitting below the deck on the lawn.

"Trixie, tell me again what you saw, but slowly so we don't miss any details. The police will probably ask you the same questions. Over and over. Boris, how soon were you aware of the situation?"

Trixie's earlier account was about all she could remember, and Boris was aware seconds after Trixie. He just wasn't at the window looking at who was driving in the driveway. Did they have security cameras? No, not at the driveway, just at the fence line, but he would check them at daylight.

Finally the late shift officer was back and some of the others had cleared out. A core group took charge of the scene. A commitment was made to overnight surveillance, and the officers were asking Boris and Trixie the same questions again.

After conferring with the officers and the Shiraz family, Dick felt comfortable leaving for town. He could see the entire area was now taped off in yellow.

Pulling out of the driveway, he strained to see the print on the tape.

Caution   Wet Paint   Caution   Wet Paint Caution   Wet Paint

FORTY-SIX

···

Again with the dog nose. Dick had finally fallen deep asleep after a fitful night of getting up and making notes to the myriad thoughts spinning through his head. Arise, write note, back to bed, hit delete.

Today was intended to be routine. Drink some coffee, check on the businesses, catch up on the internet, and think about the pending cases. And now this. Shots fired. But not any little old shots taken at Dick and Kate, no matter how ill-intended those may have been. The shots that hit Jay Boyd IV were part of a real plan, one whose target might have been someone else, one whose planners had automatic weapons. Woodstock, Wisconsin?

Dick put himself together. Jung was already down the stairs to the back yard, and Dick decided it was time to employ a new investigative tool in the Truth Is Strange arsenal.

A new lounge chair.

New to him, that is. An Eames lounge chair, with footstool, found on craigslist. The thing had hardly been used. Teak with black leather, it was competing with his red leather Stressless Recliner for comfort.

Dick found it when a young doctor at the nearby Medical Center got married recently, and his upper end apartment had given way to the country girl, a country look, in a country style house, in the country.

Half price chair. A bargain, thought Dick, and perfectly comfortable for whatever studying was required of a professional detective. The red chair had been taken over by dreams and daydreams, and surely this chair would keep thoughts professional. Jung, for his part, liked the footstool.

Moments into the process of parsing the previous evening's story into meaningful investigative pathways, Dick's cell started to dance.

"Dick Stranger."

"Hi Dick, it's Jean. Can you talk?"

"Sure. Can you?"

"Of course. That's why I called. Jeez, Dick."

"Sorry."

"Right. Anyway, Lars just called Ricky and Juan in for a trip to Chicago. They leave about four PM, so they won't be back for twelve hours easy. It'll be safely past three AM. I'll leave the gate open."

"Thanks a million. Remind me to give you a raise if you're ever on my payroll."

"Yeah, right Dick. See you later."

Dick knew he needed staff for this visit.

"Hi Dick, it's Jack."

"I know. I called you. I think you all are in on a conspiracy to gaslight Dick Stranger with that stuff. Stop that."

"Okay, okay."

"Jack I think we need to take a look inside Life's a Blast. Tonight. Late. Are you in?"

"Between Otis and me, we will be."

"Poetic. I'll let you call Otis. Let's meet at Miracle about nine PM to finalize plans."

"So, do we dress all in black with a turtleneck and long sleeves?"

"Got it, second story man. Bring your own lunch."

FORTY-SEVEN

Dick, Jack and Otis sat in the Miracle Motors office, making plans. Drive something inconspicuous. Just one more middle-aged pickup truck. Park in the row of Libre Autos vehicles nosed in behind the warehouse. Pull a front advertising plate from one of the other units and put on the back of the getaway truck. Just to fit in. Cut the lights while on the state road and use the parking brake instead of the brake pedal. No telltale taillights. Turn off the interior lamps.

Presently the three were outside the overhead door. Dick threw the valves on the air system to re-energize the door opener. Keeping all the electrical and pneumatic equipment for the unit outside was a definite fireworks safety feature, but without someone inside to "open the gate," they would be faced with no power and a deadbolt. Jean had done her part.

Now the only impediment was the opener itself. Back at the car lot, Otis swore he had an opener that would work. Now, he pulled an electrical gadget out of his pocket that looked like an iPhone, pointed it at the opener, and pressed the "enter" icon, which was a graphic of a swinging picket fence garden gate. A whoosh of air discharged from the pneumatics, and the door rose silently except for the faint clatter of wheels in the tracks.

"It works kind of like a commercial universal remote for the TV. Runs a transceiver with a series of scanners to sort out the system, and runs a code program for the right combination in 'opener' mode. It even resets the combination like any other rolling code opener. So when you exit the system, you can keep using it as an opener, but the original ones work too."

"Where did you get that thing? Late night TV?"

"It was crammed into the overhead sunglasses holder in the cab of the rollback. Thank you, Buddy's Recovery Service. He must have bought it for repossessions, but then forgot to check all the cubbyholes in the cab when he bailed on the truck loan. Lucky for us. These are probably kind of pricey on repo-stuff.com."

"Or detectivestuff.com. Or wherever you shop. Otis, you're a piece of work."

They disabled the security system with "trixie123" and used flashlights to navigate the warehouse. Pallets of boxes, shelves, receiving and shipping areas, all squeaky clean.

The laboratory was the heart of the action. Here is where the load was unloaded. No wonder the safe was so prominent a feature. On the big central work island were several boxes in progress.

Seeing no obvious sign of a paper trail or inventory accounting, Dick thought they should do some on site research. The glue on the flimsy fireworks packaging was weak to start with, so unwrapping the bundles without any rips or tears was a piece of cake, even wearing nitrile rubber gloves.

In one carton lay row after row of Statues of Liberty, each turned opposite so they interlocked for maximum shipping space utilization. Dick picked up one and gently shook it. The contents were loose, unlike the normal practice with gunpowder. Maybe it was the streamers and colored sparkling chemicals and other typical fireworks producing elements.

He carefully cut the seam and slowly lifted the front half off the statue as if it were about to blow. Inside, a white powder. Dick knew it at sight but did the taste test to be certain. Cocaine.

Jack was silently busy with another box. It was that cheap overseas pasteboard and it was lightly stenciled with "Explosive Fireworks. Handle with Care. Keep away from heat and flame. Giant Atomic Cherry Bombs. M80 & M160." The box was a cube about twenty-four inches to a side, and was divided internally into two sections. One half was ping pong ball sized cherry bombs. The other half held two sizes of traditional looking M80s.

M80 and the double sized M160. Tiny sticks of dynamite, bulk shipped.

Jack carefully picked out one of each type, and slowly shook each. A muted rattle indicated something other than explosive powder, but was indistinct enough to pass a cursory inspection as fireworks filling. Taking out his small knife, Jack methodically cut the thin paper seam until he could simply twist open the firework.

Inside, pills. Assorted colors. Ecstasy, in your choice of flavors. Marketing is everything, right?

Otis's eyes widened in amazement at the entire process. He handed Dick and Jack plastic bags for samples. Together they buttoned up the lab, but not before Jack took a good look at the safe.

"When the time comes, I can get us into that thing if the police can't, or won't."

"Easy to crack?"

"My remote looks a lot like Otis's. The wild card is usually a separate security system, but I see this doesn't have one."

The money was so big that a careful inventory apparently was not an issue. Ricky and Juan could skim the top off some boxes, or even take a few boxes themselves. The inspected fireworks could be refilled and sold retail, or wholesaled for completion. Presumably, some boxes must contain more thinly disguised, or more easily buried, contraband in bulk form. At any rate, there were a lot of boxes that were earmarked for Boris or Lars to "inspect" before stocking for sale.

With tons of photos taken on each of their phones, and with everything back in its original place, the three moved toward the overhead door and an easy escape. But Dick had one more thing on his mind.

"Let me take a second over here."

He walked over to a 2010 F150 Supercrew parked in the loading dock stall. It was a very clean truck, in excellent physical condition. The instrument panel was disassembled, and the instrument cluster was hanging loose, with an identical part lying on the seat. He knew what was going on. Most salvage yards were very careful with instrument clusters because of odometer readings. The most scrupulous kept airtight records.

Dick turned the key of the truck to the "on" position. The odometer flashed on when the cluster illuminated. 141,680 miles. Wow, a ton of miles for a three year old truck, yet the truck really did not look the miles. He glanced at the other cluster. The back panel had a sticker, Carl's Used Auto Parts. Wrangling a bit with the wiring harnesses, he unplugged the original and put the power to the replacement. 38,812 miles. Ricky Torres, Juan Rios, and Libre Autos were still at it.

Dick reconnected the original cluster after taking appropriate photos, including of the vehicle VIN. Opening the overhead door, Dick, Jack, and

Otis prepared to exit. They froze, seeing a marked City squad car crossing the Interstate on the state highway right next to them. Hitting his transceiver, Otis watched the door closing, waiting to shut off the air supply. Dick shouted,

"Otis, let it go. Get in the truck."

"I gotta shut off the air."

"Don't worry about it. They'll think someone else forgot it."

They dashed into the truck, Otis was last to arrive, and slouched down as the police cruiser's spotlight swept the area, stopping on the closed door, finally pulling up with its high intensity headlights on the door area. Hearts beat wildly in the truck.

The white Crown Vic was a circus of reflective tape, antennae, and lamps. Each with a serious purpose, no doubt, but collectively quite a sight. Of course, that was the idea, right? Presence as deterrence.

The officer was clearly experienced on the bed-check beat, as he walked immediately over to the air valves and took note of their positions. He then performed the normal door knob checks for the shift, finally getting back in the running cruiser.

He flipped open a cell and punched in a number. After a short conversation, he backed the car out and swung around to exit, the headlights playing over the extra truck in the Libre Autos inventory. Finally the car pulled out the drive.

Otis was out of the truck in an instant, almost rolling onto the ground from the cramped legs caused by his crouching on the floor boards.

Hunched over, he ran over to the air valves, pulled out a rag, and wiped the handles clean of prints. He was back to the truck in a flash. With plates correctly reshuffled, they crept out of the parking lot and back out to the highway.

Cresting the overpass, their headlights met the glare of Lars Lundstrom and the HID lamps of his Volvo, with Lars hitting the brakes and signaling for a turn into Life's a Blast.

Directly behind him, Kidd O'Connor's Silverado prepared for the same turn.

FORTY-EIGHT

....

Dick waited until nine AM to call Ian. By that time, the early morning job plans would be in place, the day's café.com would be churning, and Ian should be on the road. A safe and productive time to call.

He was trusting that Kidd's smart Hibernian mouth was running by now. Too much happening for him to contain it, especially after some social lubricant.

"Ian."

"Ian, it's Dick. Can you talk?"

Dick heard the rumble of the diesel semi-tractor, and Ian going through the gears. Thank you, Bluetooth.

"Sure, I've got a tractor on the lowboy going up to Pete's Equipment, bringing back a rental. I'll, uh . . . be here a while."

"Any news yet?"

"Well yeah, what about that deal up at Boris's farm the other night? Sounds kinda big city. It's all everyone is talking about. I think that was out of Kidd's league, of course. Plus I'm his alibi. We had darts night before last, so everyone saw our team at the bar. And as usual, Kidd got a little hammered. He's definitely driving for Schwartz, like I told you, and undercover for the PD at night. Sure likes to brag when he gets a few beers in him. Now that he's hooked up with Jay – well, I mean as long as Jay is around – yeah, with Jay and Schwartz on the liquor and cigarettes, he's also in on the crop. I assume you've heard about the crop."

"The marijuana crop?"

"Yeah, that's the one. It's all over the bar scene already. We have our own version of café.com, you know."

"Stands to reason. Every good rumor needs a mill."

"So it sounds like his piece of the action is going to be sales."

"You mean that big crop is staying local?"

"You've seen all those sheds? They're half empty."

"So they'll be their own supplier."

"Dick, it's like that business book you gave me to read. I think the term is vertically integrated."

"I'm pleased you remembered. Still got time to talk?"

"Doin' great."

"So anything else?"

"Well yeah. Now it sounds like he's also going to sell some powder and pills for somebody, but I don't know who. I don't know how he's going to spend all the money he's gonna make."

"Maybe lawyers."

"I told him that! He's taking all the risk. But he thinks like he drives – bulletproof."

Dick knew who the pharmacist was. Lars. But was the grass-in-the-corn crew keeping their gig from Lars? And how did Boris fit into all this?

"But, yeah, hey Dick. The best part? He said he's seeing Terri Moody. Just been a couple of weeks or so. Last night I went to his Facebook page to see if he had photos of them together. Sure enough, one arm around her, bottle of beer in the other hand."

"Terri Moody, eh? Maybe Boris introduced them when Kidd still worked for him. But she hangs the bar scene, so what's so surprising about that?"

"Nothing except the car they're leaning on in the photos."

"He's got a Silverado. She's got a G6. Not one of those?"

"Think sports car."

"No . . . "

"Yes. Silver Ferrari. No front plate. It has to be yours."

No front plate. Ian remembered. Dick did not like the way the domestic plate looked on the Ferrari, so he carefully removed the bracket and stowed it, plate attached, in the trunk. If questioned, it just fell off.

"So he's the thief? Or one of them?"

"I'm not sure how it went down, but we've got pool tonight, so I'll work on it. I've got some other ideas, too, about the car, but they've got to cook a little first."

"Anything on the street about a mailbox and playing cards? Another case."

"I don't know what it's about, but I've heard guys talking about the mailbox. But these aren't your average darts and pool players. These dudes are the source, and I'm worried about Kidd stepping on their toes."

"Let's talk tomorrow at this time. Thanks for all your help, Ian."

"I owe it to you, Dick. I'd never be racing if it wasn't for you."

"I have faith in you, Ian. One more thing. Do you know where Kidd is today?"

"Run to Chicago. The liquor is sold out."

Jung was fast asleep, stretched out in a square yard of morning sunlight coming in one of the east windows, with his head on his favorite stuffed animal, his bulldog.

Unlike every other stuffed animal he'd ever had, this one had not been torn open by Jung. The ones with squeakers were a no brainer. No self-respecting terrier could let an hour go by without killing the prey and removing the squeaking heart. Maybe it was because Sigmund the stuffed dog was about the same size as Jung. An occasional hard shake by the neck, to assert pack leadership, but no destruction.

"Jung. Car ride!"

The dog twisted up off the floor with his front and rear halves moving at different rates, creating more commotion than confusion. Sigmund went flying and Jung bolted for the back door.

Dick had on a blue paisley patterned cotton shirt, dark blue chinos, and his Ecco deck shoes. A leather-banded Skagen graced his wrist and the Baloramas were eyewear. Kinda retro. Jung wore a minimalist print bandana to highlight his new beige woven collar with a Taliesin-inspired pattern in Cherokee Red.

The 300C exited the garage and began the rounds of Kidd O'Connor's favorite haunts, with Dick looking for the Silverado, hoping for clues. Common sense said it would be parked near where the semi-truck and trailer were stored. Besides Kidd's normal sites, such as the apartment and taverns, empty parking lots and truck stops were on the agenda.

Finding nothing, Dick thought about the semi-truck's history. Where would I be if I were a cattle truck? With the other cattle trucks, of course. Parked in back of the old City of Woodstock warehouse on the south edge of town.

It was an obscure location, to be sure, but convenient to the highway, and the structures were about as run down and seedy as the city would allow. Low old garage buildings with semi-tractor doors took two sides of the lot, an alley for the third, and corn on the fourth. Dick hated to dirty up the car on the ancient and rutted gravel lot, so he parked at the curb and brought Jung along on the retractable leash.

There stood Kidd's truck: a black Silverado Z71 Extended Cab with aftermarket wheels, stainless tube steps, and dual exhausts. Like its owner, it had been in a few tussles. Seeing no spectators, Dick put on rubber gloves and tried the door. Unlocked. Typically careless Kidd. The interior reeked from a forest of tree shaped air fresheners hanging about the cab. Pine Tree, Vanillaroma, Cherry, New Car Vinyl Petrochemical, and Patchouli. All trying to compete with a layer of tar and nicotine that hazed the windows.

Jung backed away when the door was opened and the inside air rushed out. He sneezed once, with the circular motion of his snout spiraling all the way back to his tail. He barked and barked, skidding about in the gravel.

"Quiet, Jung. We don't need guests."

Without knowing exactly what he was looking for, Dick examined all the storage areas, map pockets and pouches, armrest compartments, glove box, and behind the backrests of the rear seats. He stuck his head low to see under the front seat, same with the rear.

Finished but empty handed, Dick closed the doors and stood with his fists on his hips, thinking. This was a basic information gathering episode with no tangible results. Jung stared at the extended cab door of the truck, and then barked twice. Not madness, two barks. He looked at Dick, looked back to the truck, and barked twice again.

"Don't like the truck, eh? Smells pretty funky in there, I'll agree with you. Nothing unusual, let's go."

Dick turned and began walking away, but Jung did not follow. He stared at the truck door and barked twice again. Dick pulled; Jung barked.

"What is it Lassie? Huh? Okay, we'll look again."

Dick opened the front door so he could flip open the rear-hinged extended cab door. He looked in, under, flipped seats up and down. He thought twice about the covered jack under the rear seat. The fastener was unhooked and the cover askew.

He pulled off the cover to find a greasy cloth bag, with a crude drawstring, the kind of bag that sometimes held heavy equipment parts. There was no mistaking the shape in the bag. Dick opened it and pulled out a 9mm Beretta Semi-Automatic.

Loaded.

Dick closed up the compartment and shut the doors. Bag in hand, he moved quickly to the car, this time with Jung happily in tow.

"Thanks, buddy. Good call. We'll borrow this for a few minutes."

The 300C roared to life and they hurried beyond the city limits. Pulling into a deserted woodlot, Dick took the bag and proceeded to exit the car.

"Jung. Hang tight. I'll leave on the air and Public Radio."

He walked out of sight into the oaks and fired two shots. Putting the warm casings in a cloth, he hopped back into the car. Waiting for the casings to cool, he wrote down the serial number of the weapon. The casings, still in the cloth, went into a plastic bag.

Back to Kidd's truck. Drop off the gun. Get out. Simple. As the car pulled away from the curb, a semi rounded the corner. Black Peterbilt cowboy truck. Cattle Drive trailer, empty, sides splattered with manure. Wrong trailer. Not Kidd's truck.

"Jung, how about a baby cone at the Dairy Queen?"

FORTY-NINE

....

Jung ended up with a chili-dog kid's meal with a bowl of water on the side, and the baby cone substituted for the fries. All that plus the customary dog biscuit. They sat outside at the pre-stressed cast concrete picnic tables, to avoid having to put on the Service Dog vest. Dick had a fish sandwich and fries, diet cola back.

After the meal, they made a quick trip west of town to check on the mailbox. Approaching it from the opposite direction as last time, Dick was face to face with another vehicle already stopped. He slowed as much as practical, and he knew the blacked out windows of the 300C would give him an anonymous and unobstructed view of what was happening at the mailbox.

A tricked out Hummer H2, in black, idled at the shoulder, and a man about 30, muscular build, with a white t-shirt and blue jeans, purple hi-top sneakers, and bleached blond spiked hair, was shifting his weight from foot to foot in front of the mail-box. He fished a playing card out of his wallet and placed it inside the box.

Dick managed to get a photo of the front plate, and a fleeting shot of Spikey, as they rolled past to the thump-thump-thump of hip-hop vibrating out of the Hummer. It would be a little too obvious to stop dead.

Gears spun in Dick's head as the 300C coasted to the bottom of the hill. How did the card thing work? What kind of business did young guys in customized cruiser have with Feckenmeyer's Mail-box?

As they turned onto the state highway into town, the integrated Bluetooth in the car flashed a call on the navigation screen: Jack Bluhm.

"Hi Jack, it's Dick."

"Okay, okay, I deserve it."

"Good. What's up?"

"You idiot. You left a message for me to call you."

"Just testing you, Jack. Question is, Do you have a scope good enough to compare those shell casing I told you about? I have a couple more to match up."

"I do. But it's not portable. All leveled up and balanced out on the bench."

"When can I come over?"

"Right now work?"

"You bet, partner."

Dick and Jung drove into town, opening the sunroof and rolling down all four windows. Country smells turned to city smells as they slowed down to make the trip north up Main Street to work their way to Jack's home in cranberry country.

Jung's nose picked up fresh flowers, just clipped grass, the musty odor of the freshly watered clay soil in the boulevard planting beds, the maple and oak and ash tree leaves, various plant and animal material flying off vehicle tires, smoke possibly all the way from Berg's smokehouse, bakery and candy essences from the Anderson Baking Pie and Candy Company, and the fryers and grilles operating at the several restaurants and taverns up and down the street.

Balancing these were the gas and diesel exhaust, fresh tar repair strips, new crosswalk paint, creosote-soaked railroad ties from the plantings and from the rail yard with its own aged oil dump smells, the burning of brake linings from the dump-trucks plying the street like ferries, and the chemical air from a flat roof job.

Dick, on the other hand, picked out a few choice smells of summer, and enjoyed the ability to put one's elbow out the window at the wheel of a cool car.

Ten miles northeast of the city, they swung up a slight incline from the low lying cranberry bed territory. Jack's house rested at the top of this rise, overlooking cranberry beds, reservoirs, dikes, sand pits and piles, and outlying buildings. His cedar home had the soaring beams and floor to ceiling windows typical of the genre, but his was right out of an architectural and interior design magazine, with the touch throughout.

The house had been made possible by an old song from Jack's early musical years. An unscrupulous agent had tried to bury Jack's copyright on a song that the agent's group had taken to the top ten. Jack prevailed on appeal, and the back payment paid for the house, and the continuing residuals covered the taxes year to year.

The 300C pulled into the circular driveway.

"Let's go, buddy."

Jack answered the door chime and they entered the cherry and oak and cedar enclave. Now those are smells, thought Jung.

"Jack, thank you so much for letting us drop in for you to check these out."

"I'd love to do it. Let's run over to the shop."

They entered a shop divided into a working area and laboratory area. Dick was amazed the first time he saw how Jack separated the research, drawing, and planning part of the shop from the area for construction sawdust, grease, and debris.

Attached to the research table was a 400x microscope with Carl Zeiss optics and complex leveling system. Jack took the two original shell casings, handling them with a forceps, and placed them on the microscope's stage. He dialed down the magnification to fit the field. They were an obvious match to each other from the firing pin imprint. He then added the newest two specimens, and it was another match. All four from the same gun.

Jack pushed a few buttons and hit a shutter button to digitally record the comparison. He then typed in Dick's email address, hit enter, and Dick's iPhone vibrated. Transmission complete.

Dick and Jack exchanged case updates while gazing out at the gorgeous countryside from Jack's deck. Jung's nose was up at a forty-five degree angle, taking in the cranberry country.

FIFTY

....

Dick sent an email to Otis with the serial number of the gun, plus the photos and the evidence of the match, and asked Otis to check the gun in his database.

Fifteen minutes later, Dick's phone rang. Otis.

"Dick Stranger."

"Hey boss, I have the gun info."

"Quiet day at the shop?"

"Priorities – this has got to be more important than fixing cars. This is actually registered, and registered to Lars Lundstrom, Woodstock, Wisconsin. Reported stolen about a year ago. It's routine. If you want to deny possession, it's stolen. If you want to show it's yours, just say you found it and forgot to report the good news."

Dick imagined Lars's short, fat fingers trying to hold the gun. Lucky it's not a .357. Lars wouldn't have enough leverage.

"There is a previous owner in the system. Nicola Lombardi. Lars provided a bill of sale from Lombardi when he registered it. Fishy?"

"I don't know, but I would put nothing past them, Otis. Significant information. This links Lars to Kidd. Now we need to make sure Kidd is the trigger man. At least for this job. I believe he is, but we have to tighten it up."

Dick looked at the messages on his phone. Anna Lundstrom. Uh-oh. She was kind of paying for this. Melissa Schwartz. Another sort of paying customer.

Three PM. Whatever happened to calm afternoons in the loft reading and solving crossword puzzles? What about the days buying and selling cars, providing income?

Bzzt. An email. Giovanni is working late. From his personal account.

"Buonasera. Client has accessed account and received notice of 14-day waiting period. The clock is ticking. Ciao. Giovanni."

Dick tapped back.

"Bene, grazie. Car may be found but not recovered yet. I will keep you informed. Grazie, grazie, grazie. I owe you una bottiglie di Strangere. Dick."

Dick mustered his courage and pressed in Anna's number.

"Anna"

"Hi, Anna. It's Dick. What's up?"

"Oh, hi Dick. I just wanted to find out what you've got so far."

Dick could hear the clanking of ice cubes in a glass. Mid-afternoon and probably not iced tea. How could she be so calm with the great Jay Boyd IV episode hardly in the taillights?

"I think we could meet at the office to discuss it. How does late this afternoon sound?"

"Okay. How about . . . oh . . . I've got a break between classes at 5:30."

Perfect. Cocktail hour.

Jung played catch, or was that keep-away, with a tennis ball thrown by Dick. Racing and skidding around the loft, Jung staged several long runs before wearing out. Still, he sat erect, ears perked and tweaking up and down, and turning his head to the side, as his master spoke.

When Jung twisted his head from side to side and held it at an angle, it was a fine line between indicating that he already knew what Dick was saying, telegraphing "I know that, you idiot," and on the other hand indicating "I don't know that word yet, can you please rephrase that."

"Okay Jung. Ball time is over. Just about time for company."

The squeegeeing footsteps once again graced the terrazzo in the hallway, foretelling Anna. Dick met her at the door, and Jung, still winded from the game, barked and wagged and finally sat and gave her a doggy smile, panting. She held her green sports bottle.

Anna was attractive as usual. Hair mussed from exercise class, and damp around her temples and the nape of her neck, yet casual and stylish. Her black exercise shorts were bicycle length, with a very cropped white t-shirt over a pink sports bra up top, baring her stomach with a small silver ring in her navel. Dick was always a sucker for accessories.

The white exercise shoes were over white golf socks with a pink band at the cuff. She wore no jewelry of note except diamond stud earrings, sold to her by Dick, and a few rings with a notably missing wedding set. Probably just removed for workouts.

The scent of lemon and lime again was paired with whatever the green bottle offered, and it all seemed very tropical. She was warm.

"Remind me to cool down before I come over here next time."

Right.

"Anna. Can I get you a drink?"

"Too early for a gin and tonic?"

"Be my guest. Make yourself comfortable and I'll assemble one for you."

Anna paced the loft during this cool-down period. Jung trotted behind her, wondering if this was all leading up to a walk outside.

"So Dick. The Transcend Mental Meditation is really taking off. Fills in the slow times and is all prepaid. I'll be getting current with everything soon. So what do you have for me?"

"Anna, I'll get to that in a minute. How are you doing with the Jay Boyd shooting? You know I know, don't you?"

"I thought so. I think he's going to be alright. The clay saved him from bleeding out. Nothing was serious after all."

How could she be so calm about all this? Proceed with the meeting.

"Glad to hear it. Anyway, on to business. First of all, forget about the idea of a reward from the time in Chicago. That chapter is over."

"Dick, I was just hopin'. A little bonus, for both of us, you know."

"Sorry. Anyway, it doesn't look like Lars is involved with anyone or anything other than work. That's where he goes."

"Not even that tramp, Terri? What about the Harley chick, Jean?"

"Terri is involved with someone right now, and there is no evidence of anything other. And Jean – totally not a chance."

"Totally?"

"Totally."

"Dang. I was looking for some great grounds for the divorce. Desertion, another woman, you know."

"Well, he does have some potential issues. The sudden source of his big money is not very legit, and beyond that, it might even make the wrong people mad."

"Oh, not that again. Anything like what happened out at Boris's place?"

"Possible."

"Anything else I can use?"

"Sorry. That's the overview. But Anna, you'd better be careful he doesn't find grounds on you. Your boyfriend isn't a private subject anymore."

She took a strong glug from the sports bottle. Hydration. Very important.

FIFTY-ONE

....

. . . Dick sat at the baby grand, entertaining a loft full of guests. They had pried and prodded and weaseled their way into getting him to perform. He just wrapped a warm-up ballad of "Wild World," and it seemed to make sense to transition from Cat Stevens to a cat song. A few verses into a best-ever rendition of "Year of The Cat" and the guests were speechless. The phone started to ring, and ring, and ring . . .

Crap. Another perfectly good nap ruined. He grabbed the phone without even looking at the screen,

"Dick. It's Kate. Cat news."

"Funny. I was just thinking about that. I think."

"The PD believes they have the burglar and the cats. They want me to identify the cats. Will you come along?"

"Sure. When and where?"

"Right now. A few blocks away. It's weird. They're holding the guy at his apartment. They need a positive cat ID to keep him."

"Meet you downstairs in five."

Kate and Dick walked two blocks south and two blocks east, into an average neighborhood of well-kept single family homes from the 1930's and 40's. Two city squad cars at the curb showed them a white two story traditional with an enclosed outside stairwell up the rear wall. Now a duplex.

An officer leaned on the hood of a squad, with aviator sunglasses in a failed attempt to make himself look experienced. On this tree lined boulevard at seven PM, he just looked like he was late for a poker tournament.

They followed the officer to the stairwell and he pointed to it. Their lead. He would cover the front in case of a violent escape attempt by the cat-napper.

Ofc. P. Justus met them at the top of the stairs.

"The perp's in handcuffs, so he's not dangerous, but he's a little upset. The cats are down that small hall in the first bedroom."

The perp? What about innocent until proven guilty? The alleged burglar sat in a straight backed desk chair in the dining / living room. He looked twenty-five, and like a charter member of Geeks International, Dweeb Division. Stereotypically scrawny, he wore cuffed corduroys, a button-down oxford cloth shirt with long sleeves, and Hush Puppies. It was unclear if he realized these were cool shoes.

His hair was long and straight, plus a wispy goatee, wire framed glasses – the whole package. Long fingers and long nails, with no stains from smoking.

Other than smelling a little musty, the place seemed spotlessly clean. Sparsely furnished, with homemade block and board bookcases. Yards of them. And books. Books, books, books.

Dick inched further into the room, focused on the open areas of the concrete blocks forming the bookcase. Almost every one held at least one deck of cards some in their cases, many just wrapped with rubber bands. Dick turned to Kate to point out the cards, but he was interrupted by a commotion in the room.

The suspect, seeing Kate and Dick, jumped out of the chair in a rage, shouting.

"You . . . you. She . . . she's mine, not yours. I've seen you trying to take her away from me. She's mine. I'll . . . I'll get you. Stay away from her."

Kate and Dick froze in their tracks.

"And you. Kate. Don't think you can . . . you can . . . ignore me in that bookstore. I bought all those books and you hardly even wait on me anymore. It's all . . . it's all . . . it's all because of him."

Kate inched toward the hallway and the cats. Dick braced himself and stared as Ofc. P. Justus shoved the suspect back into his chair, linking another pair of handcuffs down to a chair leg.

"You were . . . you were never there for her, like I was. I saved the cats after the burglary."

Another Officer took over perp watch, and Justus hustled Kate and Dick into the cat room. A cat paradise, rather, with two large cat houses, cat climbing structures, catnip mice, two littler boxes, elegant feeding bowls, and thick towels on a hope chest by a low window with a bird-filled tree outside.

"Gerald! Doug!"

The two cats charged over, winding around Kate's legs as she crouched down. Doug hopped up on her shoulder and leaned down to nip at her ear.

"Looks like a positive ID."

"These are my boys, alright. They haven't been suffering, though. Does he have other cats?"

"No. Look at the cat houses."

Each had a small brass plaque above the entrance. "Doug." "Gerald."

"Do you know this guy?"

"I see him in the bookstore all the time. I don't know him except as a customer, and certainly not enough for him to know my cats' names. I see him working in the Chinese restaurant at night."

"Typical stalker. Thinks he can be your hero after staging the burglary, then taking the cats that he will save from sure destruction. Thinks he possesses a little part of you having the cats, so he doesn't have the guts to come forward and prove to you that he's the hero. Textbook case, Chapter 89.

His Facebook page even lists him as 'In relationship – with Kate.' Curious, eh?"

Kate blew out a puff of air from her lips and inhaled deeply again, blowing this one out of her nose.

"Curious? I'll say. I never made more than normal eye contact with the guy. Helped him with a few books is all."

Dick couldn't stand it.

"You charmer. I always knew you had it for the young ones."

"Dick, this is serious."

"Plus, working in the Chinese restaurant. Do you think the cats . . . ?"

"Aw, Dick. Yuk. Quit it."

"Ma'am, he has not admitted to the burglary yet, but we expect him to soon. He sold us the iPad undercover, and the jewelry and the cats are here. I'm sure we have him."

"Can I take the cats? That is, if they want to go. Nicer place for them than it is for him. I'd loved to have had a cat-cam on them in here."

"But no original artwork or designer furniture like home. I'm sure their cultural orientation has suffered."

"Ma'am, let me check with the Captain. I'll have a decision in a few minutes. I recorded your reunion on my cell-phone camera, so I'm sure we have enough evidence."

Five minutes passed and they were free to take the cats home. Grabbing two new cat leashes from a hook on the wall, they clipped up Doug and Gerald and went back around the front of the house. The cat man sat in the back of a squad and started to yell and kick the prisoner partition as the two homeward bound cats walked past, heads and tails high, eyes straight ahead.

For cats, it was a long walk home, and while elated to be back in their own space, Doug and Gerald were beat. Dick couldn't stop egging on Kate about the boys' timely escape from tomorrow's "Major Pao's Special Tiger" entrée.

In further trying to keep Kate's mood light, Dick made a bigger than big deal over the younger man angle. Finally, he had Kate in a giggling fit and they crossed the street to the Library Café for a late snack.

Dick digested a long day, sitting in the new lounge chair with a large glass of Chianti on the side table, Luther Vandross on the CD, and Jung enjoying the late evening smells and sounds in the back yard.

The playing cards were on his mind, and he pondered the potential relationship between the people leaving cards at Feckenmeyer's Mailbox, and the cat burglar.

The cell rang. "Private Caller." Okay, roll the dice. Answer it.

"Dick Stranger."

"This is your little font of information from Chicago."

"Hey, what's happenin'?"

"Dick, you know it's almost like we know each other, with you calling me all the time for backgrounds. You know, I kind of like you. Of course, the case of Strangere didn't hurt anything either. Thanks."

"My pleasure. But is this a social call?"

"I don't know how mixed up with these guys you are, if at all, but I just got word today that some people down here are not too happy with

Woodstock, Wisconsin. Some toes are being stepped on."

"Like how?"

"Easy one first. Schwartz's cigarette thing is someone else's territory. Period. The booze is okay since Chicago wholesales it to him. But the cigs from Out East is a no-no."

"Understandable. In their world."

"Second, Lundstrom. That snake. Boris had a nice deal going with the fireworks from Chicago, and now Lars is bringing them in from Mexico. And they know it's Lars, not Boris, running that side of things, side-stepping Chicago."

"You can't tell that around here. Someone just strafed Boris's pottery barn, and I'm not so sure they didn't think Boris was in it. As it stands, the guy's gonna be okay, but it was the delivery man and partner to Schwartz. Maybe he was the target. It was the black car with gun blazing thing. Like The Untouchables."

"The purpose of my call was to tell you a warning shot is coming. Maybe I'm too late. Are you in on any of this?"

"I'm just tailing everyone for everybody else. If Schwartz wasn't a crook himself, I'd have this all in his lap. So far beside the pottery bust-up they've stolen my classic car and taken a couple of pot shots at me to warn me off."

"Anyhow, I just didn't want you to get in the crossfire. They don't know who you are."

"Thanks, friend."

"You still have a half-case credit balance."

Dick made two important late evening calls, brought in Jung, and continued contemplation with his Chianti.

FIFTY-TWO

··

The day arrived rainy, on that kind of morning that just turns a lighter grey, with no real daybreak, no real dawn. Good day for the Library Café, good day for Stranger Than Fiction, good day for a nap.

Dick sat by the window to the west, and read in the grey illumination. Breakfast in the loft, a quick review of case notes from Jack and Otis, and now some hot tea and escapist literature. Time to turn off the private detective for a few hours.

Jung moped around, upset that his outdoors was wet. When he ventured out to the back yard, he returned quickly, wet, and stared at Dick as if it was his fault.

"Sorry, buddy. Mother Nature."

Dick flipped Jung a dog treat from the chair, and in time the dog also settled in for study, contemplation, and a nap.

The cell rang. Dick looked at the screen, determined to be unavailable. Ian Jackson. Oh man, must mean Kidd talked some more.

"Dick here."

He could hear the semi-truck roaring and Ian shifting.

"Hi Dick. Me again. I'm on my way north to pick up building material for inside one of the sheds at the farm. It's going to be almost like the old tobacco barns, for drying. Nothing suspicious, right?"

"No joke. Hey glad to hear from you, Ian. Who has you on the lumber run?"

"Jay Boyd set it up for me a few days ago, but now he's not been around for a couple. Wayne Nelson told me just to do whatever Jay asked. So here I am."

"You're right, Jay's out of it for a while. I'm sure Boris will be needing some more lumber, but not a full truck load. So, learn anything new last night?"

"Oh yeah. Plus, I have another idea I want to check on when I get back. How about I meet up with you guys late today?"

"How late?"

"Six PM."

"Meet us at Miracle Motors. I'll call Jack and Otis."

"10-4."

Rainy days at Miracle Motors brought good and bad. Good – anyone looking at cars in the rain was serious, and might even overlook some minor imperfections. Bad – it was always a mess in the shop. Nothing a hose and mop couldn't cure. Good and bad both – if you chamois off the trade-in to look it over beneath the shop lights, you probably will have to do the same with the prospective purchase.

Dick dropped by the lot, put the 300C indoors to dry, got Otis to agree on the evening, and then called Jack. Also a go.

Bored, Jung spent the next couple of hours in the shop, sniffing. Otis had a strict no-antifreeze on the floor policy, same for open pans or containers, so the shop was completely non-toxic. Regardless, it was hard to get away without four greasy paws to clean.

Dick caught up with Giovanni again, this time during working hours. The client was still checking the account.

Jack rang in with another sighting at Jesse's Well-Rested.

Kate called to say that charges were being filed against the dweeb, and mentioned that this might take Terri Moody off the burglar suspect list.

Finally, a customer call to Miracle Motors. Dick thought he was working the phone bank at a telethon.

"Miracle Motors, Dick speaking."

"Hi Dick, it's Josie from The Hotel Woodstock."

"Oh, hi Josie. How can we help you?"

"Do you still have rental cars?"

"Not exactly, but what do you need? We'll help any way we can."

"I've got two guys here who just flew in on business and came in at the big airport. The airport rental agency stiffed them on their reservation. Hey, remember that Seinfeld routine on the rental cars? What a riot! Oh, back to business. I wanted to call my friends before I called anyone else. They took a cab all the way over here. Expensive. But they said they have a big expense account."

"Josie, we just rent cars for service loaners. I've had good luck with the local place. If that doesn't work, call me. I'll work something out. Thanks for thinking of us."

"Thanks, Dick. Say hi to Jung."

The Hotel Woodstock was a city landmark, occupying exactly one half square block just two streets north of A Stranger Place. A grand old building, over a hundred and twenty-five years old, the Hotel had been rescued by two professors from the College, one a historian, one an economist. Additionally, they were life partners who had an antique store in a huge Victorian near the College.

Well-tenured, Lance Rembrandt, History Professor, and Leo Chartres, Economics Professor, bought the Hotel about fifteen years ago, thinking a larger antique shop, maybe even an antique mall, was in order. The College brought a lot of people to town, as did a few manufacturers in the industrial park, the cranberry industry, and general tourism.

The building originally housed a strip of stores at street level, such as a tailor, florist, barber, and news stand. These businesses faced both Main Street and a wide inner hallway, all in brick. Inside, another row of shops faced this hall. It was just like one of those "Streets of Yesteryear" reconstructions you see at attractions such as The House on The Rock.

But shopping habits had changed, and the downtown was already strained with available storefronts. Lance and Leo decided to fill that space all with antiques, set in vignettes, and to refurbish and modernize the upper floors, furnished with antiques. The entire contents would be for sale.

The main floor at street level also included the front desk, a magnificent walnut and marble and brass edifice. Joining it were a coffee bar, banquet and reception rooms, and The Florentine Italian Restaurant. Renovations included an elevator to the additional three floors, and the antique but functionally updated guest rooms.

The rear opened to a medium sized parking area, once the Livery Stable area for Hotel patrons. Luckily, a municipal lot was across the side street.

Dick's favorite feature was downstairs, accessible from an inconspicuous stairwell in the Lobby, and from an outside entrance slightly removed from public view. A twelve-stool bar, a few stand-up cocktail tables, and a small dining area offering a sandwich menu. Subterranean, with thick stone, brick, and concrete walls, The Hotel Bar prospered in the 1920's with supplies from Kate's forebears.

A renovation during the 30's had added signage made from walnut boards with the ends cut in zig-zags, and the lettering painted in script with yellow paint, all topped off with varnish and brass hardware. Such signs hung on chains over the indoor and outdoor stairwells to The Hotel Bar, along with a wide variety of witty sayings and directions scattered throughout the cave-shaped atmosphere.

The concept, the timing, the location, and the hospitality all worked together to make a local success story. The businesses at A Stranger Place had eagerly set up reciprocal discount coupons with The Hotel Woodstock.

When Dick and Jung walked to Miracle Motors, they passed The Hotel, which was pet friendly, and they always stopped in for a doggie treat from Josie at the Front Desk. Stepping into the lovingly restored Lobby was a trip back in time, and Dick never missed a chance to enjoy the ambiance, and to maybe even catch up with Lance and Leo.

FIFTY-THREE

It was nearly noon, and Dick and Jung headed back to the loft. Stopping downstairs first, they decided on a short stay in the Café, including Dick's usual business check-in with Kate, Sage, and Pearl. He relaxed with some bar food and iced tea, and Jung nosed around a customer plate of dog snacks provided by Pearl and the impulse food inventory at The Liquid Muse.

Jean Paradise called.

"Hi Jean."

"Hi Dick. You just like that caller ID thing, don't you."

"Tech keeps us old guys young."

"Oh yeah, Dick, you are so ancient. Where are you? I need to talk to you."

"At The Library Café. Let me know what you want for lunch for you two and we'll have it ready."

"We were planning on grilled cheddar cheese sandwiches with jalapeno spread, pickled cucumber slices, and homemade potato chips. Can you come close?"

"Pastrami with mustard on caraway rye, cole-slaw, fries. For two."

Dick walked over and managed to purloin Giorgio for a lunch meeting, with the agreement that Kate got to trade with him for the dessert course.

Jean pulled up in front in the Corvette, parked, and strode in. Blue jeans, cowboy boots, a black cotton turtleneck that accentuated her long neck and arms, and a big belt buckle with a Mack Truck bulldog. She looked great, and Giorgio beamed. Jung jumped around her shins until she reached down to greet him.

Giorgio had on his usual work clothes. Flat front khakis, blue long-sleeved work shirt, Bass Weejuns in oxblood with a matching belt, brass buckle. Not very Italian, but very bookstore-ish. He was a good looking guy and they made a handsome couple. Seeing them together made Dick smile.

Soon the sandwiches had come and gone. The talk all had been about the pottery barn shooting. Black car, automatic weapon. Not a sight of the car since. Jay Boyd was getting along alright. Who was the real target?

Café.com had been going bananas, and the PD was keeping a seal on whatever evidence was not already public. But the general agreement on the hotline was that someone had made someone mad, and the rumors were crazier than when Dick crashed the Probe.

Finally, Jean got around to her matter at hand.

"Dick, I think I found what we were looking for. It's a file with a separate purchase and sales record, by vendor and retailer. Lars has it, and I see that he emails it to Boris each day."

"Jean, that's great. What do you see overall?"

"Here, I copied it to this thumb drive. I didn't want to email it. Not from there."

"Jean. Wow. I'll look at this right away."

"Something you'll notice. On the list of sales, he shows 'Ship' and "Will Call.' We have no commercial 'Will Call' customers. These are delivered some other way. Just an observation, if it's useful."

"Got it. Thanks, Jean. Well worth lunch for three."

Jean left for work, Giorgio got back to his post, and Kate came for cheesecake and coffee.

"Dick, the cats are going wild. Happy to be home. And I'm happy to have them back. I was so worried about the little guys. And our burglar admitted to everything, according to Ofc. P. Justus. Bizarre. Just a stalker, I guess."

"Of course. Sounds like a closed case to me."

Dick left the Café, parked Jung in the loft, and headed over to the Justice Center. Now that charges were filed in the wake of the confession, Dick hoped to drain a little information out of Ofc. P. Justus.

Indeed, it was P. that was at the reception desk, and Dick detected a certain camaraderie with the young officer in the wake of the burglar's outburst at the apartment. Now he deigned to let Dick in on a few secrets.

"So I hear that the cat case is closed."

"Well, we have a signed confession, and charges filed."

"Anything public I can see?"

Ofc. P. Justus scrounged in a basket marked "Current" and pulled out a pile of paperwork. He laid it on the counter in front of him and Dick, in plain sight, easy to read.

"This isn't for the public yet, but if it is something generic I can tell you."

"What did he tell you?"

"Just what you heard at the apartment, plus the fact that he broke into the apartment and took the cats, plus the merchandise."

"What did you find at his place?"

"Mostly what you saw. He was a big online gamer, played with one of your former employees, Kidd O'Connor."

"What about all the playing cards?"

"I noticed those. Can't figure them out, and he won't say. But everybody in town is talking about cards and some drug deal. Rumors are rumors, though."

"So does my name come up as anything more than 'the guy who stole Kate'?"

"He said he was warning you off. But he won't say beyond what he said to you at the apartment. Mr. Stranger, this is part of another investigation. I, for one, am trying to figure out if there is any connection to the shooting at Mr. Shiraz's farm."

"Thanks, Officer. Let me know what you hear."

Dick opened the door to the loft and headed to the green chairs. He sat gazing out the window, regretting that he was a topic in an investigation, but pleased that he now was an insider with Ofc. P. Justus.

Plus, maybe it was a positive to be part of an investigation. Maybe the very fact that he was no longer considered opposition led to the consideration of consequences for Mr. Stranger. How can we protect this citizen?

And the cards. There had to be some set of signals. But the thought of Kidd and the burglar, and shots fired, and Kate. It was starting to swim a little.

With a plan to clear the head with other information, Dick grabbed the laptop. The file from Jean was marked simply "Sales," which was an understatement. Vendors and purchases, retailers and wholesalers, and sales, shipped or will call, type and size of firework and packaging style. A fairly anal analysis.

Dick was sure Lars planned a big spreadsheet presentation, or at least intended to determine which products have the highest velocity and most profit. It would take weeks or months to track down which companies really existed, which belonged to Boris or Lars, and which had offshore accounts.

Dick emailed copies to Jack and Otis, suggesting they brainstorm on it a little late in the afternoon before meeting with Ian.

Jack was on a reconnaissance mission for the bookstore. A local family wanted a bid on a book collection, as the matriarch was moving to a nursing home. He had a good chance on this collection, because the mother had worked with Dick at the College, and she liked the idea of a local bookstore in a small town.

Jack would have to catch up with the Life's A Blast file later in the afternoon. Otis, meanwhile, was already looking it over.

FIFTY-FOUR

....

At five PM, Otis and Dick were at Miracle Motors. Otis was developing charts and graphs of the sales segments, vendors, and customers. The wild card remained the Will Call category, which likely stayed local. How was the merchandise delivered or picked up if Jean was right, that Will Call did not exist at Life's A Blast?

Jack arrived and looked over the data. He reasoned that the largest customers may indeed be local, as well as the Will Call category. Maybe it was just an artificial distinction in case the information fell into the wrong hands. Which it had.

Dick agreed, there was still sleuthing to do. Ian rolled in, and broke up the conversation.

"Hi Ian. How was the trip?"

"Another day, Dick. Someday, I'll be full time in NASCAR, and I won't have to be doing this. You'll be driving my hauler."

"That's the spirit. Have a seat. What did you find out last night?"

"Well, it took a while. I may have to apply for expenses. Kidd didn't really start to babble until he got into the tequila. I stuck with light beer. It sounds like he was definitely involved in the car. He gained access for them into the building, got the car running, and had it for the night to use as he wanted. That's why it's in the photos."

"That takes guts. A lot of people know that car around town. Maybe not in his group, though. Or maybe people thought it was me."

"He makes it sound like Lars was behind the car thing. Wanted to warn you off snooping around."

"Kind of the reverse effect, wouldn't you say? But at least I appreciate a warning instead of an elimination."

"I think maybe Lars is the powder and pill guy, and this had something to do with you checking out the store. Or so it sounds. Kidd gets a little fuzzy when it gets too late."

"My, my. But he was a talker, wasn't he."

"But Dick, there's more. Jay Boyd is, or was, also paying Kidd to scare you. So I don't know who was directing those shots. They both think you're getting too close to them."

"We have a good idea, but we're doing some checking."

"So what's with the shooting at Boris's? Is Jay going to be okay?"

"That's what we hear. The wounds weren't that bad and the clay clogged him up. He's out of danger."

"Hey, can I have a beer out of the fridge? I'm dyin' after today."

"Help yourself. In fact, get us all one."

Two round's worth of general conversation later, Ian blurted out what had been eating at him for two days.

"You know, guys, Kidd and I worked for Boris's development company. He worked electric and all while your back shop was being rebuilt. I wonder if that was Kidd's way in."

"Meaning?"

"When we worked on all these kind of jobs, Kidd was always the one with the blueprints, the schematics. Said he was responsible at the end of the day for getting them back to headquarters."

"So he kept them? Wouldn't the foremen see they were missing?"

"I don't know. I never saw what he did with them. But I'm worried because I worked on this job too. And the PD might suspect me. If they ever found out, that is. In fact, if such an idea even occurred to them."

"Highly unlikely, with the high level of investigation by the Woodstock P.D. Plus, maybe the Chief was in on it. Possible conflict of interest, eh?"

"Anyhow, this is what I was thinking. I want to look in Kidd's apartment for the plans. I still have a key he gave me one night when he was drunk and I hauled him home. I'm sure he doesn't remember. He's gone tonight and I want to do it. Like right now."

"What do you think, Jack? Does having a key get him off the breaking and entering hook?"

"Breaking and entering? With a key? Just dropping off a twelve-pack for a friend? Are you kidding?"

"I know we can't all troop in there. Dick, what do you think?"

"I'll go in with Ian. If you two want to ride along, just stay in the truck. Jack? Otis?"

"I'll go for a ride."

"Might as well. Lost my harmonica and it's too late to golf."

They took the short ride in Ian's truck. Ian and Dick walked up and in as if they were just getting home late from work. Inside, there was surprisingly little clutter, except for a second bedroom that doubled as an office.

Ian had never been in that room, as it was always locked when he was here, and Kidd chalked it up to storage.

Now it was open. Rolls and rolls of building plans filled tall boxes lining the walls. All very orderly, from a storage standpoint. But plans were scattered all over the floor and the desk, like a busy office with too many projects going at one time.

All the copies were made on a large format copier just for items like blueprints. Kidd must somehow have gained a way back into the construction headquarters to make copies. It looked like he had the raw material for a lengthy career of burglary and theft, unalarmed and undetected.

On the desk lay the unrolled electrical and security system schematics for "Dick Stranger Shop Project." No wonder Kidd could come and go without a trace. Use the properly coded remote, and reprogram the security system. Unknown to Dick, the blinking alarm probably had been on alert hiatus ever since the initial intrusion by Kidd.

"Shall we take 'em along?"

"Might be a little forward of us. Let's use the miracle of photography instead."

Lots of photos, all over the room. Job title after job title.

"Ian, you left the twelve-pack in the fridge?"

"Oh gee, I forgot it in the truck."

The already grey day darkened by the time they unloaded back at Miracle Motors.

"Jack, I apologize. How was the book outing?"

"I'm still putting dollars on the collection. Mostly salable stuff. A few for the Café program. I'll put the finals on it tomorrow."

"Jack, you work too hard."

"I'll say."

Dick's phone rang.

"Hi Dick, it's Josie again from The Hotel Wood-stock. I'm not having any luck on the rental for these guys. Is there anything you can do? They're here for business, have credit cards, federal employees."

"Sure we can help, right Otis? Tell you what. I have to go back to the loft and let Jung out. Then I'll come by the Hotel. Tell 'em to have a couple of cool ones on Obama."

Dick brought Jung along and pulled into the rear parking lot at The Hotel Woodstock with a four year old Ford Taurus. Silver. Looked fairly Government Issue, but maybe the upgraded model was a bit too ritzy. Oh well.

Josie greeted Dick and pointed to the stairwell to The Hotel Bar. Jung wagged and leapt up to catch the mini dog treat she tossed.

The cavern-like feel of The Hotel Bar was accentuated by curving plaster ceilings that dipped and dripped like a natural wonder. Dick nodded to the bartender and threw a twenty-dollar bill on the mahogany surface, polished by so many bar rags and worn by so many elbows, the smooth hazy finish of an old unrestored Chris-Craft.

He looked into the tiny dining area, and there in an alcove sat his rental customers. With ties loose, coats flung on a third chair, and sleeves rolled up, the two had a good collection of empties before them.

A field trip to the country. Recently post-military haircuts and dark blue suits said Federales; the empty plates of fried foods said frat boys. At least they were at their destination for the night, and Dick did not have to worry about them driving his rental car.

As Dick and Jung approached the table, both men stood up. Jung froze, his tail stiff and quivering on high alert, and ears twitching to hear every word of his master's command to attack if needed. The men smiled a bit glassy eyed, and extended their hands to greet Dick.

"Mr. Stranger? Dick Stranger?"

"Why yes, gentlemen. Your names?"

"Cody Doane."

"Will Byrne."

"What? Doane? Byrne?"

"Live and in person, Mr. Stranger. We meet at last."

Cody Doane, DEA Agent. Will Byrne, ATFE Agent. Dick's contacts at the federal level, always a call or email away and now faces to names and voices.

Will Byrne spoke first,

"Dick. Is it okay to call you Dick? It's like we're good buds already. We were bowled over when Josie said you were the guy to help us on the rental."

"Yeah Dick. I know I'm late to this party, but always happy to be invited. Will and I work together a lot."

By now Jung had thoroughly sniff tested them, and was wagging his tail. The overly polished oxfords had some funky smells, petro-chemicals, waxes. Overall, though, the men passed, confirmed by Dick's tone of voice.

"So when were you going to let me know you were coming to town?"

"We were hoping to look around for a few days then hunt you up. But here we are. Small towns. So much for stealth."

"So much for 'we'll be in contact as soon as we need to be.'"

Incredulous at life's daily maze, Dick filled out the rental paperwork, checked Government ID's and driver's licenses from McLean, Virginia, and Gaithersburg, Maryland. He opened an app on his phone and blocked $1000 on the Government credit card, hoping that the U. S. Government would have a high credit limit.

"We could tell from your calls that a lot is going on here. Thought we'd better be first hand."

Dick looked at Doane and Byrne and their table's detritus, and thought the visit to Woodstock was more like an excuse for a road trip, G-Man style.

"Guys, I'd love to chat a little longer, but Jung and I have had a long day. Contact me tomorrow, and we'll catch up. By the way, I gave you a break on the rental and set it up to start tomorrow morning at five AM. The front desk will have the keys available any time after that."

Suddenly sounds filled the outside stairwell. With voices racked in laughter, wild hand gestures, and the thrill of victory in their blood, in walked the women's bowling team from The Woodchuck Café, savoring a hard fought league triumph.

All eight members of the team were present, each in the team embroidered silks and tight blue jeans. A few were already carrying bar glasses. Ages ranged from nineteen to about thirty-five. Drinks all around were in order, and as the bartender promptly had his hands full, the team members started to whisper to one another.

Several greeted Dick and Jung as regulars at the Café, but Dick observed this social grace as merely a doorway. He watched eight pairs of eyes move beyond himself to the two handsome new gentlemen in town.

Cody Doane and Will Byrne gave the team a small wave of recognition, and possibly honor, and returned the girls' stares with huge smiles full of straightened and whitened teeth. Two star quarterbacks and eight cheerleaders.

Dick looked down at a sitting Jung, who had twisted his ears back and forth from the girls to the G-Men. Returning Dick's look, he blinked his eyes twice at Dick, stood up, and shook himself off, ready to leave.

They began the short stroll back to the loft.

FIFTY-FIVE

....

. . . Dick was back at The Crowbar, wheeling around in front of the old piano on the round stool with the spin-up and spin-down stem, summoning his reediest James Taylor voice for his covers of "Smiling Face" and "How Sweet It Is." Sensing that the ballads were becalming the crowd, Dick kicked away the stool and dove into "To Be Real" . . .

Jung's jump onto his master's lap woke Dick. Four-thirty AM. Still in the lounge chair, one half-full Peroni on the side table. Stereo still on the all night rhythm and blues station, which now was broadcasting the Morning Farm Report with agricultural markets.

Jung kind of likes these nights. It was sort of like a vacation day, although he did not think much about deferred leisure travel. As a terrier, each day was an adventure in "what's next?" But this was something different, more like camping out, and Jung enjoyed rucking up the throw rug that became his bed when Dick took these long term naps.

Unfortunately, the morning light roused Jung a little earlier than normal, so it would have to be for Dick too. Dick executed the morning routine, and decided to make a breakfast trip to The Woodchuck Café to capture the overnight café.com rumblings surrounding the two strangers at The Hotel Bar.

The weather had cleared overnight, and Dick wore dark blue jeans, a white with fine red stripes Wisconsin Badgers golf shirt, and black penny loafers. It was a beautiful early morning for a walk to the Café, and as he approached the restaurant, Dick saw the rental car. Six-thirty. Good job, guys.

The two Easterners stuck out more than most tourists to the area. Each was a plate right out of Orvis or Eddie Bauer, their Ivy-League blood showing strongly. No paperwork? Not here on business. No maps? Not tourists. Very hung over? Yes.

Dick and Jung stopped to greet a table of regulars: the RV dealer, one fireman, two HVAC contractors, one plumber, a short-haul trucker who ran restored classic trucks, and an appliance dealer, all in various states of retirement, and as a group giving off a strong shock of skin bracer.

Jung got all the special attention, and Dick got a few nods and head jerks toward the boys, each gesture a silent inquiry on who the two were and what was their business. Finally Dick rolled his eyes, told the table that the two men were here on business, and that he had met them renting out the car.

The Government men's food was arriving as Dick and Jung visited the table, both Doane and Byrne eyeing Jung with the "what is a dog doing in here" look. Each man had an overfull plate of breakfast rejuvenators and hangover busters: bacon, sausage, eggs, potatoes, all fried up in just the right mixture of oil, bacon grease, and butter.

Doane had the Woodchuck Surprise, which this morning was a cooked whole tomato with cheese in addition to the usual litany, and Byrne had the Woodchuck Logjam, featuring extra sausage and potatoes. Jung's nose was going wild.

"Well, when I left it looked like you were launching the Let's Meet Woodstock tour. How'd that go for you?"

"They may have kept us out a little too late. At closing time we had to go up the street to another bar. Went a little overtime for us."

"The Woodstock Girls are in constant training, guys. You were in over your heads. You'll notice they're all at work this morning, lookin' good."

"Agreed, you're right. Let us get our feet on the ground today. We won't ask a lot of questions. Then how about we get together tomorrow."

"Call me and we'll meet at my office. By the way, you should try The Library Café. Food is great, plus they've got a bookstore and a liquor store."

Dick and Jung walked down to the favorite park and bench to watch traffic. They had a box of pastries from The Woodchuck. Jung likes the ones cut out like little woodchucks.

An early call came in from Jack.

"Hey Dick, sorry to bother you so early, but last night I heard some interesting ideas on the card trick at the mailbox."

"Go ahead."

"I tell you, why don't we meet up? Where are you now?"

"Central Park. You know the bench. Drop by the Library Café and bring coffees. And a water in a plastic soup bowl."

Jack blatted up in a 1965 Datsun 1600 Roadster. With this car he was reliving his youth, as one of these had been his first car. Along the lines of an MGB, these cars were fun to drive, not very fast, and simple to work on. The Japanese promotional name of "Fairlady" was never a player in the USA, though, and was usually hidden among paperwork and not adorning a fender. Light powder blue over a black canvas top and black fine grain leatherette interior.

He threw his sunglasses onto the dash and cap over the shift lever, and brought the beverages over to the bench. Coffee for him and Dick, water bowl for Jung.

"Otis and I were in The Sand Bar late last night, and Jean and Giorgio came in after his bike club meeting. Apparently a couple members of the group are into independent sales, not to typecast anyone."

"Giorgio told me about those guys. Person-to-person retailers."

"Uh, yeah, that's it. They got to talking about the farm at Feckenmeyer's Mailbox, and the mailbox. It's a favorite on café.com right now, but very few really know about the cards"

"I'd think they would want to keep it quiet."

"Human nature, you know. Evidently, Boris has these guys set up shell fireworks companies to use for his billings and payments. If the, uh . . . vendor or client does not have a credit standing yet, they are C.O.D. All their orders are by playing card. Boris gives each of them a particular deck, so he knows who is ordering what. As far as the shipping and will call, Jean is thinking it indicates an existing customer, but maybe what kind of 'fireworks' they purchase."

"Is this overly complicated, or blindingly simple?"

"To me, the card thing is a little eccentric. I did read about a card passing system in a Mafia history once, but it was not integral to their existence. Today, why all the bother when untraceable cell phones are available. Untraceable if you set up the proper identity, that is. Giorgio went on and on with it. The private bar at their club had truly loosened some tongues."

"Okay. Makes sense. The mailbox is the order taker. Now what do we do with that bit of knowledge?"

"You got me. One other thing, Dick. I know Schwartz is crooked. So what are we doing with the product of all this detective work?"

"Good question. Give me a couple of days to think."

"Perfect. I've got books to buy. Oh, and I have to tell you about when we were leaving The Sand Bar. The entire Woodchuck Café bowling team came in, well into a victory dance. There were two young guys from The Hotel with them. It was a riot. The girls were educating them in the fine art of holding your beer."

FIFTY-SIX

....

Miracle Motors was quiet when Dick pulled in with the Chrysler 300C. Jung hopped out and headed for the front door, but paused to carefully sniff a trail leading up to the entrance and back to customer parking.

"Morning Boss."

"Otis, you kidder."

"Your twin was here this morning. Car, that is. Same look, black but maybe the windows were even darker, a handful of bumper scratches from life in the city, Illinois plates with those plastic covers sprayed with the coating to blind the red-light cameras. I'm guessing Chicago."

"Where was that?"

"Right here in the executive parking stall. Two big hunks in synthetic slacks and rayon shirts stopped to ask directions to Life's A Blast. They were headed north instead of south. But they asked me my name, and peered around like they were looking for something."

No wonder Jung was sniffing Chicago smells. Bits of Chicago Vienna hot dogs in the underfoot debris, highly bred designer dog leavings in the curb, Chicago River water – those soles left a trail of exotica.

"Thanks, Otis. I'll try to keep to myself today. This can't be the same car that made the stop at Boris's the other night, unless asking directions was to throw us off the scent."

"Maybe just the second shift."

Dick sat at the desk while Otis stepped back into the shop to finish maintenance on the College Development Director's BMW M5. Otis loved these cars, and the opportunity to make a living playing with them. Jung took a similarly serious approach to work and settled into his pillow on the chair in the sun, falling immediately to sleep.

Dick performed some actual business, completing the purchase of vehicles online from some trusted sources. He was catching up, in fact, with a low inventory due to his own neglect. Otis had continued to sell cars, as Stranger the Private Eye was Private Eyeing around. Time to re-stock.

Eight late-model Audi A4's were the best buy. If he bought the whole group, he saved enough on the purchase, plus group shipping, to almost pay for one car. Dick suddenly knew what the most popular car would soon be among the College professors.

A call was placed to Melissa, whose call to Dick had been ignored too long.

"Hi Melissa, it's Dick Stranger."

"Well, hi there, Dick. What's goin' on?"

"You called a few days ago, uh . . . "

"Oh that. You know, I decided I don't much care about that friend and her boyfriend. Let her do what she wants."

Understandable, since café.com had reported a decisive selection by Jay Boyd of Anna over Melissa. Then, too, Jay Boyd had become more suspicious than delicious these last few days.

"So should I wrap up my file?"

"Oh yes, Dick. You are such a sweetheart."

"I'll get the sweetheart's bill to you soon."

"Oh, Dick, you are so funny."

Feeling less guilty after doing some actual work, Dick gazed out the plate glass office front, across to the Public Library, past the Focus that Otis had parked for the crossing guard, over to the muffler shop, out over the car and truck inventory.

Was Woodstock losing its innocence? Corrupt Police Chief, drug-wholesaling business owners and managers, tradespeople breaking into patron's past projects, guns going off, G-Men in town, and an independent detective taking it upon himself to sort it all out.

Dick wondered if thoughts such as these could have been going through Reuben Roth's head in 1962 as he sat approximately in this seat as CEO and Chief Gas-Pumper at Roth's Conoco. Dick hoped that this was just an incredible spike on the graph. A time when, for some, Woodstock had become much more complicated than just cheering on the Winning Woodchucks.

FIFTY-SEVEN

....

Dick and Jung spent the late morning back in the Dental Office. Dick had conceded to modernity at one point, and he had purchased a large dry erase board on a rolling stand. In a nice oak finish, it was professional but a little out of place in the time capsule office, so he rolled it into a deep closet when he was out of the suite. As if it made a difference; he and Jung were the only ones ever there.

On the board he had made a grid, with criminal activities across the top, and the players down the left side. Then he put an "X" under the corresponding activity. It became the only way to keep things straight, and, like a director, he revised the chart daily to adjust people to their apparent roles.

Dick swung his feet up onto the corner of the desk and thought through the revelations of the past few weeks, and how many trajectories intersected. Not always clearly, mind you, but much like a New York Times Weekend crossword puzzle, in which many a fitting word can take you down the wrong path.

Today he needed to call on Lars to take another reading on that scheme, and to track down the Chicago boys to see what sort of warning they were issuing. For Lars's sake, maybe these two should be taken on in the reverse order. The shots across the bow at Boris's place were a dramatic message, maybe even someone's final solution, for a person or persons unknown.

Dick also wanted his car back. The Ferrari was still in the barn, according to Ian, who had been tasked with keeping tabs on it, both visually and through Kidd's beverage spurred boasts.

He drifted off in the office chair, feet still on the desk.

. . . Dick was in the loft, playing only for himself and Jung. Contemplative, he started with "What a Fool Believes," and determinedly continued with "Taking Care of Business" . . .

He popped awake as the second song ended, and inspired, jumped to his feet. Alas, his right leg was completely asleep from the edge of the desk cutting off all circulation. Almost falling onto Jung, he hopped about the office on one foot while shaking the other awake. Jung trotted out to the hall to observe this activity from a safe distance.

After a short lunch in the loft, Dick started his afternoon's rounds in the 300C. A lightweight pair of Maui Jim's with titanium spring nosepiece and bows, and smoked Polarized frameless lenses, was perfect for the tour. Featherweight, and clung to your head if you had to run.

First a route west of town. As he drove briskly up to Feckenmeyer's Mailbox via the back way, Anna sped past in the opposite direction with Jay Boyd in the passenger seat. Was she becoming a co-conspirator? At least he was out of the hospital.

As he wheeled past the farm entrance, Dick saw Boris walking toward the mailbox in the woods, and he swung the car around such as to watch Boris in the rearview mirror, and such as to be able to exit promptly. Sure enough, Boris opened the mailbox, pulled out the cards, and studied them on both sides, and then tucked them into his pants pocket. Boris walked the path back to the farmyard clearing.

Dick was out of sight by then, and made his way across South Bluffs Road to come out south of town near Life's A Blast and Lars.

The 300C with Illinois plates was parked diagonally behind Lars's Volvo. No Lars, but the driver's door was open, and one of the visitors stood in the doorway. He reached into his shirt pocket and tossed something onto the seat.

Slamming the Volvo's door, he got in the passenger seat of the Illinois car, and they tore out of the lot, passing Dick with an extended malocchia, or evil eye.

Obviously, they were not looking for Dick, or at least did not recognize him, which was a relief.

Dick approached the Volvo, thinking the worst, but no bodies presented in the cabin. Lying on the front seat were four playing cards. Two pair, aces and eights.

FIFTY-EIGHT

....

Dick called Jean inside Life's A Blast.

"Jean, it's Dick. Can you talk?"

"Depends."

"Is Lars there, and is he okay?"

"Just had two visitors. Movie heavy types. He passed my door about five seconds ago, white as his best patent leather belt."

"All I needed to know. Thanks, Jean."

"Am I safe?"

"Don't hang around with your boss outside of work."

"As if."

"Good girl. Gotta go. Bye now."

Next, Schwartz. How and when would Chicago meet up with Schwartz? The Justice Center was probably not the best venue. Ofc. P. Justus would come out shooting if all they did was resist showing ID. And the straps and bulges under their jackets were a bit too revealing, given their plus-size physiques.

Dick drove to his vantage point near Berg's barn. Sure enough, Schwartz's unmarked squad car was there, and Dick was just in time to see the Chicago boys arrive. It being mid-afternoon, Schwartz pulled the door almost closed behind them, and Dick was shut out of witnessing any interaction.

Dick hopped back in the car and parked directly in front of Berg's Grocery, becoming not visible from the barn. He made a quick tour of the store, picking up some smoked ham, rye bread, cheese spread and crackers, and a large bottle of ginger ale.

"Hey do you mind if I take a few photos of the smokehouse out back? It's such a classic, and I promised my brother back East that I'd sent him some shots. I'll just eat my sandwich out there. Okay? Thanks."

Dick went through the motions of taking the photos, and then leaned against the barn for a ham sandwich. The door was not shut tightly, yet he had trouble making out the conversation.

Suddenly it was clear, as the exchange devolved into a shouting match, each threatening the other with what they knew and to whom they would tell it, and with each telling the other the relative utility of such threats if the other party were deceased.

The barn talk returned to a normal level as Dick heard the whoosh of a car cover being removed. He risked blowing the operation by peeking through the open crack in the door, but he plunged ahead and saw the three men standing around his uncovered Ferrari.

The lead talker from Chicago pulled out his cell and made a call. He nodded to Schwartz, they shook hands, and Dick leaned in to hear that they would pick up the car at ten PM.

Schwartz was paying Chicago for the error of his ways – with Dick's Ferrari.

Oh well, with the future of his car in doubt, no need to starve, too. Dick wolfed down the rest of the sandwich, and guzzled the last of the ginger ale.

FIFTY-NINE

....

Dick stayed just out of sight, inching around the back side of the barn. Both cars pulled away from the barn, and Schwartz headed west, missing Dick's car completely. Safely undetected, he calmly sauntered back to the store, dropped his ginger ale bottle into the recycling bin, and went out front to get back into his car.

Dick had planned on letting Doane and Byrne wander around for a few days, mostly to keep them out of his hair, but he was reconsidering a conference with the two G-men in light of the day's events. At least by this time of the day they should be thinking straight.

Back at the loft, he played a quick round of tennis ball with Jung until on one particularly spirited run Jung disappeared out the open back door, thumping down the stairs with perfect balance and charging through the doggie door to the back yard, where the little dog repeatedly tossed the ball in

423

the air in order to catch it himself. Dick knew Jung would return soon, exhausted, dropping the ball at Dick's feet in exchange for a homemade treat.

Dick got Will Byrne on the phone.

"Hi Byrne. Dick here. I think the need to talk has come a little sooner than later."

"Okay. Where's the office?"

Explaining, Dick also asked that Doane come along.

"These things get intertwined, you know.

The two Feds found the loft and knocked. Jung was taken by surprise, still napping after the big game. They must wear rubber soled shoes. Lots of scrambling and barking later, Doane and Byrne were admitted and approved.

They still looked like two Harvard seniors arriving for a yacht race.

"So what are you finding out there in Greater Woodstock?"

"Pretty quiet place so far. Fairly closed-mouthed, too."

"They'll loosen up after the sun sets. A few drinks and everyone is an expert on local affairs."

"We'll try it. What did you have for us this afternoon?"

Dick gave them the short version of Schwartz, Lars, the Ferrari, and items of immediate import. Grabbing his laptop, Dick forwarded to their phones the complete files.

"Tonight we have my stolen car leaving town to settle Schwartz's score with Chicago. That might get complicated if Lars finds out, since he engineered the theft and is the one looking for a ransom windfall. Plus he would rather scare me out of the neighborhood."

"But if just Schwartz is there tonight, we can take him down on the cigarettes and alcohol. On the spot, in the warehouse. They call it a barn, do they?"

"It is a barn, but finished like a warehouse. And if we're lucky, we might be there for an inbound job, too. I called Ian and he said Kidd is expected back tonight."

Byrne looked at Doane.

"Do we want to lure in Lundstrom on the car deal, and see if we call pull off the drug bust at the same time?"

"I'm leery about tonight, but then again word travels fast. You would need to move on him tomorrow at the latest. And I wonder whose toes will get stepped on when you put the cuffs on the two Chicago thugs."

"Dick, who can we get for local muscle? We have to work past Schwartz in the Department."

"Guys, I've got the perfect Officer."

Dick rang Ofc. P. Justus on the Officer's personal cell."

"Hi Paul. It's Dick Stranger."

"Hello, Mr. Stranger. How may I assist you?"

"Call me Dick, Paul. Can you divert over to my office for a moment? I have some big stuff for you, but for your ears only. And it's not about catnappers."

"Sure. I'll go on break and be off the grid for a short while."

Ofc. P. Justus came through the door in full patrol regalia. Introductions were performed all around. Justus turned off his radio, and listened wide-eyed as Dick summarized what the DEA and ATFE called "The Woodstock Case." Dick kind of preferred "Operation Woodchuck," but opinions such as that were why he was not in Government employ.

"Paul. We'll need you and backup. This is federal, but the arresting Agents will need a cooler to park these guys. Are you okay with that?"

Okay? It was a career-making thrill. He might even use a couple of the new cells that had been waiting on a high profile offender for their inaugural occupation.

Jung could sense Justus's heart racing, and stood looking at the young Officer, wagging his tail. Hey mister, don't you know that a friendly dog can lower a human's heart rate? Ditch the pepper spray off the gun-belt and we'll be on good terms.

Logistics were arranged, vehicle movements mapped, expectations established. Justus was on patrol duty until midnight, and had authority to call in additional officers if needed, over Schwartz's head if the boss was out of pocket. He put the posse on confidential alert.

By this time Otis and Jack were at the office, in response to Dick's request.

Jung knew it was a party, but could not figure out why the music was not on, and more importantly, why bowls of snacks were not out and about. Dick did not entertain a lot, but normally he had things better organized.

Six people and a dog. The roof patio would have been perfect.

SIXTY

....

Ofc. P. Justus went back on duty, and Dick suggested to Doane and Byrne that they meet later for a light dinner at The Library Café, before the evening's work.

Dick texted Giovanni Corazzini in Siena to see if the Italian had caught his second wind of the day.

"They still trying the account? Car may be recovered tonight. Still working? Dick S."

"They check each day. Watch the days. Drinking red with friends tonight but working for u. G."

Then the tough call, to Kate. Dick had promised to spend this evening with her, for dinner and a movie at her apartment, all in order to help get the cats re-socialized. Kate felt the boys had a mild case of PTSD, and that they needed people around to re-establish trust and confidence.

"Kate."

"Hi, Kate, it's Dick."

"Oh, hi Dick. I am so looking forward to tonight. And Doug and Gerald keep asking about you."

Oh my. Cat lady speaks.

"Uh, I have some bad news, Kate. I'm working on this case, and I have to do it tonight, and it's with two other people depending on it."

"Dick. Really. I'm so disappointed, not to mention how will I ever break it to the cats. Come on Dick, can't the case wait until morning? I have dinner half prepared."

Guilt. Guilt, guilt, guilt.

"Kate, I feel bad. I just can't. Something is happening tonight on this case, and it is serious. Can we hold dinner and re-schedule?"

"I suppose. I even took off early to get ready."

"I'll get your boss to go easy on you."

Dick finalized some file input on the laptop, fed Jung, and left for downstairs.

He met Doane and Byrne in The Library Café. They each ordered the appetizer plus a sandwich special, and were deep in the midst of discussing the case when Kate walked in. She stared at the two G-men, and came over to the table.

"Kate, these are two men I'm working with on the case, Cody Doane and Will Byrne. Cody and Will, Kate Kaul, bookstore manager."

"Please to meet you both. Are you two the ones here on Government work?"

"Why yes, in fact, we are federal employees."

"Well, you're already all over café.com. Is this business meeting anything like last night's at The Sand Bar? Which one of you is the dancer?"

"Uh, ummm, that's not the plan, ma'am.

"Right. And Dick. Think of Doug and Gerald."

She was gone, the Earth Shoes ramping across the floor.

"Doug and Gerald? Those her kids?"

"Don't ask."

Over dinner, the plan was reviewed. Jack and Otis came for coffee, and were in the loop. Otis would bring the rollback for recovery of the car, but park far enough away as to be inconspicuous. Jack would co-pilot.

The group broke up and planned to meet at Dick's vantage point overlooking the barn at nine PM. Dick went back up to the loft to finish notes, making an effort to stay calm. This was not his sort of outing, but he accepted that the private investigator job may reluctantly overlap with the police.

Dick changed into stealth mode. Black jeans, black cotton polo, the black Reeboks.

Jung trailed him throughout the preparations. Something was up and he needed to be there. Carefully he rolled his big kibble ball noisily over to the low table in the laundry area. In one smooth motion, he jumped and landed all four paws on top of the ball momentarily, with just enough time to snag the Service Dog vest off the table with his teeth.

Jung then trotted over to Dick with the vest in his mouth, ears perked, tail wagging, dark eyes big and unblinking. Dick could not help himself.

"Jung, I don't believe I'm even saying this. A Cairn Terrier on a stakeout?"

They went down to the car together, Jung leading the way.

SIXTY-ONE

....

The evening light waned as the group sat in two cars, waiting for action at the Barn. A full moon began to rise in the eastern sky. Streetlights and yard lamps flickered on, and patios were being tidied for the night, with the sounds of aluminum folding chairs clicking shut, patio umbrellas grinding down, and Weber Cooker lids clanging shut. Air conditioners hummed in concert with the mosquitoes.

The clatter of a small-displacement diesel broke the still, and a red rollback, lettered "Carl's Used Auto Parts," swung through the alley and backed up to the barn. At rest it idled noisily.

The Chicago boys had hired Carl to transport the Ferrari. In a moment of promotional clarity, Carl had changed his yellow pages and internet listings to "A-Carl's Used Auto Parts," edging out "Andy's Towing" for the alpha billing. Carl. Never reasonable; always available.

Blue-hued HID headlamps broke through the dusk, and the 300C with Illinois plates pulled in, discharging the two heavies. They did some chatting and pointing with Carl's man, and then lit cigarettes. Next was the unmarked Crown Vic with Chief Schwartz aboard.

Schwartz strode right past the two smokers, and unlocked the big padlock on the chain. He switched on the lights, slid the big door wide open, and then disarmed the security system. There was the car, its cover pulled off and rudely plopped on the trunk of the classic next to it.

Dick and his crew approached silently on foot, as did Justus and four young officers, who had parked two cars in two driveways a couple of blocks away. Looked normal. This was a town where Officers could take their cruisers home at night.

Carl's driver hopped indelicately into the Ferrari and tried to start it. Nothing. He jumped back out, slamming the door. Dick cringed. The guy checked that the battery charger was on, and fiddled with the cables. Back in the car. Nothing.

He walked over to the rollback, which already had the bed extended and tipped to create a ramp.

He pulled the tow cable line off the winch reel until ten feet lay on the ground beyond the ramp. Dick winced as they pushed the car out of the barn by hand, putting their oily palms any old place on the fine rear of the car. These guys did not think twice about pushing on the taillamp of a forty year old car.

The Ferrari shone in the light of the barn, standing just out the door, and twenty feet short of the rollback.

Down the residential street barreled the black Peterbilt, ready to pull in with its load. Slowing, and then taking in the scene, Kidd downshifted and powered out of the neighborhood. Justus radioed for a patrol officer to detain the truck.

Schwartz, Carl's man, and the two Chicago guys jockeyed the car back and forth, trying to get it close to the ramp and positioned to get winched onto the rollback without incident.

Ten minutes into this effort, Lars's Volvo screamed into the alley and skidded to a stop by the barn.

Dick looked at Justus, and he gave the signal.

"Rock and roll, boys."

The investigators, agents, and police all converged on the barn as the scene among the individuals pushing the car, plus Lars, deteriorated rapidly.

Lars was shouting, Schwartz was yelling, the two heavies were waving their arms and exclaiming at the top of their voices, and Carl's man was backing away with his arms extended like he was about to fall into an electric fence.

Everyone scrambled at the sight of the Law, and Carl's man jumped into his truck for cover. The two Chicago boys charged for their car as the police called for hands up.

Lars wheeled toward the officers approaching from one side, and reached into his jacket as if for a weapon.

But it was too late.

Fate's story was written.

Alea lacta est. The die is cast.

He was committed.

Jung's launch angle was set, and there was no turning back once he was airborne.

"Fucking son of a bitch!!"

Jung's teeth firmly held onto Lars's butt cheek, and Lars started to spin trying to shake him off. At this point it took on the dimension of a circus act, with Jung extended horizontally from Lars's rear end, and Lars spinning wildly with his gun going off accidentally into the air.

Justus and the officers easily took control, and the three rookies, guns drawn, stood on the other side of the Illinois car, with those thugs frozen.

The Federal Agents grabbed Schwartz, who was vainly trying to call off the Woodstock Officers. Dick stayed in the background, but was definitely involved.

Lars continued vocalizing, reminding Dick of a cartoon character with a speech balloon full of typing symbols, ranting profanity.

Jung had released his prey, but a swatch of fine summer polyester the size of a slice of bread lay at his feet. He was panting, and finally decompressed with a long pee on the rollback's tire.

Rights were read all around.

Schwartz was livid when he learned that the ATFE Agent was Byrne. His own federal contact.

"Byrne, what do you think you're doing? You had me dropping the dime on Stranger for his wine deal – no taxes, no duties. He's a crook. I have it on dash cam."

"Sorry, Mr. Schwartz. Our intelligence said you were the violator here, so Mr. Stranger agreed to test your honesty for us with one of his shipments. Yes, you thought you were to sting him. But the records show he always pays all his duties and taxes. And his GPS unit also is a dash cam."

"You're wrong. He gave me that wine to shut me up. I was about to arrest him."

"Unfortunately you acted first, and hijacking a wine shipment is definitely illegal. Plus, your expansion into contraband liquor and cigarettes doesn't help. Receiving stolen goods just does not sit well with my boss. And the car. Stealing a stolen car to fence to Chicago as an extortion payment? What were ya' thinkin', Bill?"

Cody Doane was holding onto Lars, who was still spewing invectives.

"Mr. Lundstrom. That will not help your case. And you are getting on my nerves."

Doane stuffed Lundstrom into the back of a squad car. He asked Dick to make the calls they had discussed earlier.

"Hi Jean , it's Dick."

"Oh, hi Dick. It's late. What's up?"

"We have Lars in custody. You're safe."

"What about Boris?"

"Don't worry about Boris. I'll explain later. Sleep tight."

"Sleep tight? I'm still at The Sand Bar. Kate's even here. Jeez, Dick, you are gettin' old."

"Sorry, dear."

The commotion had roused the neighbors, who peeked out their windows just as Jung took hold of the culprit. When the dust settled, they walked over from the back yard to offer Dick a shallow bucket for a doggie water bowl, plus a couple of dog biscuits. Dick helped himself to the outside faucet to fill the bucket, and Jung crunched and lapped away on his reward.

SIXTY-TWO

....

Kidd sat at the wheel of the Peterbilt, with two city squad cars and two county squad cars hemming him in on the shoulder of the road. Terri Moore sat in the passenger seat, with the recovering Jay Boyd on her cell.

"Keep your mouths shut, both of you. You're just driving a legitimate shipment."

"They want to see the paperwork."

"Play dumb. I'll take care of this with Schwartz."

Two State Patrol units converged on Feckenmeyer's Mailbox, but Boyd had gotten far enough down the road to catch the Interstate highway. He was apprehended within a half hour, still bandaged and stiff, after a brief high speed chase. He was headed north, with Canada just five hours away. His luggage, neatly and thoroughly packed as if he was expecting travel, contained false identification paperwork and a forged passport to carry this ex-felon into Canada.

"Hey, you guys really want Wayne Nelson, not me. He's running a marijuana and coke operation out of there. He's an ex-con. I just work on the corn."

"Mr. Boyd, we are aware of your record, and we are already in contact with Mr. Nelson."

Three State Patrol cars captured Juan and Ricky as they crossed the state line into Wisconsin on a trip back from Monterrey. They had taken cars to Mexico, and were bringing back a few tons of fireworks and a stolen Escalade. More than one agency was interested in their future. Federal odometer fraud, title washing, smuggling drugs into the USA, vehicle theft, and more to come.

The scene at the barn calmed down. After what seemed like five hundred digital photos, and fingerprints and handprints and footprints, and yellow crime scene tape (this time, "Caution – Police

Line – Do Not Cross), Otis was loading up the Ferrari.

He gently slid behind the wheel, reached under the dash to throw the master electrical shut-off switch he had installed for Dick, and the car fired up promptly. He snicked the shifter into gear, and after clearing out the carburetor's congestion with a few punches of the throttle, he pulled it slowly onto the rollback. Their black one, not Carl's.

Dick had to make a couple of calls.

"Kate, it's Dick. Sorry it's so late, but Jean told me you guys were at The Sand Bar."

"Yeah. What's with that, anyway? You call Jean first? "

"Uh, Kate, I, uh....."

"Kidding, Dick. It's okay, we were just hanging around worrying, trying to dull the pain."

"Well, we did have a big takedown tonight. Nobody got hurt. I got my car back. I'll explain it all later."

"Boris, it's Dick. Did Doane already call you?"

"Yes, good evening Mr. Dick. Got everyone?"

"I think so. I just want to thank you for everything you've done on this deal. Is Trixie there?"

"Yes, of course. And my compliments on your operation. I understand it unfolded a little sooner than you expected."

"Trixie here. Dick?"

"Trixie, I've got to give you credit."

"Thanks, Dickie. You too. This makes our life a lot easier. I'll call Wayne for you. Oh, and once we get the pottery barn rebuilt, you'll have to take a turn at the wheel, right Dickie?"

Dick got home about two AM, and he and Jung put on music and started to uncoil.

"Jung, let's head to the roof."

Dick grabbed a couple of beers and a bowl of snacks for himself and a handful of treats for Jung. The full moon shed plenty of light on the roof garden. Dick walked to the front edge and gazed out at Woodstock over the chest high brick wall.

He looked across Main Street at Kate's building. Her light was still burning.

SIXTY-THREE

....

. . . Do you remembah . . . Dick wailed at the piano, both hands crashing out the chords of the Earth, Wind, and Fire hit "September" . . . one of his most favorites, always good to get your blood flowing . . .

Dick regretted downloading the free cell phone app for setting up a musical alarm clock. It was five-thirty AM. "Do you remembah . . . "

Jung performed his morning yoga stretches, including where he alternately held each hind leg straight out for the duration of a long, tongue curling yawn.

Dick hit the warm-up button on the Jura Capresso and it began the process to prepare to turn simple beans and water into espresso.

First, a call to Giovanni.

445

"Pronto."

"Giovanni, it is Dick Stranger."

"Buon giorno, my friend Dick. You bring good news?"

"Si, si, si. I have the beloved Ferrari. You may cancel the special account, and I will pay you whatever the interest was to have the money in there. Plus any administrative costs."

"Mio amico, we never put the money in. The staff they know. Account number coded as 'Minimum Balance US$200,000. No way to see the money is not there. We know. The car-napper does not know. For you – no cost."

"Grazie, grazie. I will see you in Siena."

"Prego, Dick. Arrivederci."

Dick pushed two tables together in the loft to create a conference area for the eight AM meeting. A quick run downstairs scored carafes of coffee and plates of bagels and pastries.

The principals arrived by ones and twos, giving Jung a workout. Barking alarm, skittering paws, wagging, and greeting. Reset.

The exception was Wayne Nelson, a new figure on Jung's radar. Smelled organic, with outstanding soil scent on the shoes, plus a smoky overtone. Dick shook Wayne's hand professionally, and to Jung this signaled approval.

The table: Dick, Jack, Otis. Justus and his Captain. Doane and Byrne. Boris and Trixie. Wayne Nelson.

"Boris, you have to tell me. Until Doane and Byrne got to town, I had no idea you were one of the good guys."

"I'm sorry, Dick. I did as I was asked. I even had to fire a couple of blanks at the ultralights. I had a good idea what they would report. I apologize for any undue stress, Jack and Otis. I would have missed by a mile even if the shells were real."

"The cards and the mailbox. What's the deal?"

Dick detailed the rumors and the theory of the accounts, the customers, with credit or not.

Boris grinned his handsome smile.

"The cards? Pure . . . as you would say, pure . . . theatre. You and Jean were close on the accounts. I made all the customers set up companies for the sake of the books at Life's A Blast. The trips to the mailbox were, together, just a play within a play.

The new accounts thought it was very mysterious and mob-like. I finally got to put the real Feckenmeyer's Mailbox to use after all these years. I just let the drug trade version of your café.com work its magic for me."

"Now I feel like an idiot for the night we cased Life's A Blast."

"Dick, that was the best yet. Lars, that cheapskate, insisted we buy those dummy security cameras and mount them all over. You know, the ones with the battery operated red lights."

"Jean told us not to worry, that they were fake."

"Well, I agreed to provide evidence, and I wanted Lars on tape and eventually Ricky and Juan on tape, so one night I converted the internals all over to real cameras, wireless to an internet account. I watched you on my laptop the whole time. One stealthy trio, I'll say. When Lars got the ticket to Woodstock, the DEA contacted me. I might have been in their database from, well . . . let's just say . . ., years ago."

Doane broke in.

"That's right. Our Chicago source told us they were starting to muscle in on fireworks with an added feature, the drugs. Boris agreed to play along."

"So what about the Farm?"

"We wanted someone on site who worked strictly for DEA. We 'hired' Wayne directly out of Leavenworth when he turned out to be . . . to be . . . so knowledgeable. Right, Wayne?"

"Hired? More like 'voluntary community service.' And I knew this guy Boyd from my RDAP class in prison. He was a con all along. I knew he would be back to prison. You can always tell the ones who can't leave the life. He contacted me once he was on the outside, looking for a location for a grass farm. He had no idea, the idiot. So I hired him. I knew we could bust him any time."

"So the fence and irrigation. Just for show?"

"We didn't know how far we had to take this, and Boris cooperated. It was all Boyd's idea, and all our Government's money. Boris will end up with the best corn in Western Wisconsin this year."

Trixie squirmed with anticipation in her chair, briefly reaching up to touch her diamond necklace.

"And Dickie. I know you and the boys wondered about the Well-Rested. We watched Jack follow us. That's where Wayne set up his DEA office. No maid service needed, back side of the building. I went over twice a week to help with anything he needed on the case."

Dick sat blinking his eyes. Even at this early stage in his private investigator career, he had considered himself to be a sharp and observant investigator with a sound network of snitches.

"Trixie, why then did you get me involved on the case on Boris?"

"Local color. We assumed news of Boris's drug thing would get around, and we wanted it to come from you and not from Schwartz. Plus Boris and I thought you could use the business."

Some business. You couldn't bill enough hours to cover all this horsing around. After all, now Dick had staff.

Byrne took his turn.

"With Cody and me working together, we knew we could lower the boom on Schwartz if he started to hassle Boris before we could pick off Lars and Jay and the drivers."

"Juan and Ricky. What about Kidd?"

"Well, what about Juan and Ricky? They've got a few pages all by themselves. The State DMV charges, the Federal Odometer violations, the drug skim from the fireworks, plus their connections in Monterrey."

Doane added,

"We're actually hoping to get one of them to turn so we can visit with their friends."

Ofc. P. Justus broke in,

"And Kidd O'Connor. Not only did he steal the car, but he has a ton of stolen property from all over the county. Stuff he stole for himself, not working for Schwartz. When we looked around over at the old city shop where he parks the semi, we found another old trailer full of electronics, jewelry, even some art. Didn't think he had any taste. He used all those building and security system plans to break into places that Boris's company had built. And last night we got him to admit, er . . . I mean he volunteered that he fired at you out on Cranberry Boulevard, Dick. Lars put him up to it. Just to scare you, as he put it."

"Terri Moody?"

"Just an accessory. She certainly has a lot of nice things to say about you, Dick."

"Oh, I'm sure of that."

Jung's ears worked overtime and his head twisted clockwise and then counter-clockwise, staring at
each speaker.

Another round of coffees and pastries was consumed, as everyone thought through the recent
events, events seemingly impossible in Woodstock,
Wisconsin.

Dick still had questions.

"Lars Lundstrom. Why was he worth all this effort? I know he has connections in Chicago, but
they weren't happy with him. Sent their bouncers
up to give him a little scare."

Doane turned to Dick.

"Look, Dick. Lundstrom has connections all the
way back to New York, remember? And Chicago is
in disarray. The traditional mob is being challenged by the Eastern European mobs for control
of drugs. Lundstrom's choice to use primarily the
Mexican connection and to bypass Chicago alto-
gether, ruffled some large feathers in Chicago."

"Like I said. Is he going to be worth it?"

"They're all worth it. Most of them turn Federal
Witness when the heat comes on. The odds are in
our favor. And we have some very, should I say,
imaginative Federal Prosecutors."

Justus spoke up again.

"Oh, and Dick. I have to meet with Kate briefly today. The kid who stole the cats is Lars's nephew. It doesn't make much sense yet, but it looks like it started as paid harassment of you, Dick, which never panned out. It turned into a weird crush on Kate and stalking. Plus he thought he could turn into some kind of drug kingpin, with the connection to Lars. He thought he was gaining control by holding the cards – literally. Strong imagination, but weak on the brains front. But he has been talking a lot, so he's proving productive for us. Sounds like he doesn't care for the idea of prison."

Dick tipped back on the rear legs of his chair, letting it all sink in. This was going to take the rest of the day just to type notes into the laptop. Right up there on the tangled web scale.

The meeting broke up about ten-thirty, as all the Officers and agents had reports to finish, calls to make, suspects to shuffle. Jung watched them file out, getting the occasional good bye. Regardless, he stood and wagged his tail at each as they passed by his spot near the door.

Their echoing chatter and clattering foot-steps on the terrazzo hallway sounded like a party breaking up.

SIXTY-FOUR

....

High seventies, sunny, cloudless. Dick and Jung repaired to the roof garden. Dick sat in a multi-colored Adirondack chair and intermittently pecked on the laptop, then stopped to glug sun tea he had drawn from a two gallon jar with a spigot.

He called Ian to give him the ten minute version of events, and to thank him for his help.

Dick's mind wandered as he pictured those arrested being deposited into the squad cars, and pondered the continuum of prisoner travel.

One day at the wheel of a Lamborghini or Escalade, the next peering out the rear windows of a fully marked Crown Victoria. Then the transfer from City Jail to County Jail in the Prisoner Van, all steel grids over the windows. On to Federal Prison in the Prison Bus, shackled and chained to the floor, stepping or sitting in the stink of whatever flowed from the prisoners before. Not a road one wants to travel.

Jung chased a ball around, amusing himself, and periodically watering the greenery. He rested in the ample shade provided by the cedar plank benches. The remains of Dick's cheese, meat, cucumber, endive lettuce, and pumpernickel bread lunch sat on the table.

Dick could not shake the thoughts that kept bobbing up in the front of his mind. How did the big bust change Woodstock? A few transplants would exit the scene, not to be missed. Fireworks would be sold, corn grown, books and coffee and liquor consumed, restaurant meals eaten, hotel nights slept, and Woodchuck Teeth would still be worn in the stands, the only reasons for removal being stadium dogs, cotton candy, and peanuts thrown from a vendor. The opposing fans had become accustomed to, in fact envious of, the lisp the oversized plastic teeth created in the Woodstock cheers.

Jung leading the way, Dick went downstairs and sauntered into Stranger Than Fiction. Plans to type files had evaporated. Jung sported a blue and white seersucker bandana, and Dick wore light beige linen slacks, a blue casual camp shirt made out of miracle recycled wood fibers, and deck shoes with no socks. This was not business.

He flipped through a pile of new releases mostly to lure Kate into acting as if he was a customer.

"That one in your hand, sir, debuted at number three on the New York Times Best Sellers List. With your 'Library Card,' it is thirty percent off. A great read, sir, for quiet times on rooftops."

"Why thank you. It's a gift for someone I know who is taking a few days off after working on a large project."

"As it should be."

"Now then. After you ring that up, please exit the rear of the store and be seated in the vintage Ferrari in the driveway. It can be identified by the dashing private detective at the wheel and the handsome Service Dog in the rear. And lose the Earth Shoes. It's sandal weather."

"Where to, Mr. Bond?"

Dick pulled his prized Persol sunglasses out of the glove compartment and took them out of the custom leather case. The same model Steve

McQueen wore in the original Thomas Crown Affair.

"South County hills, then east to The Pen for bar steaks."

"Proceed."

The Ferrari was, in enthusiast-speak, "well sorted," which meant that it ran right, did not overheat, tracked and steered correctly, and was free of mysterious body and suspension clanks, clunks, and crackles.

Running up the tachometer in second gear, Dick blew the horn as they passed Life's A Blast and headed south on the state road. He wondered aloud if the Shiraz empire would ever include the retail winery next to the fireworks store.

The road rose ahead up to the ridge tops above the coulees south of town. County roads rook over from state roads, and then township roads overtook those. Dick loved the roads that wound through Amish country, over the hilltops and back down into the valleys created by the small river that was full of inner tube riders and kayakers and canoeists on this perfect afternoon.

Kate had dashed over to her apartment and changed into a yellow cotton print sundress and beige sandals with hemp straps. Bright yellow earrings and a matching acrylic bracelet were accenting a pair of white plastic framed sunglasses to complete the retro look.

Jung sat quietly in the small storage area behind the front seats, comfortable in his new doggie seatbelt harness, threaded through the luggage strap. With the windows open, Jung's nose took in the countryside.

A quick tour of the State Park meant a stop for the only "Dogs Invited" trail, where they walked out on a promontory to view the valley below and to consume snacks from the local convenience store.

The Ferrari was a sensation wherever they stopped, even though Dick always parked what seemed like a mile away from the other cars. On the road, the sound of the V-12 being exercised up and down the gears, the amazing handling, the spare but precisely contoured bucket seats, all defined a true grand tourer.

A swing further south brought them closer to civilization again, and they had a short burst up the Interstate before swinging off to resume the tour. A few more small towns, past corn and soybeans and hay and tobacco and grapes, then on to the dinner destination.

Gravel parking lot, block building painted a bright but fading turquoise, a set of fifties bar windows, the ones with the corners angled off to match the shape of the big glass ashtrays inside, the awning you had to duck to see out from under – a roadhouse identified by an aging Blatz beer pole sign with the name of the place completely weathered off.

In the front window was a cardboard sign, now coated with clear plastic packing tape, that read "OPEN." The O was made up of the ribbon symbol from Pabst Blue Ribbon Beer, so that locals started to call the tavern The PEN.

The PEN had the best bar grill steaks for many miles around. All cooked to perfection, along with onions and other specialties, on a single forty-eight inch by thirty-six inch char-grill behind the open end of the bar. The usual deep-fryers took care of the rest of the menu. The bar was finished in boomerang-patterned Formica, matching the tabletops.

The PEN was dog friendly, so Jung got to meet several new friends on the canine end. With a remote location, no advertising, and an understanding health inspector, the crowd for The PEN was steady and enthusiastic.

Dick had parked across the road in the lot of The Fromager Cheese Factory and Outlet Shop, just closing for the day.

Over steak dinner, Dick told Kate the whole story. She already knew about cat boy, and had speculated on a lot of the rest, some of it off base, some of it spot on. Could turn out to be a good consultant and mystic for the Truth Is Stranger Investigations team. The imagination of her literary mind, no doubt.

The juke box belted country tunes, the pool tables were backed up, darts were being thrown, and what looked to be the serious mid-evening crowd was settling in. Having feasted on the featured steaks, our trio elected to depart.

The trip home was normally under an hour, and Jung snoozed in the rear area. Dick and Kate listened to R & B on the Burmester audio unit Otis had carefully installed, inconspicuously mounted under the passenger seat, with the small remote for it loose in the glove compartment. The township and county roads back to Woodstock were all gentle curves and steep hills, making for a calm dusky ride overall.

Dick could not help but think what change the entire Feckenmeyer's Mailbox affair had wrought on their county. Any? Was Woodstock's innocence gone, or was this just going to be a news story in the regional newspaper, then gone.

About five miles south of Woodstock, a mildly curving stretch of road dropped down from the ridge-tops to town. Kate had started to doze in the passenger seat, Jung was sound asleep curled up in his harness, and Dick's mind continued to wander.

Dick was brought alert from this reverie by the bright blue headlights of a car approaching in the other lane. It wasn't dark enough for lights, but Dick was a believer in their use at all times, plus many cars now had daytime running lights. But these caught Dick's eye because they were on bright.

As the car approached, Dick could see that it was a late model Cadillac STS, black in color. Just as the cars met, the front of the Cadillac squatted down, and the rear end hiked up, signs of hard braking. Illinois plates. One car length past the Ferrari, the black car made a skidding one eighty.

Dick had been wondering who was being stirred up in Chicago. The word must have gone out: send the troops up to look for the only silver vintage Ferrari in metro Woodstock. Here they were.

The Cadillac quickly closed the gap with Dick and the Ferrari's current fifty-five mile per hour cruising speed.

"Kate. Kate. Hang on. It looks like Guido's pals are up from Chicago, checking me out."

Jung shook his head and the tags on is collar rattled as he stood on the storage platform. Dick downshifted the Ferrari and easily pulled away from the Cadillac. But what now? A forty year old classic sports car was fun and could be driven quickly, but was no longer meant for a car chase. And into town was not a great place to lose oneself and one's car.

Dick hit the brakes and took a hard left onto a township road. Amish country. This was the only chance. Old curvy roads, up and down grades, following the old property lines. Please, he thought, let there be no Amish buggies tooling down the road in the dim light with their slow-moving vehicle signs. No buggies please, just their droppings.

The chase went on for miles, with the Cadillac occasionally catching up, and then falling back as it wallowed in the turns, with a driver who was a novice to the roads up and down the ridges.

Dick pushed hard as he raced toward the object of the game: the Amish churchyard corner. On this single corner, the Amish in this synod gathered on Sundays for three hour church services, and more. Dick took the corner on the inside avoiding the horse droppings concentrated at the entrance to the yard.

As predicted, the Cadillac under-steered to the outside of the corner and the slick mess on the road. Driving at the limit, the oversized driver of the black car had no concept of what was coming. The car's low profile tires squealed going into the corner and then slid on the manure as the driver spun the steering wheel like a bumper car's. Skidding head first into the ditch, the Cadillac bottomed out and caught some air before the brush, sod, wire, and stumps of the fence line brought it to a halt.

Slightly stunned by the whole incident, but uninjured except for a couple of bloody noses, the three out-of-towners in dark suits piled out of the car, arms waving and yelling at each other, and at Dick pulling away in the distance. It was a fairly low speed crash, once the grass had scrubbed off a lot of momentum, but it was enough to bring the chase to a halt.

Dick could see that the Cadillac was immobile, and he pulled over to the side of the road to take inventory. Heart beating wildly, he was most concerned about Kate and Jung, who were much calmer than he expected. More like a great carnival ride for Kate; more like a great elevator ride for Jung.

"How fast do you think triple-A will be there for them? Or is this an OnStar moment?"

"Dick, how can you be so laid-back? Won't they come after you?"

"I think if they really wanted to harm me they would have been waiting at home. It's just another scare. But they're probably a little pissed right now. I've got to make a call."

Dick grabbed his cell and called his Chicago contact.

"Hey friend. It's your private dick up north."

"Sounds down here like it's a busy place up there."

"That's true, but it's getting quieter and I want to keep it that way. I need a favor. And I need it right away. I know you know who's who. Let them know I'm just the messenger up here. Kind of a professional courtesy, right? Ask them to call off the dogs. I just had a short chase that didn't end the way the Illinois plates wanted it to end. I'm sure Carl's towing is winching them up right now. Do what you can. Another case is on the way."

"Another case? I've got enough to do."

"Another case. Strangere red."

"Oh. Got it. I'll get it done."

"Same shipping address?"

"I'll be here."

Dick slipped the car into gear and motored slowly around a large loop southwest of town, passing the farm and Feckenmeyer's Mailbox, and coming back into Woodstock on the west side. Just for fun, he cruised past Berg's Store just to see if there was any action at the barn. Looked quiet except for police tape flapping in the breeze.

The evening closed with the Ferrari in the garage, and Dick, Kate, and Jung on the roof. Dick's cell buzzed.

"Dick Stranger."

"Hey, I want you to know things are cool in Chicago. My contact says the big guys know who you are, and that the clown car was a few jerks trying to make up for their two buddies getting handcuffed. I'm sure they're not too happy right now, but my man says they'll get the call. You're okay."

"Thanks man, you're the best."

"Don't forget my address."

Dick disconnected and topped off the Chianti in his own and Kate's glasses. His thoughts kept coming back to the case, or these cases, as it were. Tomorrow would bring a further debriefing with Doane and Byrne, and a forecasting of the fates of those apprehended as well as of the survivors.

The full moon was high, and the limoncello came out. Kate left to make a bed-check on Doug and Gerald, and then returned for the night. Jung wagged his tail, looking back and forth at Dick and Kate.

SIXTY-FIVE

....

Days and weeks and months wore on. Charges after charges were filed. Doane and Byrne checked out of and into The Hotel Woodstock, where they held court in The Hotel Bar, regaling Lance and Leo with their tales of federal Investigations, and where they flirted with anyone from the Woodchuck Bowling Team who happened to show up.

Legally, the dominoes fell. Chief Bill Schwartz turned Federal Witness, and pled out to a long probation and possible relocation.

Lars Lundstrom kept his mouth shut, went to trial, and took the biggest hit. Twenty-one years, and the possibility that his enemies might shorten his sentence unnaturally to prevent him turning Federal Witness in prison.

Jay Boyd IV healed from his wounds in time to take a trip back to Leavenworth, but this time at the Big House, not at the Camp.

Kidd O'Connor faced only state prison time, after negotiations, plus lengthy supervised release. Terri Moody was charged as an accessory, but charges were dropped in exchange for testimony. She lost her job at Life's A Blast and became a bartender.

Ricky Torres and Juan Rios had federal time to serve, plus state time not running concurrently. They then faced a deportation order.

The two goons from Chicago went through a long run-up to a mistrial followed by jury-tampering charges.

Boris and Trixie resumed life as before, but with Trixie handling the books for the fireworks store, the farm, and the new Winery, as the farm now grew both corn and grapes. The real estate market was slowly recovering, and Boris was building again.

Wayne Nelson stayed with the DEA on a consultant basis, with periodic travel, and he continued to manage the farm. He was going steady with a Woodstock girl.

Melissa Schwartz and Anna Lundstrom expanded Melanna Yoga, funded by a large cash settlement remaining from Anna's divorce, even after the federal fines. Melissa vowed to stay with Bill, but only if he stayed local, which was unlikely given the individuals in Chicago whom he had offended.

Melissa and Anna introduced Melanna Yogurt, and a line of Melanna Hydrators, which were mildly alcoholic sports drinks. Both products received popular regional distribution.

Jack Bluhm fulfilled his lifelong dream of becoming a newspaper reporter when the headline "Drugs and Alcohol Rock Woodstock" appeared over the byline "Jack Bluhm, Special Reporter to the Woodstock Tribune." For some reason, among the press he had the most detailed account of the affair.

Marian Horton and Otis Graves became an item, and Marian began to perform occasional gigs singing blues with Otis's band. Otis continued his normal routine. He also managed Ian Jackson to a strong showing in the Stock Car series.

With Chief Schwartz out, the Police and Fire Commission totally remapped the Department. Paul Justus became Captain.

Kenny and Pearl Wisdom were rock steady, holding together the food and drink properties for Dick.

Giorgio Danto took on more responsibilities at Stranger Than Fiction, and he now helped Jack Bluhm with book purchasing. Jean Paradise came to work for Dick as his bookkeeper, and she became his on-site office interface with all the businesses and with his accountant.

Jean took over the two small apartments at the top of the stairs, over The Liquid Muse. One became the office for all the enterprises, and the other became an employee rest and relaxation and conference area.

Overall, Woodstock carried on unchanged, these few lives touched by the events known to the participants simply as "Feckenmeyer's Mailbox."

SIXTY-SIX

....

. . . Dick was at the Steinway, his fingers grace-
fully tracing his own arrangement of the amazing
Van Morrison hit "Moondance," Dick's favorite
song. Kate sat in the Eames lounge chair with a
gin and tonic, double lime, in her hand. Jung lay
on his pillow enjoying the music, reveling in this
endless sleepover pizza party that was his life . . .

The cell phone.

" . . . Dick."

"Dick, it's Kate. Are you alright? We were supposed to meet downstairs a half hour ago in the
Café."

"Oh, yeah . . . I'm fine. Just dozed off, I guess.
Sorry, I'll be right down."

Jung slunk off the green leather chair he had
commandeered when Dick had drifted off.

"Jung . . . "

The little dog scurried for the back door and Dick let him out. Ka-thunk, ka-thunk, ka-thunk down the stairs and out the doggie door with a flap-flap.

Dick freshened up a bit, made sure to have his phone, and with Jung on a leash, made for the downstairs. It was Liquor Lab night and the place was mobbed. Pearl Wisdom had a classical guitarist playing near the tables, and the crowd was double the normal size.

Jung was going crazy seeing all his friends as he and Dick worked their way over to Kate at her table. Dick and Kate were such regulars that they had their own table. As it should be for the proprietor and his girlfriend.

Sage Wisdom brought two Peronis over for Dick, claiming it was Happy Hour. Dick and Kate talked over the matters of the day. The bookstore and the other properties were prospering.

Dick felt further satisfied. As a reimbursement for services rendered, Truth Is Strange Investigations had benefitted from a special one-time payment diverted by the DEA from a Federal Prison drug treatment program.

With this sudden influx of cash, Dick had given bonuses to all his staff who had worked on Feckenmeyer's Mailbox. He had spent the rest paying down mortgages and prepaying property taxes.

"So Dick, what's going on after dinner?"

"Well, I thought I would do a little Italy work while we sit here. I need to go over to Bellapendio for a couple of weeks, or maybe more. I missed a ton of harvest time."

Wine, talk, dinner, more talk and wine. Dick touched his cell phone and drew his finger across the screen, pulling up the Italy itinerary on his favorite travel site.

He typed in the dates of travel, and prepared to tap "Book It!" to finalize the travel. He hesitated, gazing across the table. He looked back at the schedule and changed it to a complete month.

In the box "Passenger #2," he typed "Katherine Kaul," and paused, glancing down at Jung.

Of course, Dick knew Jung was not going. In fact, the dog loved these pampered vacations at Kamp K-9.

Dick eyed Jung nonetheless, tilting his head to one side, then to the other.

Jung stood up, looking at Dick, then Kate, then back at Dick, wagging his tail and twitching his ears back and forth.

Dick's finger hovered over the "Book It!" icon. . .

###

ABOUT THE AUTHOR

T. E. Vernier lives in western Wisconsin where he is the Customer Care Trainer for a regional car dealership group. He is currently finishing the next installment of the Dick Stranger series. T. E. Vernier's life is shared with his spouse of 38 years and his Cairn Terrier, Makeup.

T. E. VERNIER

Made in the USA
Charleston, SC
04 February 2014